BEYOND THE DREAM

Shaudin Melgar-Foraster

Translated from the Catalan by

Caroline Roe

Originally published in Spain as *Més enllà del somni* by Edicions del Bullent SL
De la Taronja, 16 - 4610 Picanya
Copyright © 2008 Shaudin Melgar-Foraster
Cover Art by Thong Ling copyright © 2009
Map by Yotin Quibus-Melgar
Translation copyright Medora Sale Ltd © 2009
Translated by Caroline Roe

Most Trafford titles are also available at major online book retailers.

Note for Librarians: A cataloguing record for this book is available from Library and Archives Canada at www.collectionscanada.ca/amicus/index-e.html

Printed in Victoria, BC, Canada.

ISBN: 978-1-4269-0833-0 (sc)

ISBN: 978-1-4269-0934-4 (e-book)

We at Trafford believe that it is the responsibility of us all, as both individuals and corporations, to make choices that are environmentally and socially sound. You, in turn, are supporting this responsible conduct each time you purchase a Trafford book, or make use of our publishing services. To find out how you are helping, please visit www.trafford.com/responsiblepublishing.html

Our mission is to efficiently provide the world's finest, most comprehensive book publishing service, enabling every author to experience success. To find out how to publish your book, your way, and have it available worldwide, visit us online at www.trafford.com

 www.trafford.com

North America & international
toll-free: 1 888 232 4444 (USA & Canada)
phone: 250 383 6864 ♦ fax: 250 383 6804 ♦ email: info@trafford.com

The United Kingdom & Europe
phone: +44 (0)1865 487 395 ♦ local rate: 0845 230 9601
facsimile: +44 (0)1865 481 507 ♦ email: info.uk@trafford.com

10 9 8 7 6 5 4 3 2 1

For my mother, Maria Foraster i Ruiz

thank you for everything

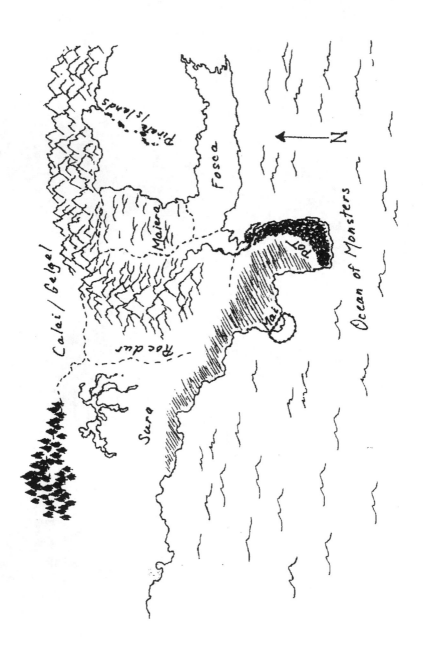

Chapter One

Interferences

*T*he valley is heavy with silence disturbed only by the rustle of tall stalks of grass shaken by the wind. The first light of morning creeps in, extinguishing the stars and driving away the darkness. Slowly, behind the hills, threads of gold and rose-coloured light appear and, in the valley, night melts away in a game between racing shadows and scraps of light. The wind tangles your hair and you push it back from your face. You don't seem to be yourself. Or is it the strange and solitary valley that upsets you?

What am I doing here? Where am I?

But you stand motionless in the stalks of grass and in the wind, remembering nothing, not knowing who you are, looking at the hills where a flock of birds has just now taken flight. Suddenly the deep sound of a horn fills the valley. On the hilltops you see thickly massed figures outlined against the sky.

"Maiera!" they shout from the hilltops and sound the horn again. The figures advance, some on horseback, others with rapid strides, the

metal of their swords, shields and stirrups gleaming. The cry "Maiera!"
echoes in the valley, along with the horn and the hoofbeats of the horses.
And you are right in the middle, standing upright in the long grass
shaken by the wind, immobile, watching as a whole army of warriors
advances.

And now the rush of boots and hoofbeats, the yells and the call of the
horn merge with the continuous loud beating of a countless number of
drums. You turn to the west and see scarlet figures with swords and
horses emerging from out of the shadows. Another army of warriors.
Both armies head for the middle of the valley. Both are marching straight
at you.

I cannot move. All I can do is look at one and then at the
other.

"Run, Anna, run! Hide in the woods under the trees! Run for
your life!"

Anna? Yes. I'm Anna. I can hardly breathe and my whole body
is trembling. The shouts and the drumbeats are exploding in my
head. My legs give way. I'm on the ground in the tall grass. The
warriors are coming closer and closer.

"Run, Anna, run!"

I drag myself along, moving toward the forest. The uproar
of drums, horns, hoofbeats and shouts is almost on top of me.
I take a deep breath and begin to run on all fours, like a dog,
faster and faster. My hands and knees are covered with cuts and
scratches, I have grass cuts on my face, but I keep running and
running until I'm in the woods.

A dense green light fills the place and the dry leaves of the forest floor
lie still, protected from the wind. "As quietly as you can, roll over
to beside a tree. From there you can see the valley." *But now the*
valley is nothing but a vast cloud of dust. From it come the sounds of
swords clashing, horses snorting and men screaming in pain.

My hands are red with blood and the cuts on my face and knees sting. I begin shaking again. My mouth is dry.

In the valley, among clouds of dust, the armies battle fiercely in a confusion of shadowy, constantly moving figures. A horseman has thrown himself at a gallop toward the forest where you are hiding. Another horseman, in scarlet leather, is following him. They have reached the wood. The one who is ahead turns abruptly and, before the scarlet horseman can react, runs him through with his sword. He falls from his horse onto the forest floor, dead, with his eyes open. At your side, Anna.

You have just enough time to back away when the other horseman dismounts, grasping his sword. His dark hair is tangled, his beard thick and his eyes are bright and alert. You stay hidden behind the tree, pressing your back against the trunk, trembling but silent. From where he lies on the ground the dead man seems to be looking at you. The warrior's boots rustle through the dry leaves; he is very close, almost on top of you, but the galloping of another horse entering the woods stops him.

"Arnom!" echoes the powerful voice through the forest.

You shift sideways a little and crane your neck, trying to see what is happening. The warrior with the tangled hair has turned his back on you. A little further ahead, the other warrior dismounts and stands still. He is very tall, and has long, reddish hair and a reddish beard. He wears a black tunic with a scarlet dragon embroidered on its breast and carries a bloody sword in his hands. You remain absolutely still watching the two warriors. The man with the tangled hair raises his arm as if to protect his face and, for an instant, the tall man looks straight at your tree. His eyes are burning red and terrifying.

He has seen me!

Anna woke up with a cry of terror smothered in her chest, her heart pounding and her mouth dry. Pale silver light leaked through the space between the curtains. She took a drink of water from the glass on her bedside table and got out of bed. Puff, her cat, stretched lazily, yawned, and went back to sleep.

She stood in front of the curtains, thinking. She didn't dare open them. If she pulled them back, she might see the solitary valley where the wind shook the stalks of long grass. And she might hear the voice that had been talking to her, the voice of a woman who was only a voice. She shuddered, took a deep breath and yanked them open.

Through the window, just like every other night, she saw the glow from the skyscrapers in the city centre, every window lit up. And from the third floor of her house, Anna could see the downtown under a cold moon and, right below, her quiet little street covered with dirty snow.

She was too old now to call for her mother, but she didn't like the idea of going back to bed. She didn't want the nightmare of the ferocious warriors at battle to return, nor the dead man on the dry leaves, nor the one with the burning red eyes... She began to shiver. She turned on the light, checked that her pyjamas weren't covered with dirt and there weren't any cuts or scratches on her knees or anywhere else, and sat down on the bed, ready to stay awake until morning. But before she knew it, she was asleep.

Anna's mother, Nuria Manent, worked at the main library at the university, where she was in charge of the section containing Catalan books. Nuria and her daughter looked very much alike, although Nuria didn't have Anna's intense dark eyes. Anna's mother was easy-going and pleasant by nature, but she found understanding her daughter hard work. Anna lived in a state of constant rebellion against injustice. Usually the slightest sign of tyranny threw her into a sudden rage, although once in a while she chose to react with silence and a frown. Recently Anna had been tending toward the second reaction, which her mother found even more disconcerting than the first.

Nuria had had a heavy morning at the library. Now, at two in the afternoon, she was sitting in an armchair in the corner of her office, settling in to a sandwich and a moment of relaxation.

There was a knock on the door. Nuria sighed and went over to open it. It was Anna, looking tousled and sulky.

"Anna! What are you doing here?"

Without a word Anna walked in, dragging her backpack, and held out a letter. It was from Mr. Skinner, the principal of Anna's school, a man who could not speak or write without being complicated and confusing.

Dear Mrs. Manent,

It is my duty to inform you that your daughter Anna has behaved unacceptably today. Let me explain. Anna has broken a window - my office window - by throwing a stone from the schoolyard at it.

When Anna's teacher, Miss Boulder, spoke to the girl - yours, let me explain, not Miss Boulder's - she, Anna, was in an agitated state, a state that, according to Miss Boulder, is not usual for her. For that reason I thought that Anna might be going through a difficult time at home. Let me explain. We have many cases like this at the school and generally that is the reason for unexpected behaviour on the part of a student. I assure you that I have broad experience in these cases as principal of this school. Well, then, as I was saying, Miss Boulder spoke to Anna and her explanation - your daughter's explanation - was not acceptable. Let me explain. According to Anna, her action was caused by some sort of vampire with red eyes and a bloody sword appearing in front of my office window. That is what she said. A vampire.

The recommendation of Hills of St. George School, of which I have been proud to be in charge for 17 years, is that you take Anna to her doctor for an examination and, if it is the case, that you inform us of any family difficulties that might have disturbed the psychic equilibrium of your daughter. I understand that you and Anna's father, Mr. Jordi Roig, are divorced.

There only remains for me to add that Anna is suspended from school for two days. Let me explain. As punishment for her behaviour.

Yours very truly,

Paul Skinner

Principal

P.S. We will be sending you the bill for repairing the broken window.

Clearly perplexed, Nuria Manent read the letter again, this

time out loud so that Anna, who was sitting in the armchair in the corner, could hear it.

"What is all this?" said Nuria when she finished reading. "I don't understand a word of it."

"No one understands Skinner," said Anna, as if there was no question about it.

"No. I'm asking you what happened?" said Nuria with irritation in her voice. She set the letter down on her desk.

"Just that I broke a window." Anna was looking at her feet and frowning.

"Am I allowed to know why?"

"What Skinner said in the letter," she muttered, her eyes fixed on her boots.

"And what family problem are you having? Your father and I got divorced eight years ago!" exclaimed Nuria.

Anna stopped looking at her boots, rolled her eyes and sighed. "Not that. What he called a vampire," she said, looking steadily at her mother.

"What insanity is that!"

"It's not insanity, Mum. I saw this really scary creature with a sword. He looked like what grandfather calls a 'bruixot.' Really. I thought he was going to attack me, right there in the schoolyard, in front of Skinner's window."

"Quiet, Anna, please. Stop saying stupid things."

"It's true."

Nuria's expression changed from angry to worried. "Are you feeling well?" she asked after a moment.

"Yes. I think so," said the girl uncertainly. Her mother sighed.

"Anyway we'll have to see Dr. Ross," she said, picking up the telephone. "Then Mr. Skinner won't have anything to complain about."

Dr. Ross examined Anna and went off to talk to Nuria. "You know, Mrs. Manent, Anna's an intelligent, healthy girl. I don't think that incident at school is necessarily serious."

"What about that story of seeing a warrior with a sword?"

"Anna told me she had a nightmare last night about some

frightening creature and it seems likely that she was still thinking about it. Anna's twelve; she probably has anxieties about growing up that could make her behaviour a little - well - disconcerting at times. Those things together could explain what she did and said. Anyway, you probably already know that Anna can't stand the principal."

"Paul Skinner irritates me as well."

"Well, then, there you have it. My advice is don't make a big issue about it. Not now. It might even be best not to discuss the subject any further with Anna." He smiled. "Of course, you'll have to pay for the broken window."

Anna decided she needed a private diary to record everything that was happening. Two days later, in the evening, she took an exercise book and began to write. Since she wasn't a particularly methodical girl, she divided it up into months instead of days.

Anna's Diary, January, 1998:
Dear diary,

I have to talk to you because I can't talk to anyone else. I've realized that there are things I can't talk about to my mother, or my father, or anyone I know at school, either. Before, when I was little, my parents always listened to me and I had all kinds of friends. Now I don't have anyone. My parents are always at work and, besides, there are things they don't believe even though they're true. The adult world is so narrow. And the kids my age have all turned into idiots and can't see what's in front of them. All they talk about is actors and what they'll do when they get out of school - and they're totally boring things. And there's Alison Walnut and her little crowd of stupid idiots. I can't stand her. The truth is that I don't have any friends and I don't like anyone, anyone at all.

Maybe my grandparents would understand. Grandma Maria always listens to me, even when she's cooking or doing other things, and she hardly ever gets mad. She's a lot like my mother, except my mum never listens to me. But they live in Catalonia and I won't see them until I go to visit in the summer and until then who can I talk to about what has happened to me? I have to act as if everything is "normal" so they don't bother me. Especially at school with Skinner. I hate him!

I don't understand what has happened, but I know that I am not imagining it. I'm really upset because I don't understand. Where did the 'bruixot' come from? I see him in the dream, then he goes and appears in the schoolyard and yesterday, in the library. My father thought I was sick when I went to his place last night. I had to pretend that I was coming down with flu. I told him that I'd caught cold and that was why I was shaking. How could I tell him that the 'bruixot' had appeared again?

Oh, diary, I am so scared! Yesterday my mum took me to the library with her because Skinner doesn't want me at school until tomorrow and my dad was teaching classes and working at his university all day. Since my mum had a lot of work to do in her office, I just walked around the library. There were a lot of students there and they stared at me because I'm so young and so I slipped in between the sets of shelves with thousands and thousands of books on them looking for someplace where there weren't any people. I found a space that was sort of dark with rows of huge books on each side. Since I didn't have anything else to do I started reading the titles - they didn't tell me much. Lots of them seemed to be in other languages. Then suddenly I felt - I don't know what - a sensation that all at once I remembered because I felt exactly the same in the schoolyard. I looked down toward the end of the row and there he was. Really tall, long hair and beard, a black tunic with a scarlet dragon embroidered on the chest, a bloody sword and those awful burning red eyes! I was terrified. I began to run. At the end of the row I turned without looking and crashed into a bunch of students loaded down with books. I kept on running to the elevator. There, I felt safe because there was a lot of light and lots of people. I turned around. The 'bruixot' was nowhere around. He hadn't followed me. He just appears. Then he's gone.

Now I'm almost always scared. Last night at my dad's place I wasn't, because it's a small apartment and it doesn't seem to me that the 'bruixot' could turn up there; although I wasn't really sure of that. I was in the living room watching television while my dad worked in his little study, and later I slept on the sofa-bed with Juli, my father's old cat, and there *was light and noise from the street because he lives right in the centre of the city and I felt almost completely safe.*

Today is different. My mum's house is on a quiet street and it has three storeys and a basement and corners filled with shadows. I always used to like my mum's house better. It's where I usually live and besides I have the third-floor bedroom which I really love. But right now I'd rather be in a small place, like my dad's apartment, where I don't think the 'bruixot' could get in. Tonight I'll leave my light on and the light on the stairs, too, and hope that I'll be able to sleep. Puff will keep me company.

Back soon, diary.

Anna found a safe hiding place for the diary under a loose board on the floor of her closet and climbed into bed. She was nervous and uneasy, but fell asleep almost at once and slept until midnight when the noise of a cat-fight in the street woke her up. Puff, who was lying at the foot of the bed, raised an ear and opened an eye. Then Anna fell asleep again for the rest of the night, not knowing that the cats in the street had taken fright at the sudden apparition of a tall figure with burning red eyes.

The next morning nothing else happened in Anna's life, if you don't count classes at school and having to go to Mr. Skinner's office and listen to a half-hour speech on behaviour. It was punctuated, like everything else the principal said or wrote, with his constant, predictable 'Let me explain.' From time to time Anna nodded her head, while managing not to listen to a word he said.

The 'bruixot' hadn't shown up again. He left nothing behind him but endless little jokes the other students in Anna's class made about him. And, of course, Miss Boulder's comments on the subject of Anna breaking a window.

That afternoon Anna was in the school's computer room, surfing the web, trying to finish an assignment for class, when the text she was about to print disappeared. The entire screen went grey. An open hand, palm outward, hit the glass, as if someone inside the computer was trying to get out. As soon as it touched the screen, the hand disappeared.

Anna pushed back her chair and jumped to her feet. Fear kept her eyes glued to the computer, even though her text was back on the screen again. Her moment of terror passed and she ducked under the table to see what was behind the computer. There was nothing but cables and connections. She looked at the screen again. Her text was still there. She hit a few keys, moved the mouse, and still nothing strange happened.

Anna was so absorbed in examining her computer she didn't realize that the other students in the room had noticed what she was doing. Then the ripples of laughter got so loud that she knew what was going on around her.

"Hey, Anna, did'ja you lose your marbles under the table?"

"Anna! Any vampires back there behind your computer?"

The feeble jokes and laughter went on. But Alison Walnut wasn't saying anything or laughing. And Alison Walnut not saying something cruel and not laughing at someone when she had a chance was really weird. She sat quietly at the computer next to Anna, pretending that she was listening to music on her *discman*, but one glance at Alison and Anna knew the other girl had seen something.

"What's with you guys?" said Anna to her classmates. "Idiots. My computer froze, okay? I was checking the connections to see what was wrong."

She sat down again with great dignity in front of her computer, even though her heart was racing. She glanced at Alison; but she seemed to be caught up in her damned *discman* with no expression at all on her face.

Anna printed her text, read it and re-read it without knowing what she was doing - she could think of nothing but the hand on her computer screen. When the bell rang she had to run for class with the others. But as she reached the door, she turned back to look again. Alison had changed places and was using the computer that Anna had just left.

Chapter Two

ANNA AND ALISON

After school, as Anna was putting on her scarf and hat, Alison Walnut came over. The mixed group of kids who always surrounded Alison watched her, looking surprised. Everyone knew Anna and Alison couldn't stand each other.

"Anna! I want to talk to you."

"And I don't want to talk to you," said Anna, picking up her backpack and going out into the street.

Alison stopped dead, apparently struggling with wounded pride. She overcame it and went out after Anna. "Just a second, Anna."

Alison's little crowd couldn't believe it. Most of her schoolmates admired Alison Walnut. She was the girl with golden hair and deep blue eyes, stacks of clothes, and better than that, rich parents who threw spectacular birthday parties for her to which most of her classmates wanted to be invited. She hardly ever studied, but was clever enough to keep passing and, as well, to hang on to her group of admirers by tyrannizing over them without them realizing it. Anna Roig-Manent had never been invited to her house, nor would she have gone there if she had been. She couldn't stand Alison any more than Alison could stand her. But now, as soon as she asked to talk to her, Anna knew why she had changed. She was sure Alison had seen the hand on the computer screen. As a matter of fact, Anna wanted to know if Alison had seen anything else when she was at her computer.

"Sure, Alison. Come up to my place and we can talk."

"The chauffeur is waiting for me," she said, batting her eyes as she always did when she wanted to establish her superiority.

"It's up to you."

Anna kept on walking up the street. Alison went over to a parked car, dark in colour and shiny, and spoke to the driver. She was hurrying after Anna when a boy stepped in front of her. It was Charles Garland, older than she was and from a private school. He usually turned up after school to hang around with Alison and her friends.

"Why are you chasing after that dumb twit, Alison?" he said, grabbing her arm.

"Let go, Charles. I have to talk to Anna. I said, let go of me!" She jerked her arm away and ran after Anna.

"Are you crazy?" he yelled after her.

Alison's group found themselves alone on the street with Charles, silenced at the sight of Alison racing after Anna.

"Hey, Anna," gasped Alison, "why are you going so fast? Slow down."

Anna stopped for a second, giving Alison a scornful glance. "I'm not walking fast. I'm walking normally. This is my usual speed. You're the one who's slow. You move like a little old lady in those uncomfortable boots."

"Everyone loves them," she said, glancing down at her expensive beige boots with their little heels.

"Well, I don't. They make you walk like an old lady and if you're coming with me you'll have to slog through dirty snow. They'll get totally ruined."

Alison shrugged her shoulders and batted her eyes. "Who cares? I've got others."

"Of course. Sure. You have more, just as stupid as the ones you're wearing." And Anna started walking again.

Alison stayed where she was, as if deciding whether she could stand one more minute of Anna. But she had to talk to her about something that might be too important to let slide and hurried after her again. Neither one of them said a word. They just walked. Anna was completely wrapped up - all you could see of her were her eyes and her red nose; Alison in her cute jacket of thin leather with no hat or scarf was trembling with cold. As almost always, a freezing arctic wind was blowing straight through the city.

They arrived at Spadina Avenue, crossed at the lights and followed a narrow street toward Anna's house. All the way, Anna brooded about the strange situation. There was no doubt that she and Alison both had information the other wanted, but then what would happen? Anna didn't trust Alison one little bit. Who knows what the spoiled brat would do with it all? Maybe she could keep her mouth shut - anything was possible - but Anna could feel her stomach twisting in a knot just thinking about sharing a secret like this with Alison.

And so they walked along without saying a word until they came to Anna's house. It was narrow and three storeys high, like so many others in the city. The two girls stood in the tiny front garden. Anna noticed that Alison was very pale: in fact, her eyes were watering and her teeth were chattering from the brutal cold and freezing wind. But Alison didn't show the slightest sign of wanting to come inside. Paying no attention to her shivering, she said, "I saw the hand." She batted her eyes and icy tears escaped down her face.

"What hand?" said Anna casually, although she was desperate to know more.

"You know what hand I'm talking about. And I've seen other things."

"So? What do you want from me?" she said, hiding her burning curiosity.

"I want to understand it."

That was the last thing Anna expected. Alison was superficial;

usually she skipped lightly over almost everything. All that interested her was being the centre of attention and finding things to laugh at in other people. And, here she was, saying that she wanted to understand, simply understand, and to understand was what Anna wanted too. She opened the front door of the house. If she left Alison outside a moment longer she was going to freeze to death. Anyway, Anna was too frightened even to think about being alone in the house before her mother came home.

"Come on in and we'll talk. It's too cold out here."

When they came in, Puff appeared, miaowing and waving his huge tail.

"You've got a cat? Cool! He's really cute. What's his name?"

"Puff," said Anna dryly. She didn't like Alison getting to know Puff.

They left their boots and jackets in the hall and Anna took Alison into the kitchen. It was where she and her mother spent most of their time when they were at home. Not only did they cook and eat in the kitchen, but it had a sofa and a television set and a little table for the computer. It was a large, pretty room, painted white and yellow. Its window, rounded off on top by a half-circle of stained glass, looked out onto the street.

"Sit down," said Anna, pointing to a chair beside the table, while she put a kettle on the stove. "I'm making hot chocolate - can I get you some?"

"Yes, thank you," said Alison very politely, batting her eyes; Anna could have cheerfully hit her. She knew her too well to be fooled by that well-brought-up girl pose of hers.

"How about an apple?" she added shortly.

"No, thank you," said Alison, batting her eyes again.

Anna took one for herself. Out of the corner of her eye, she watched Alison. She was sitting stiffly upright in her chair. She must never sit in kitchens, thought Anna. At Alison's house, the kitchen was probably for servants only.

Puff jumped into Alison's lap and began to purr, something Anna didn't like at all. But after thinking about it, she realized he would leave those beige pants she was wearing covered with grey fur. You could already see it. But Alison didn't seem to be thinking about her pants while she was stroking the cat and smiling. When Puff jumped down full of playfulness, bringing her a little ball so she could throw it, Anna had had enough. Putting the cups of hot chocolate on the table, she said, "So, Alison. Do we talk or not?"

Alison drank some hot chocolate and its warmth brought the colour back to her cheeks. She blinked. "Sure. Let's talk," she said, fixing her blue eyes on Anna.

"What do you know?" asked Anna abruptly.

"What do *you* know?" said Alison quickly.

"Uh uh, sweetheart, not a word. Not until you tell me what you know."

"Okay. I saw the hand appear on your computer."

"You mean the palm of a hand."

"Yeah, sure," said Alison impatiently.

"You said that you'd seen other things." Anna drank her hot chocolate without taking her eyes off Alison. "What else did you see?"

"You said that you saw some kind of vampire, right?" remarked Alison, swallowing more hot chocolate, not looking at Anna.

"Not exactly a vampire. A really scary-looking man."

"What do you mean exactly? You tell me and I'll tell you."

"Come on, Alison, stop haggling, eh?" said Anna, almost jumping out of her chair with annoyance. She sighed. "Okay, the scary-looking man in exchange for what you saw on the computer."

Alison thought for a minute as if she were calculating how much she would gain from the exchange. "Done," she said.

But Anna didn't want to explain the apparition of the 'bruixot' in the library and even less the dream of the battle in the valley, so all she described was the apparition of the 'bruixot' in front of Mr. Skinner's window.

"And there was nobody else in the schoolyard?" asked Alison doubtfully.

"No. I already told you. Everyone had gone into class!" Anna truly loathed Alison. She wondered uneasily if it had been a good idea to let this rich, stuck-up girl into her kitchen.

"What were you doing out there in the cold?" said Alison calmly.

"I had to finish reviewing for the test. There was nowhere else to do it. Don't you believe me?" Anna was going to add the word, "stupid" but held back. First she had to find out what information Alison had.

"You wouldn't be inventing all this, would you?" Alison continued with doubt on her face.

"And why would I invent it, eh?" Anna could feel her cheeks turning red with indignation. "Now you tell me what else you saw."

"Not a lot, but enough so I can believe what you told me about the man," said Alison cautiously, since it was clear that Anna was angry.

"Which was?"

"Well, after you left for class I went over to your computer..."

"I saw that. And?"

Alison batted her eyes and sighed patiently, irritating Anna. In spite of it Anna said nothing, waiting for Alison to carry on.

"After I'd been hitting keys for a while, the hand came back, the palm of a hand," she said precisely and looked at Anna, who was listening impatiently, "but now the screen wasn't grey like first time. It was in colour and the palm was covered with blood - I think it was blood. It didn't stay long at all and it didn't come back."

Faced with this information, Anna could contain herself no longer. "Wow!" she said, and frowned in concentration.

They remained silent staring into space, each one lost in thought over what the other had said. Puff carried his little ball from one girl to the other, but when it didn't work he left at last, miaowing disconsolately. The light coming in through the window was beginning to fade and it had started to snow. "What do we do?" asked Alison at last.

"We can't say anything to anyone," said Anna flatly. "No one would believe us. We'd only get a lot of grief over it."

"You're right. We can't talk about it. We'd only make ourselves laughed at," said Alison with a shudder. For her, to be laughed at was the worst thing that could happen. "So, aside from not telling anyone?"

"What do you mean?"

"We have to figure it out," said Alison.

Anna didn't know what to do. She didn't like Alison, had never liked her at all, and now, here she was, mixed up in a weird happening with the very last person she would have chosen if she'd been given a choice. She resisted getting tied up with her any more.

"How about trying the computer?" said Alison, pointing to the one in the kitchen.

Anna still hesitated, even though she had to find out and the computer seemed to be a good place to start. She would have gotten rid of Alison and tried it by herself, but the idea scared her out of her mind. Actually, she realized that inviting Alison to come home with her had been a way of having someone around more than anything else, because she went hot and cold at the thought of being alone. The 'bruixot' might appear with his sword and those eyes...

A loud noise outside the kitchen startled the two girls. In a panic Alison grabbed Anna's sweater. Both of them were staring at the dark hallway on the other side of the open door through which the noise had come. Neither one of them moved. Suddenly Puff came through the door, his back arched.

"Puff," said Anna, hardly able to speak, "what's happening?" Then she jumped up, grabbed the broom from the corner and dragging Alison - still hanging on to her sweater - went to turn on the hall light. There wasn't anything there, but at the end, beside the staircase, the little sitting room remained in darkness. The two girls advanced slowly toward it, clearing a path ahead of them with the broom. Puff was behind, bringing up the rear. Anna turned on the light in the little sitting room and quickly moved the broom from one side to the other, the way she had seen it done in the movies. The sitting room was deserted but on the floor was a broken vase next to Puff's toy ball.

"Puff! Bad cat! What have you done?" said Anna; Alison was still glued to her and Anna removed her hand from her sweater. "It wasn't anything. Well - yes, it was. This little monkey broke the vase."

"It's a very pretty vase," said Alison in a tiny voice, looking at the pieces of china scattered over the floor.

Anna broke into laughter. "Sure. As you can see, very pretty."

Alison giggled.

"You were scared, weren't you?" said Anna.

"You were too. Don't try to pretend you were all brave."

"I had the broom and you were hanging on to my sweater."

"Did you think you could attack a huge warrior who carries a sword with a broom?" said Alison seriously. Anna realized that she had upset her. "I think it's time I went."

"What about the computer?" asked Anna, her uneasiness returning.

Alison shrugged her shoulders.

"Hey, come on, why don't we get it over with once and for all," said Anna. "Let's go back to the kitchen."

Alison followed her reluctantly. Anna turned on a light on the table and switched on the computer.

Time passed and nothing seemed to bring them nearer to what they were looking for. They tried the same website Anna had visited at school and Alison tried to reproduce the pathway through the 'net she had followed that morning on Anna's computer. Nothing weird turned up. Outside, the early nightfall of wintertime was already enveloping the city in total darkness, and the snow continued to fall rapidly in tiny, frozen particles that smothered all the noise from the street. And inside the pleasant kitchen of that ordinary house, the two girls kept on trying to find something strange on the computer.

"I'm fed up with this," said Alison, looking tired. "There's nothing else we can do. I'm going to call for the chauffeur."

Anna rolled her eyes. Calling for the chauffeur! Why she has to come to our public school when she has all that money - a chauffeur to drive her home from school! Well, she thought, she must do it all to make herself noticed. And now she'd go and leave her here with no one else in the house, but there was no way she would tell her she was afraid to stay alone.

"Whatever. The telephone is over there," said Anna, but Alison had already taken her cell phone out of her pocket.

Before she could phone, she screamed. Her high-pitched cry was followed at once by Anna's. For there on the computer screen was not only the blood-stained palm of a hand, but the hand belonged to a man with long hair and a beard who was looking straight at them. The apparition lasted only a moment and then disappeared. Even so, the girls ran, screaming and getting themselves tangled up with Puff, toward the front hall. On the other side of the door stood a figure, white from head to foot. They kept screaming.

"What's going on here? What's all this racket?" said Nuria Manent, turning on the light and brushing the snow off her coat.

Chapter Three

ROCDUR

On the side of a rocky peak deep in the mountains rises the dark and sinister-looking Castle of Rocdur. Time has blackened the enormous stones that make up its walls and since the grand entrance is its only visible opening, it appears to have been carved from a single huge block of stone. Following its smooth surface all the way up to the top, the eye can see battlements where the soldiers of the Castle stand guard day and night. On one side of the Castle rises a tower. In front, the walls of this tower are as smooth as the rest of the building, but in the back there is a large window, the only one in the Castle. From it you can see the mountain range and down below, the Town of Rocdur, spread along a valley, creeping up into the hills around. A banner with a scarlet dragon on a black ground waves from the top of the tower.

Inside the Castle, beyond the enormous entry doors reinforced with iron, is a great hall. Its walls are made of stone and its floor of black marble tiles that reflect the torchlight. It is cold enough inside to make anyone tremble, but more intimidating than the cold is the silence.

In the middle of the hall there rises a majestic black marble staircase. A very tall man has suddenly appeared in front of it. His long hair is reddish and his red beard touches the scarlet dragon embroidered on the front of his black tunic. His black leather boots are covered with snow. He casts aside the bloody sword he carries in his hand and, in loud commanding tones, cries: "I am here!"

Down the stairs come six men in scarlet tunics embroidered with black dragons; their hair and beards are reddish in colour, but on some the red is mixed with white. All of them are tall, but none as tall as the one wearing the black tunic and standing at the foot of the stairs. Nor do any of them have burning red eyes that strike fear in the heart of those who see them.

"Lord!" exclaims one of the men coming down the stairs as fast he can and falling on his knees at the feet of the tall man.

The others follow and they kneel, too. All bow their heads.

"Where were you, Lord?" asks one, raising his head and then quickly lowering it again, terrified by the burning red eyes.

"Who gave you permission to speak?" The Lord's baleful voice resonates through the hall.

There is total silence. The six men on the ground remain kneeling with their heads bowed. The Lord looks at them with his fierce, beast-like red eyes.

"Out of here, cretins. Let me by!"

The men crawl backward over the floor to make a passageway for the Lord. He heads up the stairs, leaving a trail of melting snow behind him. At the top, he walks along a torch-lit passage with a floor of black tiles so highly polished they reflect his image. A small man, with long, curly green hair and wearing a short ragged tunic, is polishing the tiles. He sees the Lord's shadow, huge on the wall, drawing near and backs away at once. Trembling with fear, he stays on his knees with his head bowed until the Lord passes through an arch at the end of the passage.

The Lord has arrived at the tower and climbs another staircase that winds its way up to the top, where there is a room with swords hanging on the walls, a table of dark wood and a chair of scarlet leather. The large window in the wall across from the door looks out over the Town of Rocdur and the mountains.

As soon as he enters, the Lord claps his hands and at once two small green-haired men, like the one polishing the tiles, come in. They kneel at once, their heads bowed.

"Bring food and wine! What are you wretches waiting for? And tell the Secretary I want him!"

A few moments later, a man dressed in a scarlet tunic with a black dragon, like those who had welcomed the Lord, comes into the room.

"You sent for me, Lord?" he says. His words glide smoothly from his mouth. He kneels, but does not bow his head. There are two scars where his eyes should have been.

"How went the battle at the Valley of Can?" asks the Lord of Rocdur, standing directly in front of him.

"We won," he answers, his face impassive.

"Were they all exterminated, then? Our enemies?" Curiosity burns under the commanding tone of his question.

"No, Lord, they retreated eastward."

"You just said we won!" he shouts, his red eyes glittering with rage. The Secretary remains silent. "Why weren't they exterminated?"

"They fled." The expression on the Secretary's face is unreadable.

"And why were they not pursued?" asks the Lord angrily. The Secretary does not answer. "I asked why were they not pursued. Answer me!"

"The Chief of the Army would be able to answer you better than I, Lord." The words creep slowly out from his mouth.

"Perhaps, but right now I am asking you. What do you know about it?"

"It would seem your absence rattled them. They were not sure what to do."

"My absence, eh?" The Lord turns to the window overlooking the mountain range. It is already beginning to get dark and lights from houses in the Town flicker in the dusk.

The two small green-haired men come into the room, their heads bowed, and leave food and wine on the table.

"That'll do!" snarls the Lord. "Get out!"

The Lord and the Secretary are alone again. The one with the burning eyes is outlined, tall and heavy-set, in front of the dwindling light coming in the window, clenching his fists impatiently. The other remains kneeling, wary and unreadable.

"Tell me. Where did you think I was?" says the Lord, leaning toward the expressionless face of the other man.

"We did not know, Lord. No one knew. There was great confusion at the Castle. The wise men consulted the mirrors day and night, but there were no clear answers."

The Lord looks at the Secretary who is still kneeling, his face as unreadable as ever. The burning red eyes concentrate on the blind man's two scars.

"And you?" he asks at last. "What did you do?"

"I looked deep, Lord," he answers, the words creeping out.

"And?"

"Nothing, Lord. I did not find you."

"It wasn't much use, then, that I took out your eyes?" says the Lord coldly, all the while caressing a pendant he wears under his tunic.

The Secretary remains silent and without expression. At last, he says, "But I saw things, Lord."

"What did you see? Answer me!" he asks impatiently.

"Well..." He drags the word out.

"What?" snaps the Lord, irritated.

"When I looked for you, I saw a girl."

"A girl! What was she like?" He comes closer to the Secretary. "A girl of around eleven or twelve? Hair and eyes dark - like some of the rebels? Indescribable clothing, clean face?"

"Clean?" he asks, perplexed, even though his face continues to be expressionless.

"Not dirty?"

"Yes, indeed, Lord. Like that."

"Where was this girl?" The Lord's voice echoes around the room.

"I do not know. I could not see anything else."

"Are you saying they consulted the mirrors?" he asks, trying hard to repress the rage growing inside him.

"Yes, Lord, but the result was confused. They saw the same girl as well as another, a blond with blue eyes."

"Girls? Just girls?" he shouts.

"Yes, Lord."

"Tell the Keeper of the Mirrors to bring the wise men together." The Lord swallows a mouthful of wine and sits down to eat. "I'm going down. I want to see them all."

While that is happening, near the foot of the mountain a family huddles in front of the fire in a small, wretched hut, one of many huts like it leaning together, miserably, in a clearing in the forest. They are Potians, immigrants from the country of Pot to the south of Rocdur, a race of small people with curly green hair and eyes the colour of honey, able to endure heavy labour and exploited by the Rocdurians. In the hut a man is talking to his son. "I said you can't keep it and not to mention it again."

"But, Dad, I'll keep it hidden here and..."

"By the sacred hair of Nana! That's enough, I said."

"No one hides anything in this country," his mother nods in agreement, while stirring the soup cooking on the fire. "Try it and they'll put out your eyes."

"Or cut off your hands or even your head if you're no use for anything," adds his grandmother's tiny voice. Her hair is more white than green and she's so little and shrunken you could almost fit her in a basket.

Tam, the boy, is stroking a kitten with a yellow coat, glossy like a ray of sunlight.

"He's so beautiful," he says, "and so small he'll die if I abandon him."

"He doesn't look that small to me," says the grandmother.

"You don't think that anything looks small, grandmother."

"But she's right," says the mother. "He's a big kitten, and strong. Look at those huge paws."

"Big, little, what difference does it make!" interrupts the father angrily. "I said I don't want to talk about it any more. Take that cat away from here before they kill us all! It was a cursed day when that beast turned up, as if we didn't have enough headaches already." The father is in a corner emptying out a little basket with a cover. "Take this. Put him in it and get him out of here."

"But Mau," says Noa, his wife, "it's already dark and the Watch will be out patrolling. Maybe you ought to take him."

"If they catch me they'll certainly arrest me, but you know the Chief of the Army protects Tam."

"If he finds him with a cat that won't help him."

"You'll be able to get it away from here, won't you, Tam? If you run into a patrol tell them that you're going to collect leftovers from the Chief's kitchen and don't open the basket." He keeps looking at his son. "But stay away from the patrols whatever you do, just in case."

"Take him to the river," says Noa. "No one goes there."

"That far?" cries the grandmother.

"For you, everywhere seems far, mother," says Mau. "Come on, Tam, look sharp."

They open the door very carefully and Tam, carrying the cat in the basket, slips out into the shadows, much against his will.

There is no moon and in the forest, the road is dark and the wind howls through the trees. Tam walks quickly, stumbling at times, looking now and then at the twisted branches crowding in on both sides of the road. The massive block of the Castle of Rocdur on top of the mountain seems more the ghost of a building than something solid. Now in a sharp turn in the road a patrol appears out of nowhere: tall soldiers with reddish hair, in scarlet leather with a black dragon outlined on their chests. All of them carry swords and some have torches as well. Tam has no time to flee.

"Hey, you, piece of filth there, stop!" shouts one of them. He steps forward and seizes Tam by the scruff of his neck.

A soldier with a torch grabs the basket and opens it. "It's empty," he says, moving his torch to light up the boy's face. "Tam! What are you doing here?"

"I'm going to the Chief's house to see if there are any leftovers."

"You know going out at night is prohibited."

"Yes, but I have a new story the Chief will want to hear."

The patrol huddles together, whispering.

"Good, then," they tell him. "To the Town. Come with us."

Still holding the basket, the boy runs alongside the long-legged men. The flames of the torches flare up in the wind, lighting up the road in moving patches. Tam is silent but he is thinking fast. He needs a really good story to tell the Chief of the Army. It is unbelievable luck that he was stopped after hiding the cat and not before.

Poor little thing, Tam is thinking, how will he get along by himself in the cave behind the waterfall? Maybe I could come by often and bring him things to eat. He's so young he doesn't know how to hunt. At least no one else knows about the cave, and if the cat doesn't come out, no one will find him. If they do, they'll kill him.

Tam is the only one who knows all the hiding places in Rocdur because Tam roams everywhere. Rocdurians follow orders and never do anything forbidden. Potian immigrants, like Tam's family, are too afraid to go beyond the edge of their settlement. But Tam has the good luck to have an imagination that never fails him, and his stories delight everyone who hears them, especially the Chief of the Army. The Chief suffers from terrible insomnia and constant agitation of his nerves that can only be soothed by listening to stories. Tam started telling him stories some time ago; he was only eight when, as a result of a chance meeting, he told him the first one, and now that he is eleven he enjoys the Chief's protection, a protection that in spite of being rather precarious gives him more security that any other Potian immigrant has.

The patrol and Tam finally arrive at the soldiers' barracks. They enter through a great archway and walk along a corridor, through a dining hall full of empty tables, and come out into a huge flagstone courtyard where the dogs sleep. As they walk, Tam fishes around in his head for a story. Nothing comes. Anxiety about hiding the cat and weariness from all the walking have clouded his mind. Maybe he can rescue himself by using one of his grandmother's tales from Pot, told in his own way.

The trouble with that idea is that Rocdurians aren't interested in Pot. As far as they're concerned, Pot is an insignificant country filled with inferior, miserable people. They provide cheap labour, but give them headaches controlling the entry of illegal Potian immigrants.

But as he and the patrol walk out of the other side of the courtyard, Tam decides that he has no choice. He will have to tell a story from Pot. They enter the stables where hundreds of horses are sleeping, and with each horse, there sleeps a Suran.

Tam has never spoken to a Suran but, like everyone in Rocdur, he knows that they are immigrants from the country of Sura to the west. He also knows there are more Surans in various places in Rocdur where there are other Rocdurian troops and more horses. The Surans are slender with long black hair and are superb horsemen. Their skill with horses and knowledge of horsemanship give them certain privileges in Rocdur, because the army needs them. They are, you could say, well treated. Not like Potians, thinks Tam with envy. We do the heaviest labour and are daily victims of the rage of the Lord of Rocdur and his people.

At this moment, in the stables, a Suran lies in the straw beside the horse in his care, his eyes open. He is a young man named Tajun, who arrived in Rocdur a couple of years before from the lands far beyond the Suran lakes. He left home, one of Sura's most remote regions, when he was just an adolescent, because grass was sparse and the antelope were dying off, leaving the people with nothing to eat. Tajun's whole family was dead - his father killed fighting in the north against the Gelgelians, the rest from starvation.

During the long journey from his home all the way to Rocdur, Tajun saw a great deal, met many people and listened to what they said. Vegetation and animals were disappearing and all Sura seemed condemned to disappear as well. Only in the north did the woodlands still stretch out thick and full of life, but the lands of the north were dangerous because of the constant incursions of Gelgelians. It was risky to live there.

In spite of the danger, many Surans moved north, facing the risks. Others emigrated to Rocdur, even though it was clear that Rocdur, by hunting and logging, was to blame for the miserable condition of Sura. The Rocdurians killed off all the wild animals they could and then cut down the forests they lived in.

Tajun considered joining the Suran guerillas to fight the Rocdurians who were destroying their country, but decided it would be better to get to know the enemy first. And so at sunset one day, watched by the border guards, he rode up to the border between Sura and Rocdur on a horse so weak it seemed more dead than alive. But Tajun, although he was thin, looked strong and arrogant. He held his head high and his long black hair hung down his back. He was bare-chested, the arm holding his lance was steady, and there were two blue horizontal stripes painted under each of his forceful-looking dark eyes.

As soon as he arrived, his horse fell to its knees and died of hunger and exhaustion. Instead of falling with it, Tajun leaped off and stood fearless and confident in front of the soldiers. They seized him and brought him to an officer.

Although Rocdur needs Surans for the army not all Surans are acceptable. They must be young, healthy and strong, speak the Common Language[1]and be excellent horsemen, not only knowing how to look after horses but also to ride them with skill in battle. Bringing their families into Rocdur is difficult. After a Suran has lived in Rocdur for a long time and has demonstrated his value, he can ask for his wife, children, or brothers and sisters to join him - if they are healthy, speak the Common Language and can, now or later, be of use to the army. Parents are never accepted. Rocdur does not want old or feeble Surans. When Surans living in Rocdur fall ill or grow old, they have two options: return to Sura or be executed.

Not only did Tajun have the qualities necessary to immigrate to Rocdur, he also spoke the language of the Gelgelians, a

---

1   Catalan

language so difficult that no one in Rocdur knew it well. That made him very useful. And so, after passing the tests at the border, he found work quickly.

Now, two years after his arrival, Tajun does not sleep. He lies in the stable observing the patrol pass by.

The patrol and Tam leave the stable and go out once more into the night. Ahead of them lies the Town of Rocdur. Close to the barracks is a big house with large windows and balconies filled with flowers - the house of the Chief of the Army. The men from the patrol knock at the door and a trembling servant of the same race as Tam opens it.

"Tell the Chief Tam is here with a new story," says a soldier.

The servant comes back at once. "The Chief says to come in."

Tam, still carrying the basket, enters and follows Ep, the servant, up a broad stairway of polished wood. The servant opens a door at the top of the stairs and takes Tam in. It's a big room the boy knows well - the Chief's bedroom, with a bed, comfortable chairs by the fire and a table set with candles and dishes of fruit. A map of the entire known world hangs over the fireplace. Every time he comes here, Tam's eyes are drawn to his family's country, Pot. He cannot read, but he can recognize the pot-like shape of the land his parents and his grandmother came from.

The Chief is in one of the armchairs. Like all Rocdurians, he is tall and, like the soldiers, he wears scarlet leather with a black dragon. His hair and beard are a reddish chestnut in colour mixed with a few grey hairs. His discarded boots are lying in a corner and he is clutching a cup of wine in his hand.

"They tell me you have a new story," he says to Tam, and the boy sees that his dark blue eyes are dulled, with swollen eyelids and dark circles under them.

"Yes, Chief," says Tam, leaving the basket near the door and kneeling in front of him.

"A good one?" says the Chief, sighing with exhaustion.

"I think so, Chief."

"Sleep escapes me. I've hardly slept at all since the Battle of the Valley of Can. The disappearance of the Lor..." He stops and looks suspiciously at Tam. You don't speak about happenings at the Castle to Potians. He brings the cup of wine to his lips but his hands shake, infuriating him. He throws the cup, spilling all the wine. "Hey, you, Ep, come on," he says to the servant who is kneeling close to them. "What are you doing stuck here like a idiot? Clean it up."

The servant moves rapidly, putting salt on the wine stains.

"Enough!" roars the Chief. "Do it later. Come on, Tam, start."

Tam is used to dealing with Rocdurians. You do what you're told and pay no attention to anything that's going on. He settles down to begin the story, hoping that the Chief will like it, since otherwise something rather disagreeable could happen, but before he can say a word, the door opens. A slender girl with dark blue eyes and long bright red hair pulled back and hanging loose comes into the room. She is wearing a long dress, pretty and elegant, the same blue as her eyes, and riding boots that look rather out of place with the rest of her clothes. She smiles at the boy.

"A new story, Tam?" she asks him.

"Yes," he says, pleased that the girl will be there.

"Father," says the girl to the Chief, "why didn't you tell me? You know how much I like Tam's stories."

"It's late for you to be up, Tariana. You should be in bed."

"No, Father. No sleeping when there's one of Tam's stories." She sits down in an armchair.

The Chief says nothing more. He's probably too tired to argue with his daughter, and anyway, he knows it's useless. Tariana always wins.

Chapter Four

THE LORD OF ROCDUR

The Lord of Rocdur is in the Hall of Mirrors of the Castle, where he has been for some time, walking up and down while he talks to the Keeper of the Mirrors and his team.

"We're not hitting it because you're not there," says the Keeper of the Mirrors, a very old man, his hair and beard pure white.

"Nonsense," says the Lord of Rocdur. "There has to be some way to see it again."

Half a dozen tall men, all wearing scarlet tunics embroidered with black dragons in front, are kneeling in the hall. They are the men who met him on his return, the Wise Men of the Mirrors, the most important men in the land, except for the Lord, the Secretary and the Chief of the Army. In spite of that, not one of them can bear to look directly at the Lord. No one in Rocdur can look him in the eyes. The Secretary, who is also here, stays still and silent with his inscrutable face and the two scars where his eyes would have been.

The Hall is spacious and contains six mirrors at which the wise men usually work. The mirrors are used, mostly, for spying operations, a difficult task that requires great concentration on their part. They are there to watch enemies, but are also useful for finding one of their own men. In order to do this a wise man smears blood from the person he wishes to see on the palm of his hand, places his hand on the mirror and concentrates. If he's lucky, he will see him, friend or enemy. Of course, the person they are trying to see must still be alive.

The wise men keep samples of blood from all important Rocdurians. But when they tried to find the Lord, all they saw were two girls. Two girls, who, as the Keeper pointed out several times, looked rather like rebels.

"You didn't manage to get even a tiny amount of blood from the unknown world, Lord?" asks a very pale wise man with cold, expressionless blue eyes.

"Do you think I wouldn't have told you, imbecile? I know how the mirrors work."

"It would have been very good to have a little blood from one of the girls," says a young wise man with a long nose and an untrustworthy look.

"Damnation! I know it would have been very good! But the fact is that I didn't; moreover, toad, I told you that I only saw one of them, one girl, the one with dark hair who was in the Valley of Can. You saw the other one in the mirror."

"I could almost touch them," sighs a wise man with blue eyes like clouds in a stormy sky, "but the mirror was solid against the palm of my hand."

"And someday maybe we'll be able to touch someone in the mirror?" says the Lord. "Eh? Tell me that, nitwit."

"No, Lord, we can only see them. But this time they saw me, and that has never happened before."

"No, of course it's never happened, nor have any of the other things happened before." The Lord stops pacing up and down the Hall. "Well, then, aside from telling me what I know already, what other options are there?"

"Lord," says one of the wise men, as thin as a skeleton, who seems to have an idea and in the excitement, raises his eyes for an instant, and at once, lowers them again, "maybe we can't do anything with the girls, but... What about your sword?"

"What do you want with that?"

"The blood could help us see the enemy."

"I'll have you know, idiot," says the Lord, "that all those that my sword touched in the Valley of Can are dead. As Arnom would have been if..."

"Arnom!" say all the wise men at once.

"What stupid creatures you are." The Lord burst out laughing. "Why should we fear that flea-bitten wretch? Eh? Tell me, what can that miserable rebel Arnom do to us?"

"Nothing, Lord, nothing," says a wise man with a beard so long that he almost treads on it with his knees. "But..."

"But what," shouts the Lord, now really angry.

"He has escaped back to Maiera again," says the wise man, surreptitiously drawing his beard out from under a knee.

"Yes! He has escaped again thanks to the uselessness of our army!"

"Just as you disappeared," says the Keeper.

"I'm sick of this tale!" roars the Lord angrily and, in saying so, comes close to the Keeper, who with difficulty bows his head toward the ground. "As it seems, everyone blames me for the flight of the enemy. Isn't that it?"

"No, Lord, no. No one would ever blame you."

"Good, then. Now - I want ideas."

The wise men are silent and trembling, their minds blank. Not one of them has an idea. The Secretary stays at his place, no doubt listening to everything, but silent and enigmatic. The Lord starts pacing through the Hall.

"We know the Gelgelians are preparing a big attack," says the young wise man with the long nose and untrustworthy air.

Quick as a flash, the Lord grabs him by the hair. "And I know that your head is not safe on your shoulders, cretin. I don't give a damn for the Gelgelians."

They all remain silent. The Lord lets the wise man go and turns to leave. When he reaches the door, he turns back. "Find me the girl...or both girls," he says, and leaves.

The Lord of Rocdur is thinking, sitting in an armchair in the room at the top of the tower. The torches have burnt out and his

wicked burning red eyes move restlessly in the darkness. The
Lord of Rocdur is thinking about that other world and about
things he has told no one. What has he said to them? That he
went to stay in an unknown world and that he saw a girl who
was in the Valley of Can. That was all; now that fistful of toads
who look after the mirrors have enough to think about. The only
thing he hasn't told them is that it was because of the girl that
he did not finish, once and for all, with the cursed Arnom. As
he was about to say it, he realized he'd had enough of watching
them all tremble at the sound of the insolent rebel's name.

The Lord gets up from his armchair in a rage. The apparition
of the girl in the wood made him lose the opportunity to kill
Arnom! That girl! The same girl who threw a rock at him in the
other world! At him, the Lord of Rocdur! He takes a sword from
the wall and seizes it by the hilt in a powerful grip. He could cut
her in two with the sword; he could strangle her with a single
hand. But how does he find her? He throws the sword on the
table and sits down again, uneasy.

The Lord of Rocdur remembers the unknown world and the
emptiness that surrounded him. It left him baffled for a long time
during which he saw nothing, as if he were made of fog within a
fog, but knowing he was in another world because suddenly the
air cleared and he could see a city with streets filled with snow
and strange carriages moving quickly without horses, and people
dressed in a way he had never seen before... Different kinds of
people, mixing together! Some could even have been Rocdurians,
others looked like Surans, many were like the Maieran rebels,
and many had dark skin like the Foscans. Although he isn't sure
that he saw any Gelgelians, everyone in that world seemed to
use their language - he couldn't speak it, but he could recognize
it. Still, he didn't see anyone with green hair like the Potians,
although some were little and looked like them. And no one
saw him when he came briefly out of the fog and the emptiness,
except for that accursed girl from the Valley of Can, the girl who
threw a rock at him, the girl, right where he was, in the castle
filled with books. Each time he could sense she was around,
almost smell her, even at night, that time in the garden, he knew

the girl was inside the house. If only there hadn't been cats. Cats everywhere. Cats, a whole city filled with cats!

And now the idiots working with the mirrors tell him that there is another girl, who also looks like a rebel, this one blond, and that both of them can see them in the mirror. He takes the sword again. He cannot tell them what he has seen - people mixing together - nor what has happened, and, especially, he can't mention the cats. He must keep exercising absolute control in Rocdur. He strokes the pendant that he wears under his tunic. He has to retain his power.

He turns toward the window and looks at the Town below. It is still in darkness, except for the house of the Chief of the Army where a window is lit up, the window in the Chief's bedroom. That nitwit who allowed the enemy to flee, thinks the Lord, that nervous fool with incurable insomnia! He could get rid of him, but he needs him. In spite of everything, he is a good strategist and leader of men. The Lord is aware that the situation in Rocdur is not as good as it seems: there are constant Gelgelian raids, the lands of Maiera keep up their rebellion, guerilla activity continues in Sura, and illegal Potians arrive by stealth in Rocdur in spite of the executions. He knows that Fosca is arming itself for war more and more by the day and although the Foscans have not said anything to the Rocdurians, in Rocdur it is suspected that they are preparing strong defences against a possible invasion.

The Lord smiles evilly; the Foscans are not wrong. As soon as the Rocdurians crush the rebellion in Maiera they will invade Fosca; they need those prosperous agricultural lands and a sea filled with fish.

And what was that unknown world? Where is it? In the south, beyond Pot and the desert, going far into a turbulent ocean filled with sea-monsters? Or farther than the Sea of Maiera, Fosca and the Islands, navigating toward the east where they say there is nothing but water and stormy raging seas. Or in the west, far to the west, crossing the lakes and the great expanses of Sura to the fog-shrouded ocean that hides no one knows what? Or perhaps far to the north in the land of snow beyond Gelgel? That, if you think about it, seems most likely, since after all the city in the unknown world is filled with snow and its people speak Gelgelian. But, even though not much is known about Gelgel, it is known that no one can live further to the north. It is too cold, even colder than Gelgel. Where is that world? The Lord gets up once more from his chair and goes back to looking out the window. The Chief's bedroom is still lit up.

The Lord strokes the pendant, mentally leaving the unknown world and plunging back into the political complexities of his own. He has to talk to the Secretary and make plans. The Secretary ought to be asleep but that doesn't stop the Lord. He never sleeps and the fact that other people do irritates him. He claps his hands. The two Potians who sleep huddled on the other side of the door appear at once and the Lord tells them to fetch the Secretary.

"Is it true what the wise men have said," the Lord asks the Secretary as soon as he is kneeling in front of him, "that the Gelgelians are preparing a great attack?"

"Yes, Lord. The Keeper saw a meeting of a number of Gelgelian chiefs in the mirror."

"How did we manage to see them?"

"We wounded Calpor and got some of his blood."

"Calpor!" The Lord seems surprised. "When did that happen?"

"During your absence, Lord."

"Why was I not told?"

The Secretary says nothing about the Lord not wanting to listen to the wise men talk about the Gelgelians preparing to attack, preoccupied as he was with finding the girl. He explains diplomatically, "They will have forgotten, Lord. They were very worried about what had happened to you." The words slipped smoothly out.

"How have we managed to get Calpor's blood? We have never been able to wound him."

"You already know that during the battle of the Valley of Can we had army battalions in the north stopping a Gelgelian advance. One of our Surans displayed great valour against the

Gelgelians, even wounding Calpor with his lance. When the news of that deed came to us you had already disappeared."

"Is this Suran alive?"

"Yes, Lord, he survived the battle and is quartered with his horse in the Town stables."

"Let the Suran be given a good meal," says the Lord generously, thinking all the while.

"Yes, Lord."

"So the Keeper of the Mirrors saw a meeting, and with several Gelgelian chiefs, but we do not know what they were saying, since no one understands Gelgelian well enough."

"But yes, we do know, Lord. The same Suran who wounded Calpor was present in the Hall of Mirrors."

"Damnation! No filthy Suran has the right to be present at a reading of the mirrors!" The Lord explodes with rage. In the still dark room the reflexion of his burning red eyes intensifies.

"Lord, his eyes were covered, he could see nothing, he could only listen to what the Gelgelians were saying. The Suran has a perfect grasp of Gelgelian."

"What is this Suran's name?" The Lord seems to have calmed down.

"Tajun."

The Lord says nothing for a moment or two. Tajun can be extremely useful to them. "And the Gelgelian attack. What are they planning?"

"Various Gelgelian clans have united: the *BlackWolf*, Calpor's *OldLand*, the *Newborn*, the *RedSword* and some others unknown to us. They said they hoped to convince other clans to join in on a great offensive against Rocdur. We don't know when or where it will take place."

"Do you have writing instruments with you?" asks the Lord while he thinks.

"Yes, Lord, I do," the Secretary replies, taking sheets of parchment, a pot with leaf juice and a writing stick from under his tunic.

"It's time to start making definite plans. Take down everything we discuss," says the Lord while the Secretary prepares to write. "The Suran, Tajun. We will keep him here to spy on the Gelgelians. When we find out the time and place of the Gelgelian offensive, we will send a large army to the north. The Gelgelians won't expect us to know. The Suran, Tajun, will go under the command of one of our best officers. If this Suran has the skill to wound Calpor, he is indispensable. Let him be treated well until he dies in battle."

"How do you know he will die? He is a skilful warrior."

"He will die. He will be sent to fight at the front and, with luck, he will kill Calpor or another Gelgelian chief. If he comes out of it alive, we will execute him. It is not convenient for us to keep Surans who are too clever. With all his success, he might decide to join the Suran guerrillas. We don't know. In addition, even if his eyes were covered, he knows too much about the mirrors. Is all that clear?"

"Yes, Lord, it is."

"Good. Now, let's move to Maieran rebels and to Fosca..." He stops for a moment. "We need the pirates."

"The pirates, Lord?" The Secretary lifts the writing stick from the parchment. "The pirates from the Islands?"

"And what other pirates are there? Tell me that, dolt?"

"No others, Lord, but how...?"

"They can help us against the Maieran rebels and later with the invasion of Fosca."

"Lord, you can't trust pirates. They go their own way and never collaborate with anyone."

"They will collaborate. We will tell them that they can sack Fosca if they help us first against Arnom. Naturally," he adds, his nasty smile lost in the darkness, "we will never allow them to sack Fosca. They will be exterminated before that. Are you getting this down or what?"

The Secretary goes back to the parchment and suddenly asks, "And how do we get in contact with the pirates? We would have to cross over Maiera first or go by Fosca."

"Which seems easier to you?"

"Going through Maiera is absolutely impossible, Lord. The rebels will never allow us to get to the sea."

"Well, then. What is the answer?"

"Through Fosca? We don't have any treaties with Fosca. They will never allow Rocdurians through their country. As you know, they don't trust us."

"If you think about it, you're not much use, are you? Tell me, what is the only danger that Fosca faces?"

"Us."

"You're right, but up until now nothing has happened, nothing has ever happened between Rocdur and Fosca. It will, of course. Obviously. We will invade them, but they can't be sure of that. Up to now we're not bothering them."

"The danger they face, then, is the pirates."

"Ah - you aren't as dumb as I thought. Exactly. The only obvious danger that Fosca has is the pirates. And it seems they bother them pretty often by attacking the towns on the coast. Although they can't do a lot of harm, since as we know Fosca is well organized, they irritate them and Fosca will never be able to get rid of them once and for all, because they haven't the military power for it."

"We know that they are arming rapidly."

"Because they're afraid of us, not because of the pirates. And more than that, what are they arming themselves with?" The Lord laughs. "Bows and arrows!"

"They have great skill with them, Lord."

"If they aren't much use to them against pirates, they won't be able to do anything against us. Have you got it all down?" he asks impatiently. The Secretary nods "Yes," and the Lord continues. "This is the plan: we will send a delegation to Fosca to convince them that they ought to allow us to travel to the Islands with their ships and thus exterminate the pirates."

"And our supposed motive," asks the Secretary uneasily. "What would that be?"

"That we need the Islands to defeat the Maieran rebels."

"Won't they suspect that we want an alliance with the pirates and not to get rid of them?"

"As you said, you can't trust pirates. The Foscans won't suspect that we want them on our side."

"And if they do suspect?"

"Damnation! Enough!" The Lord slams the table with his fist, making the swords on the wall rattle. "Is that all you're going to do - make difficulties?"

"I am trying to help, Lord."

"All you have to do, idiot, is take notes. The complete plan: we go through Fosca to the Islands, we ally ourselves with the pirates, we fight the rebels in Maiera from Rocdur and from the Islands, we finish off Arnom and his men, we invade Fosca and annex it to Rocdur, get rid of the pirates and everyone in Fosca who isn't any use to us. The fishermen have to be spared. Potians don't know anything about fishing at sea. At the same time we battle the Gelgelians, destroying the offensive they are preparing. Then later we'll see about finishing off the problem of Gelgel once and for all." He made an irritable gesture. "And those tiresome Suran guerrillas. Yes - we'll step up security as of today at the Potian border. I don't want one more miserable Potian in Rocdur!"

"Wouldn't you like to incorporate Pot and extend Rocdur even more? And while we're at it maybe incorporate Sura as well?"

The Lord looks at the Secretary. It is impossible to see what he is thinking behind that impassive face. "No," he says, indignantly. "Certainly not. You don't enlarge a country with rotten territories. Let Pot rot all on its own. Its lands are good for nothing, except for a few plantations in the north; and we really don't want inferior people forming part of our country. That applies to Sura, too. We've taken almost everything from it that we want. But Fosca, now. Fosca will give us wealth, great wealth, and the lands of Maiera with the Islands and the sea - You have all that written down?"

"All, Lord."

"Let the Chief of the Army know that we will need him to finish up things and let him know about the Gelgelian invasion. Also, tell him that..."

There is a knock at the door. The Secretary gets up and goes to open it. Outside is the Keeper of the Mirrors, panting from climbing the stairs all the way up to the tower. "We have found a way of seeing the unknown world," he says breathlessly.

Chapter Five

TAM TELLS A STORY

"Many, many years ago," Tam begins, trying to concentrate. He is tired and the fire in the Chief of the Army's room is making him drowsy. "When Pot was a new country..."

"Why are you messing around talking about Pot?" says the Chief in an angry voice.

"Papa!" Tariana exclaims. "Let him carry on."

"I'm not interested in knowing anything about Pot. Nothing at all," he adds stubbornly.

"Well, I am," says Tariana and Tam notices that she looks annoyed. "I don't care where a story takes place. Keep going, Tam."

The Chief wants to say something, but decides to keep quiet. He may be thinking that Tariana is right and if the story is good - and Tam's are always good - it doesn't matter where it takes place. The important thing is to relax.

"Shall I go on, Chief?" asks the boy. He doesn't want any problems with the Chief of the Army.

"Yes, come on, but it had better be a good story."

"Well," Tam continues, "when Pot was a new country, so new it didn't have a name..."

"It certainly didn't," the Chief interrupts. "We gave it that name."

"Now, Papa, that's enough interruptions," says Tariana.

Tam pulls himself together again and carries on. "In those far-off times, the whole country was covered with jungle and little lakes and marshes up to far away where the desert began, and not like now where there is a lot of desert in Pot. And there were animals everywhere: monkeys and fish and water rats and birds, and there were also little red and yellow fruits like the ones sold in the market in the Town, but there were hardly any people. Just one small group. Those people were like us, the Potians, but they didn't have any hair."

"Ha, ha!" laughs the Chief. "Potians without hair. That's a good one! Ha, ha!"

"Well," Tam carries on, looking at the fire, "those people, the ancient Potians, had a lot of problems because they didn't have hair. Animals spotted their bald heads right away through the green leaves and the Potians found catching them hard work."

The Chief of the Army is smiling. He takes a drink of wine, puts his feet up on a footstool and relaxes, closing his eyes.

"The ancient Potians ate fish and fruit and hunted water rats to eat and also to make clothes from."

"What did they hunt with?" asked Tariana. "Did they have weapons?"

"They weren't actually weapons, because they didn't know anything about weapons. They hunted with ropes made out of water rat skins and fished with nets made out of the same material."

"You didn't know how to make weapons, eh?" says the Chief, while signalling to Ep to fill his cup with wine.

"Well, it would have been hard because the tree branches were either very thin and bent too easily to use or so thick and strong that they couldn't be cut, and in the jungle there wasn't anything to cut them with." Tam waits a moment. Since no one asks anything, he carries on with his story. "They lived in huts made of branches and leaves. It was never really cold at all and so that was enough for them."

"What did they sew their clothes with?" asks Tariana.

"Oh, they were very skilful with little things," he explains, very proud of his people. "They could make needles from the tiny bones of water rats and they used them to cut skins, too, even thin enough to make ropes and nets."

"Since you were so primitive, you must have eaten your meat raw, right?" says the Chief taking a drink of wine.

"Yes," says Tam, feeling his cheeks redden. "In those days we didn't know how to make fire."

"Long ago," interrupts Tariana unexpectedly, "in Rocdur people didn't have metal and were afraid of the dark."

"Tariana!" says the Chief angrily. "What kind of nonsense is that?"

"I read it, Papa."

"Lies out of books. We have never been afraid of the dark and we have always had metal. It's your mother's fault. I used to tell her that you didn't need to learn to read and fill your head with nonsense. Carry on, Tam, and pay no attention to what my daughter says. Women don't understand anything."

Tariana chooses to be quiet, but her eyes are burning with anger. Tam pretends nothing has happened and continues. "As I was saying, the ancient Potians had problems with that business of not having hair because they also had very delicate skin on their heads. They tried to make themselves hats out of skin or from leaves, but the hats bothered them. They only put them on if they were dying of hunger, which was often."

"Things haven't changed much," says the Chief, completely relaxed in his chair. "Potians are always dying from hunger. That's why you annoy us coming into Rocdur like a plague."

"Papa!"

"What, Tariana?"

Tam cuts off the argument at its beginning by continuing his story. "But one day something happened that was worse than not having hair," he says, shutting his eyes to concentrate. "In a small lake in the middle of Pot, near where the Potians were living, there appeared a dragon."

The Chief opens his eyes and sits up in his chair, suddenly tense. "There are no dragons in Pot," he says categorically.

Tam doesn't know what to do, since he doesn't want to infuriate the Chief. "In those faraway times," he points out, "there was a dragon..."

"There have never been dragons in Pot, only in Rocdur," insists the Chief with irritation in his voice.

"Papa, if you don't like the story, I will take Tam to the sitting room below so he can tell me," says Tariana, getting up from her chair.

"No one is going anywhere! And there have never been dragons in Pot," says the Chief again stubbornly. Tariana sits down angrily.

"It was a green dragon," says Tam in a trembling voice, "not like the Rocdur dragons."

"You see, Papa? It wasn't like the Rocdur dragons. It was really different, wasn't it, Tam?"

"Very different. It didn't breathe fire from its mouth and it had black eyes..."

"Did it have horns?" asks the Chief suspiciously.

"Yes, it did, only one, like dragons, but it didn't fly and it lived almost always in the water."

Tam and Tariana look hopefully at the Chief.

"Good," he says at last. "And so it wasn't a dragon."

"More a big green monster that lives in the water and looks like a dragon," says Tam, optimistically.

"A big green monster that lives in the water and looks like a dragon," repeats the Chief, thinking. "Fine, go on."

"That...big green monster seemed very fierce because it had an enormous mouth with a lot of teeth and a huge tail that it smacked down on the water, splashing everything far and wide. The ancient Potians were very afraid and so they ran from there to escape from the... from the big green monster. But they couldn't escape."

"Why?" asks Tariana, intrigued, while grabbing a handful of raisins from a plate and offering some to Tam.

"Because the... big green monster followed them and kept turning up right next to where they were," says Tam while happily chewing the raisins. "People couldn't sleep and spent their nights in terror, and they couldn't hide because the big green monster could see their bald heads. They couldn't hunt or fish either, not even with a hat of green leaves, because the big green monster was faster. He ate the game and the fish with those huge teeth that he had. One day he ate a Potian."

"Ah," says the Chief, slapping his thigh. "The solution to illegal immigration. Big green monsters at the border."

"That isn't funny, Papa," says Tariana.

"Why not? It's the great solution. Come on, Tam. Continue."

"After the big green monster ate a Potian, the Potians decided to go live in the trees with the monkeys and the birds. There they could sleep without being afraid, but they couldn't find food, because even the little fruits were down below. They tried eating leaves from the trees but that gave them stomach aches, so they had to climb down from the trees to pick the fruit. They tried that, and one day the big green monster ate another Potian. And now the ancient Potians had a big problem, worse that not having hair. And even worse, the big green animal spent its nights singing."

"Singing?" says Tariana while setting the dish of raisins between her and Tam; Ep, the Potian servant who is still in the room, no doubt listening to the story, is watching with envy.

"Yes, always the same song, all through the night, so no one could sleep," says Tam rapidly chewing some raisins. "The song goes like this:

I'm the biggest,
I'm the greenest,
I'll eat you
Whatever you do.

That, along with everything else, made the life of the ancient Potians a nightmare. They decided the best thing to do was to head for the desert. The big green monster needed to live near a lot of water and so the desert seemed to be a secure place."

"But in the desert they wouldn't have anything to eat," says Tariana. "Less than when they were living in the trees."

"Maybe not, but they wouldn't be eaten, either, and not being eaten was what they wanted most. And so, the Potians began to cross Pot toward the west, toward the desert. It was what the Potians call The Long Trail." Tam changes position a little and glances at the Chief who is still sitting relaxed in his armchair, taking a drink of wine from time to time. The Potian servant is listening very quietly and Tariana keeps her dark blue eyes fixed on the boy, waiting. "During The Long Trail the women and children went first and the men came behind to protect the weaker ones. From time to time the big green monster, who was following them, ate one of the men, but the group continued forward. One morning, the Potians finally saw the yellow earth of the desert further ahead, and with the feeble strength that remained to them, ran straight for it, leaving the jungles and the water behind. And the big green monster."

Tam takes a drink of water from the cup Tariana gives him and goes back to his story. "There were mountains on the horizon. The Potians put their hats made of leaves on, since the sun was very strong, and walked toward them. When they arrived, they rested in the shade. There were no trees, but there were huge rocks that cast shadows over them. And after resting, they walked around the place and found something that really pleased them. The mountains were filled with caves, some of them very large. They had smooth walls and level floors that weren't too sandy, and they were even quite cool. And besides, they found the best thing of all..." And like the good story-teller that he is, Tam pauses to create suspense and in passing take the opportunity to eat some raisins. When he notices the Chief is shifting anxiously about, he continues. "In a very large, dark cave there was a spring from which water dripped slowly down. They settled there in the mountains."

Tariana gestures for the servant to bring them a dish of apples from the table and gives one to Tam.

"Tariana," says the Chief with his eyes half-closed, watching what his daughter was doing. "You are spoiling the boy." He closes his eyes again.

Tam takes a bite of the apple, chews rapidly and carries on with his story. "It seemed there was nothing to eat in the desert, but in fact there were insects and poisonous snakes. There were black snakes that came out at night from their hiding places and there were yellow ones that came out during the day. Well, after everything that had happened to the Potians, eating insects and snakes wasn't so bad. At first, some Potians died from snake bites, but later they became skilled at killing them by crushing their heads with a rock before they were bitten. When the Potians were asleep they always had someone watching in case a snake came into the caves.

"In spite of the difficulties, they were very well off there in the desert, although their baldness continued to be a problem. The sun was extremely strong and everyone had to cover his head to keep it from getting burned. They did this with snake skin, the material from which they now made clothes and most other things, even though snake skin irritated their scalps, too.

"Did they have to go out when the sun was shining?" asks Tariana as she eats an apple. "Couldn't they do everything in the evening or at night?"

"No," Tam answers, taking another bite of his apple. The interruptions allow him to keep on eating. "The yellow snakes had to be hunted during the day, and they were the biggest ones, and easier to catch because there was light and they could find them in a place where there were plenty of stones. And they often had to go into the jungle as well."

"Why?" asks Tariana again. "Wasn't the big green monster around?"

"Was it ever! He was right there at the edge of the desert waiting for them. He ate a Potian from time to time, but they still had to go to the jungle looking for little fruits because they got tired of eating insects and snakes all the time. And, most of all, they had to fetch water."

"Didn't you say they had a spring?" This time the Chief interrupts Tam, looking at him suspiciously.

"Yes, but it was very tedious getting water from the spring because it came out in drops - drip, drip, drip, all the time, and there was never more than just enough to keep you from dying from thirst."

"Where did they put the water?" asks Tariana again.

"Well, since they were very skilful with little things, now they cut and sewed with snake bones. They did it so well that they could make bags to hold water so that not a drop escaped. But many years passed before they could live well in the caves - if it hadn't been for the big green monster in the jungle."

"Did it live a long time?" inquires Tariana.

"Oh, yes, of course. A very long time. So long that it was still alive when the Potians learned to make fire and built huge fires in front of the caves at night and smaller ones inside the caves, all made with branches and dead leaves that they also went to the jungle to find. And now they roasted the snakes and the insects." Tam is looking at the Chief deliberately without him, however, realizing it. "And they kept themselves warmer, since the desert nights were cold. And while they were seated around the fires, there came from far away the voice of the big green monster singing: 'I'm the biggest, I'm the greenest, I'll eat you, Whatever you do.'"

Tam notices that the Chief has followed the rhythm of the song with his hand and a little smile escapes him. "Many, many years passed with the Potians in the desert caves, having to go often into the jungle where the big green monster was waiting for them," continues Tam. "But then something happened that changed the destiny of the Potians forever."

Tam decides that this a good moment to pause and finish his apple. He chews, trying not to make too much noise since complete silence has fallen inside the room. One would say that the Chief has fallen asleep if it weren't for the wine he drinks from time to time, indicating that he is only relaxing. Tariana has taken off her boots and is sitting in the armchair with her legs crossed, looking into the fire. The servant, resigned, has stopped giving furtive, hungry looks at the dishes of fruit, and stays kneeling waiting for Tam to carry on with the story.

"And that was Nana," says Tam. "Nana was a Potian girl, very clever and very, very pretty." He pays no attention to the sarcastic "sure" from the Chief. "And in addition to that, she sang beautifully. At night, by the fire in front of her cave, Nana sang while her sister played the sweet wood."

"The what?" asks Tariana, shifting her focus from the fire and looking at Tam. "What is that?"

"It's a hollow stick," says Tam. "And it has little holes on top where you put your fingers while blowing through one end. Sweet music comes out the other."

"Give me the music of drums starting off a battle any day," the Chief is heard to say. They look at him for a second, and unanimously ignore the comment.

"All the Potians loved to listen to Nana," Tam continues. "And besides, with the music of Lula's sweet wood and Nana's voice, they couldn't hear the big green monster singing out there in the jungle. After all those years of listening to that irritating song, the Potians were fed up with it. Well, as I was saying, Nana was very clever. She even knew how to paint beautiful pictures on the walls of their caves. First she outlined them with a small stone with a sharp pointed end. Then she painted them with charcoal, snake blood and the juice of green leaves.

"They all asked her to make them pictures in their caves. One would say to her, 'Nana, make me a picture of my children' and Nana set herself to drawing the little ones playing, just as they were. Another would say, 'Nana, draw me a picture of the day we came back from the jungle with so many little fruits,' and Nana drew the group of smiling men loaded down with fruit so well it looked as if they were real. What no one wanted, though, were pictures of the big green monster. In spite of that, Nana asked to be allowed to do some in the cave of the fountain, since she wanted to draw the history of her people. Many Potians opposed it, but finally Nana convinced them all by saying that it was important to draw their history for the future, because however many times it was told around the fire, to have it drawn would mean that no one would ever forget it, even after many years when otherwise they might not remember it."

The fire in the fireplace has almost died. Tam yawns. He is very tired and knows that a good part of the story remains to be told. Ep, the servant, gets up and stokes the fire, making the flames flare up and for a moment light up the faces of Tam, the Chief and Tariana. Tam rubs his eyes and continues.

"Nana painted a huge picture on the wall of the cave, starting on one side of the entrance and continuing back to the spring which was in the middle. She said the other half of the cave was for adding the history of their people yet to come." Tam takes a handful of raisins and chews mechanically as he thinks. "The picture grew very beautiful and explained their beginnings, with the ancient Potians in the jungle, the arrival of the big green monster, the Potians in the trees, The Long Trail, life in the desert caves, the discovery of fire... It was all there. She had painted the Potians red, the caves black and the jungle green, using one green that was particularly intense for the monster. Everyone liked it a great deal, and Nana's parents were very happy to have such a clever daughter. Her mother said that she would make her a pretty dress to celebrate the picture, and her father told her that he would go with some companions to the jungle to look for fruit.

"And so he did, and never returned, because the big green monster ate him."

"How terrible!" says Tariana. "Poor Nana!"

"Soldiers don't always come back," says the Chief unexpectedly. "That is war, my child. But they are remembered."

Tam is surprised that the Chief might have considered, even if it were in his own way, the Potians to be his equals. Without a doubt, he is deep in the story. That is a good thing, a sign that he likes it. And Tam carries on.

"The death of her father caused Nana overwhelming sorrow. That night she walked through the desert toward the jungle and sat on the ground near where the trees began. There, Nana raised her eyes to the sky and began to sing a very mournful song." Tam took a sip of water. "I don't know how to sing like Nana, but the song went like this:

I have waited for you, father, looking far on top of the mountains
where the green breaks forth and light dances on the water.
I have waited for you under the powerful heat that falls from the sun
*   until the first shadows spoke of a doubtful return.*
Now it is night in the desert, and I weep bitter tears that you are gone.

Tam finishes the song and takes another drink of water.

"It's a beautiful song," says Tariana, smiling at the boy. "You sang it very well, Tam."

"I don't think so. I'm sure that Nana sang it better."

"How did you come to know it so well?" asks the girl.

"I learned it from my grandmother. Since she is very old, she knows a lot of things."

"You have a very old grandmother?" asks the Chief.

Tam bites his lip, knowing he has said too much. "Actually, only a little bit old," he says, lying.

"Does she work in the fields?" the Chief asks again.

"Of course she does," says Tariana, lying as well, as she tries to fix the problem that has been created. "I saw her the other day working with Tam and his parents when I rode by the fields. Come on, Tam. Keep going. What happened to Nana?"

The boy gives Tariana a grateful look and goes back to his story. "After singing the song Nana walked almost as far as the jungle and said, 'Goodbye, father.'

"And then, as she was heading back toward the mountains, a powerful voice said, 'Who are you, young woman?' Nana felt a shiver go up her spine but she turned toward the jungle and saw a huge form with a lot of teeth that gleamed in the darkness. 'They call me Nana,' she said in a clear voice, suppressing the trembling of her body. 'You sing very well, Nana. Why don't you sing for me?' asked the big green monster, for it was the monster who was speaking. Nana was filled with great loathing for that monster that had eaten her father and was now asking her to sing. Without a word, she turned toward the mountains, and while she was walking, getting herself far away from the jungle, she heard the strong voice of the big green monster saying, 'Turn back, Nana. Sing for me. I won't eat you. I only want you to sing to me.'"

"What a nerve that green monster had," says the Chief. "Not only does he eat her father, he wants her to sing to him. She never did it, though, did she?"

"Well, let me explain what happened," says Tam and the Chief closes his eyes again, sighing in resignation. "Days passed and then, during the nights, the green monster was heard singing, but it was a different song. Now he sang this:

Tell Nana I wish
she'd sing to me.
I'll stop eating you
if she'd agree.

With the death of her father and the green monster's new song, Nana neither sang nor painted. Her mother and her little sister, who also suffered great sorrow, were made even sadder watching Nana so overwhelmed. She spent all her days in the mountains hitting rocks with other rocks, one against the other, bang, bang, bang, all day long. Little Lula, her baby sister, thought it was a new way of making music, because as far as Lula was concerned, things existed so you could make music with them. Years later, Lula was the first to make music with stones which is a thing that Potians do, even though it's another story."

"Come on, Tam. Drop all this stuff about music and tell us what happened to Nana," says the Chief.

"Well then, little Lula, who used to follow her sister all day, realized that Nana didn't want to make music because now she was polishing a long piece of stone. She wasn't hitting it, but filing it with another stone, from morning to night, without saying anything to anyone. All she did was file the stone. Lula sat near Nana in the shade of a rock and watched her sister file and polish while she played the sweet wood for her. She thought that Nana was going to use the stone to draw with and that made her a little happier. Until one day little Lula discovered that Nana was not polishing the stone to draw with."

"Why was she doing it?" asks Tariana.

"Well - Nana kept filing the stone and from time to time she looked at it and said, 'I have to make it sharper," and sharpened it more. One day around noon, when the sun was at its fiercest, she took the stone and went down the mountain toward the desert. Her little sister followed behind her. When she was at the foot of the mountain, she told Lula to wait for her there and she carried on very slowly toward a pile of rocks. Her little sister was very frightened, because there were snakes in those rocks. Parties of men always went there to hunt and now Nana was going by herself. When Nana arrived at the rocks a huge yellow snake came out, raised itself up by half its length, and opened its mouth wide, darting out its tongue at Nana. She stayed where she was, watching with the long polished stone held tightly in her hand. She began moving extremely slowly, stopping very close to the creature. Then she reached out, inch by inch, inch by inch, until her hand with the pointed stone in it was behind the head of the snake. Lula, nearby, watched her with terror in her eyes, scarcely able to breathe."

Tam pauses for a second and realizes that they are all listening breathlessly, hanging on every word.

"Nana stayed very still," says Tam, "her eyes fixed on the snake. It remained as it was, mouth open, tongue darting out and eyes cold and still. In that exact moment, Lula, filled with anxiety, moved a little and a pebble fell. It rolled toward the spot where Nana and the snake stared at each other, disturbing the snake. In a flash it struck at Nana, but she, faster still, punctured its head from behind with the stone, leaving it nailed to the ground, motionless, dead. Soon she unfastened it, taking the sharpened stone in one hand and the snake by the tail in the other. She went to her little sister, who was staring at her wide-eyed. 'Let's go to the cave,' was all that Nana said."

"A determined girl," says the Chief. "She's like my Tariana."

Tam and Tariana look at each other for a moment and smile. The boy continues. "The Potians couldn't get over the fact that Nana had killed the snake, and like that. They asked her a lot of questions about what had happened, but she said nothing. And that night, while they were eating around the fire, Nana asked her mother if she would make her the dress she had promised her. 'Of course, child," said her mother. A few days later Nana had the dress. It was a pretty yellow tunic without sleeves, falling to the knees, open on each side of her thighs and belted at the waist with a broad black strap. The day she received it, Nana wrapped black straps around one of her thighs, and around her neck she put a thin yellow strap from which she hung the eye teeth of the snake that she had killed. That night she brought everyone together and told them that she was going to the jungle to sing to the green monster."

"No!" exclaims the Chief, sitting up. "Why?"

"The Potians said the same thing, but their protests were useless. Nana said that if she did this, the green monster would stop eating Potians. And that same night, under a sky filled with stars, Nana walked through the desert toward the jungle, accompanied by all the Potians. She walked at the head of the group, her hairless head held high and her stance determined. Her anguished mother was on one side, and Lula on the other, playing the sweet wood and crying. Further back the entire population walked in silence. When they were almost at the jungle edge Nana told everyone to stop. She embraced her mother and her little sister, sighed and advanced as far as the trees. When she got there she said, raising her voice, 'I am Nana and I come to sing to you!' They heard a violent splash in the water and the enormous form of the monster appeared between the trees. "Come here, Nana," said the powerful voice coming out of a mouth full of teeth. Nana slipped into the darkness of the jungle and disappeared from view."

"He didn't eat her, did he?" asks Tariana.

"Well - the Potians stayed there at the edge of the desert a good length of time listening to Nana's beautiful singing, and then returned to the mountains."

Tam takes a drink of water and rubs his eyes again. He is so tired that continuing takes a great effort. "Days passed and Nana stayed in the jungle with the green monster. Just as dawn was breaking, the green monster would wake up in the lake, slapping the water with his tail and singing softly. Then, right away, he would dive. The uproar and the splashing would wake

Nana up and she would kneel on the shore looking into the water. Right in front of her the huge head of the green monster with a sinister smile full of teeth would emerge. 'Sing, Nana,' he would say and she would answer, 'First I have to eat or I won't have the voice to sing,' and she would set herself to eating little fruits while the green monster grew impatient and slapped his tail on the water, leaving Nana soaking wet. When she had eaten enough, Nana would sit down and begin to sing. The green monster would lie quiet in the water, listening without moving. Only the green horn on top of his head, his nostrils and his black eyes were visible. After singing for a long time, Nana would say, 'I must sleep because if I don't sleep I won't have the voice to sing,' and curl up to sleep. If the green monster thrashed his tail around in the water, Nana grew angry and yelled at him, 'Keep quiet. You're not letting me sleep and I won't have a voice!' And the green monster would stop thrashing his tail about and go off through the little lakes and marshes to hunt for a while. Sometimes the green monster came out of the water while Nana was sleeping and stayed by her side watching her or lay down to sleep as well. When it was dark, Nana ate once more, and then sang until late in the night when she would go back to sleep again."

"And during all this time the Potians were going to the jungle?" asks Tariana. She was beginning to look tired, but with a brightness in her eyes that showed more interest in the story than desire for sleep.

"Yes, of course," answers Tam. "They went to the jungle often then, because the green monster never ate another Potian again. They never saw Nana, though, because when the Potians came into the jungle, the monster made Nana climb up on his back and he took her deep into the jungle through the lakes. And so it went until at last came what the Potians call The Day of Blood."

"The Day of Blood?" says Tariana. "I remember when I was young there was a day in the year when all you Potians, before going to work, clapped your hands and you wore green garlands, and my mother said you were celebrating The Day of Blood which was a very old Potian celebration."

"Yes," adds the Chief. "And you made an unbearable uproar. That was why the Castle had to ban it."

"It wasn't an uproar, Father. I remember that it was a very interesting celebration."

"If the Castle prohibited it, it was because it wasn't anything good," says the Chief, partly in anger and sitting up in his chair. "But come along, Tam. Tell us what else happened."

"Well, one day, early in the morning, when the monster began with his tail thrashing and his little songs, he realized that Nana was neither sleeping and nor was she kneeling on the shore of the lake waiting for him so she could tell him that she had to eat or she could not sing. Nana was beyond the shore, standing, her hands on her hips, looking over toward him. The green monster ploughed through the water until he was close to where she was and asked, 'What's going on, pretty Nana? Don't you want to eat?' 'I'm not hungry,' she said. 'Do you want to sing?' 'No, I don't want to sing. I never want to sing to you again.' The green monster slapped his tail on the water in a rage and roared in a voice as loud as thunder, 'You have to sing!' 'Well, I won't sing because I don't like you at all.' And now the monster was really enraged. He came out with a fury of blows of his tail on the water, splashing it everywhere and making the frightened birds and monkeys flee from the uproar.

"After all that slapping of his tail he calmed down a little and asked Nana, 'Why don't you like me?' 'Because you are bad. You have eaten a lot of people. You have no heart.' 'Yes, I do,' cried the monster. 'I don't believe it,' she said. 'I tell you I do have one!' And Nana said, 'Let's see. I want to listen to it.' And the green monster came out of the water and walked over to the girl."

Tam notices that there is a great deal of tension in the room. Even the Chief's tired eyes are wide open looking at Tam expectantly. The boy carries on.

"Nana put her ear on the side of the thick hide of the monster and said, 'You see, you don't have one. I can't hear a thing.' 'That's because it's under me,' said the monster. 'You have to be under me to hear it.' But the monster, as big as he was, had very short legs, and so Nana said to him, 'I don't want to crawl under you

because you'll squash me.' So the monster stretched out on the
ground and exposed his belly where his skin was much thinner.
Nana climbed up on his belly and placed her ear on it, listening
until she found the exact place where the heart of the monster
was beating. And while she was saying to him, 'Of course you
have a heart, of course you do,' Nana was slowly drawing out
the long, pointed stone that she carried hidden under the bands
around her thigh. But as she raised the hand grasping the stone,
the monster lifted his head and saw it. The eyes of the monster
and the girl met in a single moment. Then with astonishing
speed Nana thrust the stone straight into his heart. The monster
had no time to say more than 'oof' and he was dead."

Chapter Six

THE DECREE

No one says a word in the bedroom. Nothing can be heard but the crackling of the logs on the fire. Finally, the Chief applauds, breaking the silence. He is very pleased. "Well, that is something," he says. "What a girl that Nana was. If all you Potians were like her we could give you work in the army."

Tam doesn't point out that maybe the Potians don't want to be in the army and settles down to finish. "Well, after killing the green monster, Nana pulled the stone from its heart and noticed that the creature's blood was green and extremely cold. She had to cross the desert to bring the good news to the Potians and the sun on her head was going to be very hot. Since she was very clever, she put some of the monster's green blood on her head and at once felt a wonderful coolness. Right away she went to the lake to wash the stone and clean the blood from her hands, and then set off on the path toward the caves. Just as she had thought, even though the burning sun was fierce, her head felt cool.

"The Potians hadn't noticed her crossing the desert, but when she reached the mountains, they saw her at last and ran to meet her. But no one embraced her, not even her mother or Lula; they just looked at her in surprise. 'The monster is dead,' said Nana, smiling, but no one said anything. They stared at her as if they hadn't noticed what she had just told them. At last, little Lula moved close to her sister and reaching up, touched her on the head. 'Your hat is made of green eyebrows,' she said. 'Made of eyebrows?' replied Nana. 'No, that's the blood of...' and touching her head, she felt soft fuzz on it."

"It was hair, wasn't it?" says Tariana, her voice full of excitement.

"Yes. She had grown green hair on her head. Since the only hair the Potians had was eyebrows and eyelashes, Lula didn't understand. Well, when everyone understood what had happened, the Potians made a dash for the jungle where the dead green monster was. They pushed and shoved their way in to put green blood on their heads. 'Wash your hands!' yelled Nana, trying to impose order from the top of a tree, 'otherwise you'll grow eyebrows on your hands.' They all did what Nana told them. 'Go out in the sun to dry yourselves off,' she said, and they all did it. Slowly all the Potians developed green fuzz on their heads. A few youths, however, put green blood on their feet and legs as a joke and grew green hair in those places too and laughed their heads off."

"Are there Potians with hair on their legs and feet?" asks Tariana, curious.

"I don't think so. Those were young trouble-makers who ended up leaving the community afterward and were never seen again. Anyway, now the Potians didn't know which was better, the death of the green monster or having hair."

"Did they return to the jungle?" asks Tariana.

"Many went back. Others preferred to stay in the caves, especially now that they could go to the jungle without fear of the monster or the sun. In time, their hair grew long and curly, as it does now, and babies born after that had green hair."

"What happened to the green monster?" asks the Chief.

"They dragged it far away to the south. After a long journey - many days - they came to the ocean and pushed it over the top of a cliff into the water. When it comes down to it, he was returned to the place he must have come from, the Ocean of Monsters."

"And the horn?" asks the Chief. "What did they do with the monster's horn?"

"Nothing," says Tam, shrugging his shoulders.

"They did nothing with a dragon's horn?" says the Chief, surprised.

"Papa," says Tariana, smiling. "Remember that it wasn't a dragon but a green monster that looked like a dragon. There have only been dragons in Rocdur, or have you forgotten?"

"Of course. That's true. The Potians wouldn't be the way they are if they had a dragon's horn."

"Tell me, Tam," Tariana asks him, "did Nana keep on as the leader of her people?"

"Well, for a few years she did, because she had to impose a little order, but when she grew up, Lula became leader of the community. And indeed, to make things short, Nana went to live in the caves and spent the rest of her days painting pictures. She had no descendants. She lived at first with her mother, and when her mother died, she lived alone. Lula, however, had children."

"And are there still Potians living in the caves?" inquires Tariana.

"No. No one has lived there for a long time. Now there is so much desert in Pot that the caves are farther and farther from the jungle. No one has ever gone back." And Tam yawns hugely.

"It's well past time for everyone to be in bed," says the Chief, for whom the yawning is contagious. He is so tired he has trouble getting out of his chair. "It has been a very good story, Tam. Truly very good. Ep, take Tam to the kitchen and let him eat what he wishes before going home. If he's still hungry, because I saw you eating all that time."

The servant struggles up to his feet from the floor, stiff from kneeling for so long. The Chief calls the boy. 'Come here,' he says, opening a box; he takes from it a very small gold coin. 'Take it, it's for you."

"Thank you very much, Chief. Good night," says Tam, full of smiles, and leaves.

The door has hardly shut before the Chief collapses on the bed and begins to snore.

"Go to bed, Ep," says Tariana when they reach the ground floor. "I'll take care of Tam."

"But Tariana, your father..."

"Is sleeping. He certainly needs it. Come on, Ep, go to bed. Sua must be worried."

"Believe me, my wife has been asleep for some time. But, if you wish it... First I must put out the torches."

Tam and Tariana go to the kitchen and the girl puts a walnut cake and a glass of goat's milk on the table. "Sit down and eat. Tell me, Tam," she asks, sitting down beside him, "what happened to Lula's descendants? Do they still rule in Pot?"

"No, Potians have never been ruled like that. It doesn't matter who your parents are, the best person rules and that's it, even though they say that everything is going badly in Pot." Tam swallows a mouthful of cake and looks at Tariana. "All Lula's descendants are called Lula. My grandmother's name is Lula."

"Your grandmother is descended from Lula! Then you are too. And from Nana. That's why you are so determined. Imagine. A Rocdurian descendant of Lula's. How interesting."

Tam stops chewing and looks at Tariana as if he doesn't understand.

"You are Rocdurian, Tam." And seeing that the boy doesn't understand her, she explains. "You were born here, weren't you? Then you're Rocdurian. Rocdurian of Potian origin or Rocdurian-Potian or however you want to put it. There are many Rocdurian-Potians in Rocdur. But don't say that to my father. You know how he thinks."

Tam says nothing and Tariana adds, "You're dead on your feet from lack of sleep. You should go home. Finish that cake while I go down to the cellar for some provisions to take with you. A cheese, potatoes and some eggs would do nicely, wouldn't they?"

Before the boy can answer, Tariana takes a candle and goes down a set of stairs. Tam, still surprised at what Tariana has said, eats his cake. His eyes are half-shut and he's so tired that even chewing is hard work, but suddenly he remembers something. The basket! He left it in the room upstairs and it's the only one they have at home. Without thinking, he leaves the kitchen and tiptoes up to the Chief's bedroom. The Chief is still snoring and Tam retrieves the basket without any difficulty, but as he closes the door again he hears loud knocking down below. Tam freezes. He hears footsteps, probably Ep's, and the squeaking of the main door. He hears a cold voice that seems to drag out every word, saying, "Take me to the Chief's room."

Tam is panic-stricken. What can he do? He certainly can't stay where he is. Near him is a window with floor-length curtains. He hides the basket by a piece of furniture and slips behind the curtains. Through a tiny gap between them he sees Ep climbing the stairs with a candle. A tall thin Rocdurian is following him. Tam can see the scarlet tunic embroidered with a black dragon.

In the kitchen, Tariana has left the provisions on the table and is searching everywhere for Tam when he comes into the room. "Tam, where were you? What happened? Why are you so pale?" the girl asks. Tam sits down on the floor without saying anything and Tariana crouches next to him. "What happened to you, Tam? And what was that knocking? Was it at the door?"

"They have come from the Castle," says Tam in a tiny voice.

"Who has come?"

"He's up there, with the Chief."

"My father is asleep."

"Not any more. He's talking to him."

"This 'he' - who is it?"

"The Secretary."

"What are you saying? The Lord's secretary?"

"Yes."

Tariana pushes the window curtain back a bit and looks out at the street. It is beginning to get light and the girl sees a dozen soldiers in front of the house, dressed in black leather with the scarlet dragon. "Tam," she says, closing the gap in the curtain, "you had better leave right now. There are soldiers outside. Not my father's, but soldiers from the Castle. Do you have something to carry this in? Perfect - you have a basket. I won't give you anything more - it will be too heavy. Come on. Try, Tam. Get up, there now, on your feet! You need sleep. We will go together to the road by a way no one knows anything about. It's better if the soldiers from the Castle don't see you. They don't know who you are and I don't trust them at all."

Tariana lights a torch and turns back to the staircase that leads to the cellar. Tam follows. The girl carries the basket, but even so, she moves so quickly that Tam finds it hard work to keep up. At the back of the enormous cellar sits a worm-eaten cupboard. Tariana pulls it aside and they enter a passage cut out of the rock. Tariana pushes the cupboard back with a bar and closes the entrance to the passage.

"Nobody but me knows about this exit," says Tariana, lighting the path with the torch and and taking lengthy strides. "Not even my father knows anything about it. My mother showed it to me in case I was ever in danger and had to escape. It comes out in the forest near the road that leads to your village. You won't tell anybody, right?"

"No, Tariana, I won't," says Tam, following the girl as best he can.

They keep walking as quickly as possible, saying nothing. The only sound is of their own footsteps; the sharp clap-clap of Tariana's boots and the light scuffle of Tam's feet wrapped in cloth. The passage is dark, with a thick and almost oppressive darkness that is only dispelled in patches here and there by the light of Tariana's torch. Except for one wall covered with a piece of black marble on which a picture has been chiselled, all its walls and the ceiling are made of hard rock. The passage is narrow and twisting as well. One moment it seems to climb, then all at once to plunge. Sometimes it turns sharply to the right and at others to the left.

Tam tries to guess where they are heading, and even though his mind is in complete confusion, he is still able to orient himself skilfully. He knows it's been a while since they left the Town behind them and the soldiers' barracks, passing under the stables with all their horses. In spite of everything above them, down in the passage, he hasn't heard the slightest sound, and still less a voice or the bark of a dog. Right now the boy is certain they are following the road that must be up above them - who knows how far up?

"Tam," says Tariana, while walking, "I'd like you to know that I'm very fond of you and I never want anything bad to happen to you. I remember how we met as if it were yesterday. As small as you were then, you pulled me out of the river. Do you remember? I had fallen off my horse and rolled until I fell into a deep pool in the river. My skirts were wrapped around my legs and I couldn't get out. You threw yourself into the water and pulled me onto a tiny beach."

"I was right there, close by, picking blackberries," says Tam, who remembers the incident very well.

"When my father, desperately worried, arrived with the soldiers, you kneeled and told him very assuredly, 'Chief, my name is Tam and here you have your daughter.' And my father, happy that I was safe, burst out laughing and asked you, 'And what can you do, Tam, other than save girls from the river?' And you said, 'I tell stories. A whole lot of stories, really good ones.' My father had never come across a Potian like you, much less one so young. How old were you? It was three years ago. So I was fifteen and you must have been eight, weren't you?"

"Yes," says Tam, still running behind the girl, and realizing that the passage has been climbing for a while.

"Well, I'm very happy that I fell in the river, otherwise I would never have met you," says Tariana, stopping at last in front of a stair carved in the rock. "Come on. We climb up here."

The stairs end at a flagstone in the ceiling. Tariana pulls a bar and it opens. A little dirt falls on top of them and feeble light enters through the hole. "Up above is the forest. Here! Don't leave the basket behind. When you are up there, I will close it. Put a little dirt on the flagstone. Usually no one goes through the wood here, but in case they do, they won't notice the flagstone."

"Tariana," says Tam in a very low voice.

"What's wrong, Tam? Everything is fine. The soldiers from the Castle are far from here, there are no more patrols of the watch and you're just a moment away from your village. The road is down below."

"Tariana, they want to kill my grandmother."

"What?"

"Potians who don't work will have to go back to Pot."

"That's always been so but they've never worried about old people."

"There's to be a new decree. The oldest Potians have ten days to get out or they'll be executed along with the illegals."

"How did you...? Did you hear what the Secretary said to my father?"

"Yes. It's orders from the Castle," says Tam in a low voice. Tariana went pale. "They will kill my grandmother, Tariana. She can hardly walk. She could never get to Pot in ten days. And even if she did, what would she do there all by herself?"

"Those cursèd men from the Castle. They won't let my father sleep and now they want to kill old people." The girl's cheeks are scarlet with anger. "But don't worry, Tam. We will find a solution. What you have to do now is sleep or you'll get sick. And I have to run back home and see what is going on."

Tariana helps the boy get out with the basket and closes the stone cover. As instructed, Tam puts dirt on it and walks through the wood in the direction of the road. Dawn is just breaking high above the trees, but in the forest everything is grey, diffuse, and dull. Tam wraps his old cloak tight around him. Exhaustion, worry, and the chill of the early morning make him tremble and terrible visions of his grandmother being arrested and executed drain away the little strength he has left. Tariana says they will find a solution. But how? No one can do anything against an order from the Castle.

Chapter Seven

A Mirror Cracks

Anna's Diary, January, 1998
Dear Diary,
Guess what? I think I have a friend now. Her name is Alison and *we share a secret. That means we're friends, even if outside the secret we aren't friends at all.*

Remember the stuff about the 'bruixot'? Well, I haven't seen him again, but two things have happened, just as weird as seeing the 'bruixot'. First the palm of a hand appeared on my computer at school, and Alison saw one too. And the same day she was at my house and a 'bruixot' showed up on the computer in the kitchen. A different 'bruixot'! Instead of having burning red eyes, his eyes were pale and dull, almost colourless. His hair and beard were long, too, but not as red as the hair of the 'bruixot' with the sword and the burning red eyes. Alison and I were totally terrified! Even though it was only for a second, like when the other one appeared, the one with the burning red eyes - there one moment and gone the next.

Alison and I ran to the front hall and my mother had just come home, totally covered with snow. I thought she was another 'bruixot' and so did Alison. She just stood there and screamed. I screamed too, but not as much as Alison, no matter what she says. My mother was so mad when she saw the broken vase in the sitting room, but that's something else. It's not important. We didn't say anything about the 'bruixot' in the computer, because we can't. Who would believe us?

But so far nothing more has happened. It's not because Alison and I haven't spent hours and hours trying things on the computer. Maybe nothing more ever will happen and that would be awful. Then I would never know what all that business of 'bruixots' was about, and I would never be able to understand it.

Now Alison comes to our place after school every day to try things out on the computer. She wanted to get the chauffeur to drive us home but I didn't like the idea. So we walk and he comes here to pick her up - that doesn't bother me. Now Alison wears a thick jacket and snow boots, because the first day she walked over here she nearly died of the cold outside.

Alison's friends are really surprised that she comes over to my house. But that's the only time we're together - when she comes to the house. At school she hangs around with her group like before and tells them she's taking private lessons in Spanish from my mother.

Alison carries on as usual at school. Yesterday at lunch hour she was in the cafeteria with her friends, explaining that she was studying Spanish because she had to go to Mexico with her parents. Cindy, dumb as ever, said to her, "So why aren't you, like, learning Mexican?" And Alison told her she was stupid, that in Mexico they speak Spanish. Alison, actually, isn't stupid. She and the rest of them laughed at Cindy until Cindy was almost in tears and then Alison grabbed her by the shoulder and told her that, no matter what, Cindy is her best friend. And turning to the others said no more laughing at Cindy, because they probably didn't know what people spoke in Mexico either. But when she saw they were sort of hurt, she said it didn't matter, they were all her friends, and she'd bring them presents from Mexico. And turning to the other kids around, she said there'd be a big party at her house and everyone would be invited. I left because I was sick of it all.

And today she was at it again. We were in the hall waiting for Boulder, who was in Skinner's office, and we had the door to the classroom closed. There's this girl, Angela, who hasn't been in Canada long and never bothers anyone. She was at the end of the line and tired of waiting, like everyone else. Anyway, she started singing without realizing what she was doing. Alison yelled at her, "Hey, Angela, keep those tribal chants for the jungle!" All of Alison's friends split their sides laughing, but a lot of kids in the class were upset, even if no one ever stands up to Alison. Only Ryan, who's from Jamaica like Angela, went over to Alison. He was really mad, but Angela asked him to cool it. I went over to Angela and told her not to pay attention to her, that Alison was like that with everyone, and Angela smiled and said she knew that, and added, "I don't know how you stand it," because everyone knows she goes to my house after school.

So we're not really friends, except that when Alison comes to our house she changes a little, she is more normal, and when I see her playing with Puff or totally serious at the computer, which she knows a lot about, I think that maybe she is not as horrible as she seems at other times. What's clear is that I still don't understand her. Maybe she always had too much money, I don't know. Sometimes she gives me the feeling she's bored out of her mind, that she was always bored, and that all this stuff about 'bruixots' is the first time she ever found anything really interesting. When my mother comes home, Alison stays around for a while before leaving and - I don't know - she seems to feel comfortable in the kitchen with us. My mother talks to her in Spanish now, because Alison told her family that's why she comes over here. In a few days she's already learned a little, although she gets confused because my mother and I speak Catalan to each other.

So, diary, I still have no real friends, and now I'm sharing a huge secret with a girl who is impossible to understand. And there's totally nothing about the 'bruixots', and I'm behind in my schoolwork, because I spend all my time at the computer looking for 'bruixots'. Boulder has already complained to Skinner that I don't do my homework, but she hasn't said anything about Alison, who doesn't do hers either. The only person who understands me is grandfather Roger. I like him more than anyone else. He reads a lot and talks to me about stories and other things he's read. He likes taking long walks in the mountains and he always takes me with him. We pretend we're explorers. He loves the same things I do and I'm a lot like him, not in appearance, because I'm like grandmother Maria and my mother, with eyes like my father and grandmother Montse, but in disposition. The trouble is, he's thousands of miles away. Good night, diary.

When Anna got up the next morning and pulled back her curtains, the sky was gradually turning pale blue. After breakfast, it was a luminous, transparent, spotless blue, and the sun sparkled off the dirty snow in the streets. But all the same, Anna dressed more warmly than usual, because bright sunny winter days in Canada are generally freezing cold.

Anna and her mother left at the same time, and as they always did, walked together. Since it was Friday, Nuria asked her daughter what she wanted to do that evening. Usually on Friday nights they made something special for dinner and then watched a movie on video. Saturdays, Anna went to stay with her father.

"What would you like to watch tonight?" asked Nuria. She was walking cautiously, since there were patches of hidden ice.

"I don't know. You choose."

Anna was miles away. At that particular moment she was wondering whether she should tell Alison about having seen the 'bruixot' at the library. She felt a bit guilty about keeping it from her, even thinking that she should also tell her about the dream in the valley. If she was sharing the secret, hiding all that from her wasn't right.

"Anna!" Nuria grabbed her daughter by the arm and pulled her aside. "You almost landed flat on your face on that ice. Watch where you put your feet."

At Spadina Avenue they said goodbye; Nuria preferred to go down the avenue, because it was wide and had been cleared of ice and snow. Anna kept going straight toward St. George Street where the school was. When she got there, Alison's chauffeur-driven dark-coloured car had just parked in front of the building. Anna went over to it.

"Hi, Alison," she said as the other girl got out of the car and waved at her friends, who were waiting for her further away.

"Hi," she said, but she was looking at her friends with a smile on her face. She shut the door, which made that dull, muffled sound that the doors of expensive cars make when they're closed, and turned toward Anna. "I won't be coming to your place today. We're having the Garlands and some family to dinner."

"Fine. Tomorrow, then."

"It's Saturday." Alison seemed impatient to go and join her friends.

"Oh, right. And I go to my dad's, but we could meet Sunday if you want. We don't have to wait until Monday."

"Look, Anna, it'd be better.... I mean I was thinking there's no point in all this stuff with the computer. Like - nothing is happening and anyway, I think we ought to stop."

"Stop? What are you talking about?" said Anna, frowning.

"Like, I'm sick of it, that's what. And there's something else. Probably it was a government thing."

"The Canadian government?"

"Or some other government, maybe the Americans, the CIA, whatever. So goodbye, then. I won't be coming over to your place any more," and making a half-turn, she headed for the building.

Anna stayed where she was. She couldn't believe it. She watched as Alison entered the school laughing with her friends as if nothing had happened, feeling as if someone had punched her in the stomach. Crossing the schoolyard, she felt terribly alone and defeated, on the point of tears. She walked up the three steps to the entrance, opened the door of the building, and went quickly down the hall without seeing anything around her, overwhelmed by a wave of rage that smothered everything else.

Anna couldn't concentrate in Miss Boulder's class. Now and then she glanced over toward Alison's desk. Alison batted her eyes and looked away. Anna could cheerfully have hit her.

"Anna!" called Miss Boulder. "I've asked you twice if you had your homework done."

Anna came back to reality and looked at her teacher with irritation. She was a big, tall woman with a round face, and she was looking back at her, waiting.

"No." Anna almost yelled the word. "I haven't."

"And why not?" said Miss Boulder, her thick legs carrying her toward Anna's desk.

"I was studying computers with Alison," she said. The whole class looked at Alison, who said nothing.

"Oh, yes. And what exactly were you working at?" the teacher asked.

"Well - according to Alison, it was CIA stuff."

There was a moment of silence followed by an outburst of laughter. Except from Miss Boulder, who appeared furious. She put her moon-shaped face right in front of Anna's.

"CIA? And was the vampire also from the CIA?"

"I don't know. Why don't you ask Alison?"

The teacher's little eyes got even smaller.

"Alison," she said, "perhaps you would be better at explaining what Anna is talking about."

"I haven't the faintest idea, Miss Boulder," said Alison, blinking calmly.

"Have you done your homework, Alison?"

"Yes, Miss Boulder."

"Well, Anna," said Miss Boulder. "Do you have something else to say?"

"Yes. I don't give a damn!"

Anna was sent to see the principal. She listened to a speech by Mr. Skinner that made no sense at all and came out of his office into the empty hallway. She saw Alison at the end of the hall, opening the door to the washroom. Typical, thought Anna. Alison always asked for permission to go to the washroom in the middle of a class and returned with her blond hair combed, as if she couldn't wait for the break to fix her hair, thought Anna as she headed for the washroom as well. Opening the door she saw Alison in front of the mirror with a comb in one hand. Alison saw Anna reflected in the mirror and turned.

"What are you doing here?"

"Do you have an exclusive on the washrooms?"

Alison shrugged her shoulders and blinked as usual. Anna said nothing, just watching her and taking deep breaths.

"Know what?" she said finally, her voice shaking. "There is something I haven't told you. About the 'bruixot'."

"Yeah? And what's that?" asked Alison, pretending to yawn.

"After seeing the 'bruixot' in the schoolyard, I saw him in Robarts, the library at the University of Toronto where my mother works."

"And you're telling me now? Why?" said Alison calmly, even though Anna noticed that she jumped nervously for a second. "You just made that up. I can tell."

"You know it's true."

"If it's true then you are totally stupid!"

Alison's image disappeared from the mirror and in its place a hand appeared, covered with mud, the 'bruixot' with eyes like storm clouds, and other 'bruixots', including the tall one with the frightening red eyes. Anna screamed and Alison turned to the mirror.

The 'bruixots' disappeared, the mirror cracked from top to bottom and Alison was swallowed up in the crevice as if she had been made of smoke.

"Alison!" screamed Anna in horror.

Anna took a sip from the glass and pushed it away. She had never liked grapefruit juice. She left it on the little glass table and sank into a huge black leather sofa that made her feel very small. Several hours had already passed since Alison had disappeared and Anna was exhausted. She had been questioned by Miss Boulder, Mr. Skinner, the police, her parents, and Alison's parents, Mr. and Mrs. Walnut. Anna told all of them that she knew nothing about Alison, that she had not seen her since they were in class, and that there hadn't been anyone in the washroom, that she had screamed because she had seen a cockroach, (knowing, however, that it was not a very convincing explanation for her parents) and that she had no idea why the mirror was broken. What could she say to them? If she told them the truth they would think she was crazy and maybe lock her up in a hospital and everything.

Now she was at the Walnuts' house, in a room full of sofas and little glass tables and expensive-looking objects. Her parents were in another room with Alison's parents and a police inspector talking, no doubt, about the two girls, their friendship, and perhaps, even about Anna's 'bruixot,' trying to find something that would help them figure out where Alison was.

Anna didn't like Alison's parents at all. They seemed cold and full of themselves. When Jordi Roig, Anna's father, told them he was a professor of Catalan studies at York University, they looked at him as if they thought his job was weird and totally unimportant.

There was a crowd of people in the house, relatives of the Walnuts, apparently, as well as Charles Garland and his parents. They must have been there for the dinner party that Alison had been talking about that morning. Luckily for Anna, they all scattered into various different rooms in the house and left her there where she was, alone.

The girl in uniform who had brought her the grapefruit juice came in with a tray. "You look bored and you must be hungry," she said, and smiled. "I brought you some sandwiches, but I think you'd be better off upstairs. Come on."

She took her to the top floor, to a room with a television and shelves filled with movies, books and games of all kinds. It was bigger than the room below and a little messier. The girl set the tray on a table. "Tony, come out from there. Come and have a sandwich with Anna," she said and went out.

Anna was left alone and perplexed until some blond hair and then very blue eyes with glasses rose up from behind the sofa. Moments later a boy of eight or nine came out, his hands full of pieces of Lego. Anna looked at him with curiosity. Except for being dressed rather sloppily, he resembled Alison. "Do you like playing with Lego?" he asked.

"Sort of," she said doubtfully. Who was this boy?

"I love it more than anything. Come on and I'll show you what I made."

The boy had built a spaceship behind the sofa and he settled down to tell her about everything he had put in it until Anna felt dizzy, although she had to grant that the construction was impressive. "Aren't you hungry?" asked Anna, managing to interrupt him.

They ate the sandwiches. Anna said nothing, pretending to listen to Tony who never stopped talking about all the things he'd made out of Lego. "I love coming here because they have so much Lego. We don't have enough at home because my parents don't have all this money," said Tony, waving a hand at all the things around them.

"Do you come here often?"

"No. Only for Christmas and when there are special things like someone in the family dying."

"Ah. And today is special?" Anna asked, wondering if there might have been a death in this house.

"I guess so. I think it's something about money, from what I heard my dad say."

"You're related to Alison?"

"My dad and hers are cousins, but I don't think they like each other," he said, biting into a sandwich. "Are you and Alison friends?"

"Yes..." Anna felt a lump in her throat. "Why?"

"You two seem different. Are your parents rich too?"

"No."

"And you don't know where Alison is, do you?" said Tony, finishing off the sandwich.

"No, I don't." She frowned.

With that, Tony got up and went back behind the sofa. Anna had no desire to play with Lego, and so she took a book and sat down on some cushions. But she couldn't concentrate on what she was reading; she was thinking about Alison, the broken mirror and the 'bruixots', and she was seized by fierce anxiety. Was Alison still alive? And if she was, where was she right now? A prisoner of the 'bruixots'? And where were those 'bruixots'?

Tony emerged from behind the sofa. He went through a door to the bathroom and closed it. Anna put down her book, stared at the wall in front of her, and thought. She had to find something that would help explain what had happened. Over and over in her mind she saw the scene in the washroom at school, and each time she recreated it and saw Alison being sucked through the crack in the mirror, the anxiety came back. She felt guilty without knowing exactly what she was guilty of, only that it was her fault.

A loud noise of running water was coming from the bathroom Tony had disappeared into. Whatever was he doing? But she had to concentrate on the 'bruixots'. How could they make themselves appear? It had to be some device for seeing with the palm of the hand. They put the palm of their hand on some thing - did they have computers? - a palm filthy with blood and then with mud. It made no sense. And yet the 'bruixot' with the burning red eyes appeared as if nothing... The noise of water running full blast interrupted her train of thought. It sounded as if the shower was on too. What was Tony doing in there? She went to see.

"Tony," she yelled, banging on the door. The sound of the shower and the taps running stopped and a very wet Tony came out of the bathroom.

"What were you doing?" asked Anna. The boy shrugged his shoulders and disappeared behind the sofa.

The bathroom was filled with steam and there was water everywhere. The bathtub was full and in it floated a ship made of pieces of Lego. "Tony! Everything's soaking wet!"

"I had to test the ship," said a voice from behind the sofa.

"They'll be furious at us if they see all this. Get up and come here. Maybe we can mop it up."

Chapter Eight

THE SHIRT

They had mopped the water from the bathroom floor with a couple of towels that were now hanging in the shower, dripping. Tony was behind the sofa again and Anna was sitting on cushions on the floor, her socks soaking wet. A blond head emerged from behind the sofa.

"Do you want dry socks, Anna? We can probably find some in Alison's room. She has stacks and stacks of clothes. And I'd like to get myself a sweater."

Each time Anna heard Alison's name she was aware of the lump in her throat and her anxiety returned. Still, she hated going around in wet socks and besides, she was curious about Alison's room. "Okay, but won't they mind?" asked Anna.

"What are they going to say? They'll never know, this house is so big."

Alison's bedroom was quite lovely, even though to Anna it seemed cold and too silent. It was like the room of someone who has died, she thought, and realized she was covered with goose bumps. It was huge and had thick wall-to-wall carpeting, pink, to match the bedspread. The clothes closet was a whole room in itself where Tony, who had already found socks, was searching for a sweater. Anna sat down on the floor to put on the wool socks Tony had given her. She looked at the boy - he had already taken off his wet sweater and was putting on one of Alison's - and came to a decision. She couldn't bear the lump in her throat or the anxiety any longer. She had to talk to someone.

"Tony, I have to ask you something. It's just... well, I'm writing a short story - " The boy looked at her with interest. "And - uh... well, I have a problem and maybe you could help."

"Are you a writer?" asked Tony, in amazement.

"No. Not yet, but I want to be," Anna explained without lying. She had always thought about being a writer when she grew up. "Well, then, in my story there is... there is this bad guy who can see people at a distance by smearing blood or mud on the palm of his hand."

"And he sees people by doing that?" said Tony in a tone that suggested that Anna might be better off devoting herself to other things.

"Yes. No, wait, it's not exactly like that. When someone is at a computer or in front of a mirror, sometimes he sees the bad guy appear in it and his hand is placed on the glass, as if he were inside the computer or behind the mirror and there's blood or mud on the hand," said Anna, more exactly. Tony said nothing. "What I can't figure out is how to make it so someone can see him when they want to. Why are you looking at me like that? Don't you like it?"

The boy didn't answer, just kept on looking at her. Perhaps he didn't know how to tell her that the story was really weird.

"Tony, you have to help me. I need to know how to find the bad guy!"

"You have to find him? That... Does that have something to do with what happened to Alison?" he asked without taking his eyes off Anna.

"Just tell me if you can help."

"The bad guy puts his hand..." said the boy after a moment of silence. "Why blood or mud?"

"I don't know! What would you do to find him?"

"Well... Where is Alison?" he asked, looking sharply at Anna.

"I don't know that either! And I don't know how to find her!"

Neither Anna nor Tony said a thing for several minutes; they just stared at the pink carpet, thinking. Actually, Anna was figuring out what step to take next and how much money she had in her moneybox.

"Tony. Help me and I'll buy you more Lego," she said finally. The boy's eyes appeared to be more blue than ever. "No one else can help me. Adults don't understand anything and you seem to be very clever."

"Done," said Tony, smiling. He looked happy.

"Done? What?"

"I help you find Alison and you buy me Lego. How much will you get me?"

"All that I can."

"Cool. So tell me everything that has happened. I won't tell anyone else," he added.

Anna explained only the things that Tony needed to know in order to help her. Nothing about her encounters with the 'bruixot,' only the business of the computers and the mirror. Tony seemed to be very impressed. "And she went through the mirror?" the boy asked.

"Yes, she did. Come on, think. What do I do?"

"Maybe you could try to find her with mud and putting your hand on the computer," he said in an indecisive sort of way.

"Yeah, sure, muck up the computer and ruin it, probably for nothing."

Once again they were silent for a good long time. At last, Tony pushed his glasses up and looked at Anna with the expression of a politician about to announce something of national interest. "Let's go to Alison's bathroom," he said.

"What? Oh, no. I've had enough of playing with water!"

"Not to play. We have to find some of Alison's things. Like they do with dogs when they're supposed to find someone." Tony got to his feet.

Anna followed him to Alison's bathroom, which was bigger than both the bathrooms in her house put together. She didn't quite understand Tony's idea, but neither did she have a better one. Tony emptied the dirty clothes hamper and picked out a gym shirt.

"This ought to do," he said, sniffing the gym shirt and looking disgusted. He gave it to Anna. "It's soaked in sweat."

"And what do I do with it? I don't have a dog."

"It's not for a dog," said Tony with a sigh. "I said it was like what you do with dogs. You have to put it on the mirror."

It was midnight. The witching hour, thought Anna, getting dressed silently. She kissed Puff, who was still asleep, took the bag with Alison's shirt in it, a flashlight, a pair of screwdrivers and the firelighter and crept down the stairs. Her mother slept on. Anna put on her warmest things and, with great care, went out into the front garden and locked the door behind her. The bitter cold out on the street almost made her give up going to the school, but Anna wasn't a girl who turned back once she had made up her mind.

The dark and deserted road lined with bare trees and the fearsomely cold temperature were not enough to stop her. She slipped a couple of times on the ice - the streets were like a skating rink - and gave herself a real scare when she came across a solitary figure sitting in the middle of the sidewalk. It was a woman wrapped up in blankets, a homeless woman who probably hadn't been able to find refuge in a hostel for the poor. Anna thought about the Walnut's house, with so much space and so many, many things in it. But, rich or not, Alison had gone through the mirror and she had to find her, supposing that she succeeded in getting into the school and that Tony's trick worked.

Once she was in front of the school she saw that the first floor lights were on. Would someone be there? What if they had security guards or even police after what had happened to Alison that morning? Maybe they were examining the washrooms and if they were, how was she going to put the gym shirt on the mirror?

She went around to the darkest side of the building, knelt down in front of a basement window, and turned on the flashlight. The window was covered with ice and drifted snow. It was not going to be easy to get it all cleared away without making any noise, but the sooner she started, the better. She did a pretty good job of clearing away the recent snow, but the ice was a lot of work. She melted it a little with the firelighter and chipped away at it with the large screwdriver, stopping from time to time to listen for footsteps. She finished, though, and now all she had to do was take the screws out of the window. That turned out to be harder than getting rid of the ice. She warmed them with the firelighter first and then tried to draw them out immediately with the screwdriver. She had to take her thick gloves off to work, then put them back on when her hands began to freeze, and carry on like this for what seemed to be forever. After taking out the first screw she was dripping with sweat in spite of the cold. Luckily the window was flimsy and she finally opened it enough to slip into the building.

As she advanced along the first floor corridor she heard voices coming from the principal's office. The door was open a crack and to get to the washrooms Anna had to go past it. She was startled to recognize the voices of Mr. Skinner and Miss Boulder talking in a way she had never heard before. Just as Anna was crouching behind the door, Mr. Skinner was saying, "Jenny, darling, don't take it like that. How many times do I have to say it? Let me explain - it would look really bad."

"I don't know why. The fact is you don't love me," said the voice of Miss Boulder.

"Jenny. Have I explained it to you or haven't I explained it to you? Of course I love you, but I can't marry a teacher in my own school. It would look - well - bad."

"Since you've explained it so much, try explaining it better."

"It would look bad to the students and their parents. Shall I explain?"

"Yes. Explain!"

Anna could just imagine Miss Boulder's round face going scarlet with rage. Even though that was an amazing conversation and totally interesting because of who was speaking - good Lord, Skinner and Boulder - all those "explanations" were a bit sickening. And more than that, Anna wasn't there to listen to what that pair of idiots had to say to each other. She slipped by on the other side of the corridor, hoping that they would neither see nor hear her. Past the principal's office, she straightened up and going on tiptoes, arrived at the washrooms.

The light was on and the cracked mirror was still on the wall in front of the door. Seized by fear, she half-closed the door and went up to the mirror. She pushed her hat back from her forehead, undid her scarf, put her gloves in her pocket and ran her finger down the crack. It was deep and Anna could feel the roughness of the wall behind the mirror. She looked at herself and her heart skipped a beat. The crack parted her face in the mirror like a crude knife wound. She swallowed and moistened her dry lips with her tongue. She could hardly breath. But in spite of everything, and without thinking any further, she took Alison's smelly gym shirt from the bag and - her mind made up - put her hand with the gym shirt over the crack in the mirror. She closed her eyes. Nothing happened. Anna sighed, closed her eyes again and tried to concentrate on Alison's image. "Where are you, Alison?" she said softly. "Shirt, take me to Alison, take me to Alison." She heard footsteps in the corridor. Anna opened her eyes. The footsteps drew near. Panic-stricken, Anna kept her palm on the crack in the mirror, whispering and focussing on Alison.

The door opened and Miss Boulder appeared reflected in the mirror. She stayed where she was with her mouth open, staring at Anna, who was still whispering, her hand and the shirt on the mirror. At last, Miss Boulder reacted, and with two strides of her massive legs, seized Anna by the scarf. Anna closed her eyes.

"What the devil?" said Miss Boulder.

Anna smiled without opening her eyes, feeling, not Miss Boulder clutching her by the scarf, but a force swallowing her violently inside the mirror. The scarf untwisted itself while Anna was sucked further and further inside. She felt she was passing through a narrow tunnel, drawn by a force that pulled her head first. She opened her eyes for a moment and saw only her hand with the shirt; everything else was in darkness. Suddenly the force pulling her stopped, and Anna found herself lying on her stomach on the floor in someplace very dark. She didn't have the strength to move, as if that force that had swallowed her had taken all her energy. And then she realized that she was falling asleep.

Anna woke up and, for a moment, didn't remember anything of what had happened. She thought she was in bed at home, but something seemed different. She opened her eyes wide and in the dusk saw that, yes, she was in a bed, but it certainly wasn't hers nor was she in her own bedroom. The bed was actually a mattress on the floor. Close by there was a window, but its shutters were partly closed to allow only a little light to come in. Then she remembered that she had been sucked in by the crack in the mirror. She got up at once. Feeling her way over to the window, she opened the shutters. The day was beginning to grow bright. Beyond the window she saw sky and water; the air carried with it the unmistakable smell of the sea. Anna couldn't believe it. The sea! There was no sea in Toronto and more than that, at the foot of what seemed to be a hill, she could see strange houses everywhere. And it was hot! Where was she?

She turned around and saw her boots at the foot of the bed and on a sort of low wicker rocking chair were her jacket, hat, gloves, socks and thick sweater, as well as the bag and Alison's gym shirt. The room was elliptical in shape and on its white walls were little ceramic candle holders with candles, surrounded by shells set in the form of a spiral. The bedclothes were white too, and the shutters and a closed door were of light wood. The floor, very clean, was made from reddish tiles. None of it could be true.

She turned to look out the window. The sky was now covered with pale pinks, faint blues and wisps of yellow dispersed over a calm, pale green sea where boats were sailing. White birds, perhaps seagulls, soared and cried up and down. At the foot of the hill, toward the right, there was what seemed to be a port where people painted boats and mended nets. The city, or town, or whatever this was, had narrow cobbled streets and the houses were painted in pale colours. But they weren't houses like any that Anna knew. All these were round, or rounded and on top of each one there was a cupola.

She heard the door open and froze, tense, where she was. Would it be the 'bruixot' with the burning red eyes? But the person who entered, standing in the doorway, was a woman with straight black hair wearing white trousers, a yellow sleeveless shirt and sandals. Her facial features seemed oriental.

"You're awake!" she said in Catalan, although with a rather peculiar accent. "You don't understand what I'm saying, do you?"

"Yes," said Anna. "Of course I understand."

"Well - imagine that," said the woman and gestured with her hand, as if to invite someone to enter.

In came Alison. She looked well, although a trifle dazed. The two girls stood open-mouthed at the sight of each other. Then the moment of surprise passed and they ran and gave each other a hug.

"I see you know each other," observed the woman, throwing Anna's clothes on the bed and sitting down on the rocking chair.

"Yes," said Anna.

"Can you understand what she's saying?" asked Alison.

"Of course. She speaks Catalan," said Anna in English.

"Perfect," said the woman. "I see that you speak the language of the other girl. Now we will be able to clear everything up. Who are you?"

"She's Alison and I'm Anna."

"Ah, very good. Very good indeed," said the woman while she rocked back and forth on the chair. "And I'm the witch Ling."

Chapter Nine

THE KINGDOM OF MAI

Anna froze in shock. A witch! Now they were really done for! And the 'bruixot' with the burning red eyes was probably close by. Except that, if you thought about it, the pleasant-looking woman in the summery clothes who was rocking back and forth on the rocking chair did not seem in the least intimidating nor did she seem to have anything to do with the burly man with the bloody sword and the ferocious look.

"What did she say?" asked Alison in a tiny voice.

"That she is a witch and her name is Ling." Alison opened her eyes wide; the woman watched them for a moment and continued rocking. "But she doesn't look like one to me."

"To me neither. Do you mean you understand her?" Alison's voice had lost its usual confidence.

"Yes. I already said she speaks Catalan. Listen... what are you doing here? What happened?"

"I don't know." Alison looked nervously over toward the rocking chair, although the woman had closed her eyes and seemed miles away from the two girls. "Something swallowed me up through the mirror and I fell asleep. When I woke up I was in a room like this one and tthat woman was looking at me.

She kept saying things, but I couldn't understand a word. After that another woman came in bringing me oranges and saying more things I didn't understand."

"But you were well treated, right?" asked Anna. She wasn't quite convinced that the woman was a witch. Maybe she hadn't understood her very well.

"Well, yes - although they kept me in that room all day with a whole string of women coming and going and saying things I couldn't understand."

"Why are you wearing those clothes?" said Anna. She had just noticed that Alison was wearing pants and a summer shirt and sandals.

"They gave them to me when they noticed that I was really hot. The shirt and the pants are like, kind of cheap and ordinary-looking, but the sandals are cool, aren't they?" she said, showing them to her.

Anna hid a smile. She could imagine how terrified Alison must have been - swallowed by the mirror and then finding herself in a strange place surrounded by people who spoke a strange language, but even so she looked pleased, showing off the sandals.

"Later," said Alison, "they came back with things to eat; fish and something I think was seaweed that I didn't eat because I didn't know what it was. They also took me a couple of times to a sort of bathroom they have on the ground floor and they gave me a toothbrush and a comb. I have it here in my shirt pocket..."

"They have a bathroom?" asked Anna, thinking that Alison must have spent an hour in there fixing her hair.

"That's what they think," said Alison with an expression of scorn. "It has a really cloudy mirror and like, a sort of bathtub only it was more like one of those antique laundry tubs. They use it as a bathtub, a shower and a washbasin."

"And toilet?"

"Awful!" she said with a shiver. "A hole in the floor."

"Do they have running water?"

"Yes. You could call it that, only it comes out in a trickle. If you wanted to take a bath you'd have to spend all day filling the tub.

Well - when it got dark, after they brought me some fish soup," they lit a couple of candles on the wall and that woman," she said, nodding at the woman who was still rocking with her eyes closed, "made gestures at me to get into bed and sleep and went away, closing the door. It wasn't locked or anything, because I opened it later, but I went back inside because it was totally dark. I couldn't sleep and time was passing. I couldn't go out through the window either, because this house is on top of a hill and it's really far down to where there's a sort of town..."

"I just saw all of that."

"So, I was in bed hearing voices and music in some place in the town and the noise of the sea. Did you know that's the sea?"

"Yes, of course. Keep going."

"Well, then, I finally fell asleep and now that woman woke me up and... What are you doing here too?"

Anna described everything that had happened from when Alison went through the mirror until she arrived at the point where Anna and Tony were at her house and she asked the boy to help her.

"No! You told that little brat what happened?" Alison exclaimed.

"Not everything. Besides, he doesn't know that the 'bruixot' appeared in the schoolyard. And no matter what, he won't say anything and it's thanks to him I'm here," she said, looking at the other girl with an angry frown.

Alison's expression softened and her eyes seemed to turn a deeper blue, reminding Anna of Tony when she told him she would buy him Lego. And Anna continued her story explaining how she got out of the house in the middle of the night and succeeded in breaking into the school without anyone hearing her.

"Skinner and Boulder?" said Alison, laughing when Anna described the conversation she had heard at the school. "So that's why Boulder is always in Skinner's office."

When Anna finished her tale, Alison didn't seem to know what to say. "Thanks," she said, weakly, and turning red. "For...

for everything you've done. I didn't want to believe that about the 'bruixots', since nothing else had happened..."

Anna would never have expected that much from Alison. Who knows, maybe it was the first time she had ever thanked anyone. "I didn't tell you that the 'bruixot' appeared to me in the library. I'm sorry."

"Stuff happens," said Alison, shrugging her shoulders and looking over at the woman. She had kept going back and forth on the rocking chair during the whole conversation.

Anna looked at her as well. She seemed miles away in thought with her eyes closed. But she realized they had stopped talking and opened her eyes. "Who are you?" she said, out of the blue.

"Alison and Anna," said the latter.

"Oh, yes. That's right," she said as she got up from the rocking chair and went to look out the window. "It's a splendid day, don't you think?"

"Yes," agreed Anna, and asked tentatively, "Uh - where are we?"

"At my house," said the woman, surprised.

"But... where is the house?"

"By the sea. Can't you see it?" she asked, pointing out the window.

Anna, who was translating all this for Alison, tried again. "What is this place called? We don't know where we are."

"Oh, of course. I forgot you don't come from here. This is the kingdom of Mai. And you, where are you from?"

"The city of Toronto."

"And where is that city?" she asked, frowning.

"In Canada."

"And what's that?" She seemed really surprised.

"A country. Canada. You don't know it?"

"No. I haven't the slightest idea where that country is. Imagine that. I thought I knew them all. Perhaps the queen will know something about it. And what are you doing here?"

"We don't know."

"Really... Well, all I know is that you both appeared in the cellar of my house with a huge amount of noise. Just imagine what I said to myself: 'Oh, dear, the shelves in the cellar have come down.' I went down there and I found myself with a girl with yellow hair sleeping on the floor. And then at night it was you who gave me a scare with all the noise. But that's how it goes. That's why I have a cellar, so sleeping girls can appear in it." Ling gave a little laugh.

"What is she saying? What is she saying?" Alison kept asking. Anna translated as fast as she could. "Now ask her if it's true that she's a witch."

Anna did it a little uncertainly.

"Yes, of course. I'm Ling, the witch of Mai. What a strange question," she said, and right then, a couple of women who resembled Ling came in with platters of peeled oranges and dates.

"Thank you. We'll talk later," said the witch Ling to the two women and took some dates. The women smiled at the girls and went off chattering. "Come on, have something to eat. Do you like orecs and sweetfruits?"

"What?" asked Anna.

"Orecs and sweetfruits," said the woman again pointing at the plates.

"Oranges and dates?" asked Anna, sitting on the bed beside Alison.

"You're not making sense," said the witch, taking an orange.

For the first time Anna realized that, even though Ling spoke Catalan, there were things that they called by other names entirely. And by asking and asking, while translating for Alison everything the witch Ling said, she learned a lot. The country they were in, Mai, was ruled by a queen of great age. She lived on the opposite side of the sea, which was enclosed, like a lake. And Anna also discovered that the queen spent her time studying a great variety of subjects, because there was nothing else that she had to do. In Mai, things moved along pretty smoothly. Only occasionally did the queen intervene, if there was a dispute between the speakers, as the members of the government were called.

Anna also discovered that in Mai the majority of speakers,

one of whom was the witch Ling, were women. Of the ruling council of twelve, ten were women and, moreover, the majority of important decisions were made by women. According to the witch Ling, it had been like this for centuries.

"A long time ago, when men ruled, we had an army," explained Ling, "and we were always fighting with everyone. Now we have neither an army nor wars. In fact, no one knows we exist, and even if they knew, they could never reach us across the desert."

The girls were confused. They didn't know enough history to fit what she was saying into anything they did know. But they had studied a whole lot of geography and now they were trying to figure out why they had never heard anyone speak about the place; with all the satellites overhead, how could Mai hide?

"Ask her where Mai is," said Alison, as she ate an orange delicately. "North, south...?"

It was hard to translate, eat, and try to understand everything the witch Ling was saying at the same time, but Anna did it.

"In the south," said Ling.

"South of where?" asked Anna insistently.

"South of the known world, touching Pot to the east and Sura to the north, but because we're surrounded by desert no one knows we're here."

Anna translated it for Alison and neither of the two said a word, but looked at her in amazement. What was this woman talking about? Where were these places?"

"The known world?" said Anna finally while helping herself to an orange. "What does the known world mean?"

"Well - all the countries. You know - Mai, Pot, Sura, Fosca, Rocdur, Maiera and the expanses of Calai, or as it's called by those who don't come from there, Gelgel.

The two girls had a morning full of surprises. Right at the start, with everything thrown at them at once, they were in a state of total confusion, but little by little they began to relax and, without a doubt, even began to enjoy being in that strange place called Mai. Apparently everyone here spoke Catalan, although Ling told them that she didn't know what this "Catalan" thing was. They spoke the Common Language, the language that everyone in the world had spoken for centuries, except for Gelgel where they spoke something else. And Anna went on translating it all for Alison.

When they had eaten, the witch told them she was taking them to see something beautiful and then in the afternoon they would go to see the queen who, maybe, could shed some light on why the two girls appeared in her cellar.

"I didn't take her there yesterday," said Ling to Anna, pointing at Alison, "because she seemed too frightened and also, she didn't understand us."

One of the other women came in again and led Anna to the bathroom, having given her trousers made of undyed cloth that were fastened around the waist with a sash, a blue shirt with pockets like the one that Alison was wearing, sandals that were tied around the ankles, a toothbrush and a wooden comb. The place was just as Alison had described it, except that it was spotlessly clean as well.

The witch Ling's sisters - the other women who lived in the house - seemed very pleasant. They gave the girls big straw hats, saying they were pale and, without them, would get sunburnt. And dressed like that they went with Ling through the streets of what turned out to be a small city. More than once someone stopped to speak to the witch, asking her where the girls had come from, and Ling said the same thing to all of them, "From my cellar," and kept on walking.

Anna and Alison realized that everyone wore sandals, shirt and trousers, which many had rolled up to below the knees. They also noticed that many of the people looked, like Ling, rather oriental, although not everyone. There were people who appeared to be a mixture of more than one race, although there were no blondes, and so a lot of people stared at Alison. The ones they really noticed were those with green hair. Alison said it was dyed. No one seemed to them to be very strange, though, except for two boys who played the flute and a girl who played a sort of guitar. They were seated in a small plaza.

"Hey, Alison, look at them," said Anna, pointing to where the music came from. "They all have green hair on their legs and feet."

"They're wearing boots," said the other girl.

"From time to time a child is born like that," said Ling, when she realized what the girls were looking at. "According to the queen, many years ago some Potians with green hair on their legs and feet came to Mai. The other people from Pot only have green hair on their heads. And although just about everyone here is of mixed ancestry, with some Suran and Potian ancestors, no one has a characteristic personality connected with the way he looks. Except that children born with green hair on their legs and feet are always very mischievous."

Anna translated that for Alison and got the idea that the other girl wasn't particularly convinced, neither by that nor by many of the things that Ling said and Anna translated. Although Anna had no doubt that they were in a different place, outside of the world that they knew, Alison kept on stubbornly saying that they were in some hidden spot in our world and that in some way that maybe science could explain, they had managed to end up here. For Alison many of the things that Ling described were merely legends that these people must have.

Ling said that they would walk to the stable outside the city, since where they were going was too far to get to on foot.

"There must be horses. I'd love to go riding," said Alison, full of animation, and added, batting her eyes, "I'm good at it. Ask her if we're taking horses."

Anna liked the thought of riding a horse, even though she only knew a bit about it. She translated the question for Ling who just said, "What's this about "horses"? We will be going by 'raster'." And she described what seemed to be some kind of cart. "A 'raster' pulled by a mouse."

"A mouse!" exclaimed Anna, stopping and translating for Alison, who first of all opened her mouth and then broke out laughing. Anna also started laughing.

Ling stared at them, puzzled. When Anna was able to stop laughing and describe a mouse, Ling also burst out laughing.

"That's a 'queeter'," she said. "No, obviously we're not going by 'queeter'."

Once she had explained what a 'mouse' was, the girls thought that it was probably a horse. Alison didn't care much for the idea of a cart.

The road toward the outskirts was long because Ling kept losing her way. "You do realize that we're going toward the sea?" said Anna, and Ling turned around.

"We've gone by here at least twice," said Alison, and when Anna had translated, Ling giggled and changed direction.

The problem didn't seem to be that Ling couldn't find her way around; it was more that she appeared to be very absent-minded. Anyway, the long tour gave them a really good chance to see that the city was a series of little streets joining little open squares. Once, though, they came to a spacious plaza surrounded by round buildings that were very much bigger than the houses. Ling explained that they were government buildings and the yellow one was for people who for some reason or another had been left without a place to live.

"Aren't there people here living on the street?" asked Anna.

"Of course not! What are you thinking of! What a thing to say, people living on the street! Do you think we're animals here? There, you see that blue building with the garden where boys and girls are playing? That's our school." And she told them they studied a bunch of different things there, with some girls studying witchcraft so they could become witches like her.

"And what do the witches in Mai do?" asked Alison in an incredulous tone. "I don't see that Ling does anything in particular. Go on, ask her."

"We make potions," said Ling to Anna who translated it to Alison; and seeing Alison's expression of incredulity, she added, "and do other things."

All at once, she rose up a couple of metres from the ground, staying up for a little while; from there, she greeted a man who was heading toward one of the buildings. "Good morning, Speaker Ping."

The man stopped for a moment, looked at the girls, looked

at Ling up there and sighed. "Good day, Speaker Ling," he said coldly, and carried on toward the building.

When she came back down to earth the two girls looked open-mouthed at Ling.

At last they arrived at the stable outside the city and saw what the witch called 'mice.' They were donkeys, not horses. Ling climbed up into a carriage pulled by a 'mouse' and took the girls far from the city. They passed through leafy orchards where the air was filled with the smell of oranges, up to a road that took them beyond the orchards, across fields with small trees, brush and flowers toward a wall which could be seen in the distance. When they drew close, the girls realized it was not an ordinary wall. Not only was it very high, but it also stretched out on both sides as far as the eye could see, with towers built into it at intervals.

On reaching the wall, Ling got down from the carriage and, opening the door in one of those towers, urged the girls to follow her. Inside the tower was another door, as well as a staircase which they climbed. At the top they found themselves in a square room with two big windows. Through the one looking south they saw the fields they had driven through, some indistinct cupolas in the city and what must have been the sea further beyond. Toward the west there were low mountains, and to the east more fields and palm trees. Then Ling made them look through the window facing north. Beside the wall the land was filled with flowers, shrubs and little trees like those on the other side, and much farther on stretched a desert.

"Tell her it all seems very nice," said Alison. "What else is there?"

"This wall," explained Ling in answer to the question, "encloses all of Mai up to the sea."

"Impressive," said Alison, looking bored. "And now what?"

Ling reached into her shirt and pulled out a flute that was hanging from a cord around her neck. She began to play a melody. Anna thought that maybe there were more urgent things to do than listening to music while looking at a distant desert - like going to see the queen and finding some way of getting home - but she didn't dare say anything.

The girls didn't see them until they were very close. Between the shrubs and brush on the desert side lions appeared. Very yellow lions, of a yellow that gleamed like gold. There were a whole lot of them, all roaring from the other side of the wall.

"Stay here," said Ling to the girls as she went down the stairs, leaving them where they were. With a shiver of fear they saw her go out through the door on the desert side. The lions came up to her and Alison gasped in fright from the top of the tower. But the lions lay down on the ground with their bellies in the air and Ling patted them as if they were kittens. After a while she returned to the girls in the tower. They stared at her, appalled.

"Are they all lionesses?" asked Anna at last in a tiny voice without taking her eyes off the huge ferocious-looking beasts; for none of those lions had manes.

"Are they what?" asked Ling.

"Are they all females?"

"Why?" said Ling. "No, obviously not. There are males and females. The babies are farther away under the trees."

"They don't have manes," Anna said stubbornly.

"Cats with manes?" Ling began to laugh. "Where have you seen anything like that?"

"What are you saying? what are you saying?" said Alison and as always Anna translated.

"Those aren't cats," said Anna, looking at the huge animals and frowning. "They're lions."

"If you want to call them that..." Ling shrugged her shoulders. "Well, beautiful, eh? I love them so much. Right. Here we are. We have to go home before going to see the queen. I've already sent her a message."

"Why are they such a gleaming yellow colour?" asked Anna as they were going down the stairs.

"Because they accumulate moisture in their fur. So, if necessary, they can go for a long time without drinking."

On the return trip Ling told them that there had been a 'cat' that she had been very attached to, but that almost a year ago pirates had stolen her.

"Pirates!" said Anna, while Alison asked, "What's she saying, what's she saying?"

"You didn't tell us there were pirates in Mai," continued Anna.

"They're not from Mai! They're pirates from the Sea of Maiera and Fosca."

"But didn't you say that no one knows that Mai exists?"

"Pirates don't count. They don't deal with anyone except to rob them. Besides, as far as we know, they have only come to Mai twice, both times in the last hundred years. The attack a year ago was the second one. And anyway, this time none of them survived either. They all drowned in the Ocean of Monsters."

"Of monsters!" said Anna again and Alison repeated, "What is she saying? What is she saying?"

And so, at the pace of the carriage, on the return to the orange groves and the city, Ling told the story of the lions and the pirates, while Anna acted as interpreter for Alison. According to Ling, the pirates turned up from the east, where the Mai and Pot deserts meet. It was surprising that they had crossed the Ocean of Monsters, getting all the way to an inlet right by the desert, without being eaten by sea monsters. They left the ship in the inlet and equipped with swords, nets, ropes and sacks they scaled the wall and reached the city of Mai. The Maians, however, had already seen them coming and everyone went to the fortifications on the other side of the enclosed Sea of Mai, where the queen lived. The Maians had brought all their boats with them, and the pirates discovered that they had no way of crossing the sea, because they had no boats, nor could they climb the inaccessible walls that closed off the sea on each side. They resigned themselves to sacking the market, houses, government buildings and orange groves. They didn't do much damage because there weren't very many of them and they couldn't carry much back to their ship. In revenge they set fire to a few houses and a government building that have been restored since then. As well, from the wall that separated them from the lions (or 'cats' as Ling called them), somehow, maybe with nets, they captured a lioness and took her away. What they wanted to do with her, no one ever knew, but Ling suffered much unhappiness because of it, since she was her favourite lioness, and more than that, she was expecting cubs.

"Poor thing," said Ling, sighing, while they passed through the orange groves. "Probaby she died when the pirate ship broke up on the coast of Pot."

"How do you know that it was wrecked?" asked Anna.

"Well, later on I saw two pirates half-eaten by cats and I realized that they had taken away the cat. I flew over the ocean looking for them and found their ship in pieces near the coast of Pot.

"She flew?" said Alison after hearing Anna's translation.

"So she said. Maybe she has a broom."

"Come off it, don't be stupid."

"Or maybe she doesn't just rise up from the ground, but she can fly too."

"I've made a mistake," said Ling, interrupting the girls' discussion as she turned in another direction between the trees. "I was going to go straight into the city, but first we have to go to the stables. 'Mice' can't be brought into the city; they get the streets dirty and it's dangerous for people if 'rasters' go through the streets. They can only come in with goods that are being taken to the market early in the morning. Good heavens! There I go, heading back to the wall again."

Chapter Ten

THE MUSICIANS AND THE QUEEN

It was past noon and the girls had gone back to Ling's house for lunch - really good fish cooked with seaweed and little cakes made with honey and some kind of almond as well. Like everyone else, they ate kneeling at a big low table on a terrace under the cupola at the top of the house. Ling's sisters chattered constantly, and it was difficult for Anna to eat and keep on translating the chaotic conversation for Alison. They were arguing over the best way to prepare fish, along with whether Speaker Ping, who wanted to give permission for 'rasters' to enter the city any time they wished, was right or not. Anna tuned out of the conversation; Alison had already appeared withdrawn for some time. It was pleasantly cool here and there was a view of the sea. It would not be entirely bad if they could never return home and had to stay in Mai forever, thought Anna, who had been wondering all day how they would manage to get back. But she was growing sad as well, thinking of her parents.

"So," said Ling, getting up. "Let's go. Come on, we're off to see the queen."

An old man called Tian, the queen's messenger, took them

across the sea in a small fast sailboat. Alison, who knew how to sail, asked if she could help and seemed happy doing so. Anna and Ling enjoyed the crossing.

"Ling," said Anna, looking into the transparent water where from time to time she saw a school of colourful little fish go by, "there aren't any monsters in this sea, are there?"

"Certainly not. The Sea of Mai is completely closed off, except for narrow pipes that only water and tiny fish can get through. It's an amazing piece of work. If we had time I'd show you the whole thing. Where we are going now, where the queen's house is, is in the middle, but the fortifications that close off the sea stretch way out there on each side and turn to join with the wall that separates us from the desert. If you look over there, you can just see it."

Very far off, under the glare of a sun that seemed to break up the sea into an infinite number of fragments, there was drawn a dark line that followed the horizon. A gentle wind raised little waves that hit the keel and filled the sails pushing the small boat toward that dark line in the distance.

"It's a fortification that has existed from the days when we had an army," said Ling, carrying on with her explanation. "It was an idea of the men who ruled then, a brilliant idea, I must admit. The wall separating us from the desert and from the 'cats' was also one of their projects. In that case they did it to protect themselves from possible attacks from the country of Sura, but it is very good for us so the 'cats' won't bother us nor will we bother them. Not everyone can handle them, only witches. In those days though, there wasn't as much desert in Sura or in Pot. Pot in particular has suffered severely from the spread of the deserts. That's why no one comes here from those countries any more. For us, it's good, because they leave us in peace. It's a big problem for Pot, though."

"What's she saying?" asked Alison, fastening some ropes and sitting down beside her.

Anna sighed. She was tired of translating. She made a very brief summary of what Ling had said, but Alison didn't seem very interested in it all and went back to helping Tian sail the little boat.

"And...what are the sea monsters like?" Anna asked Ling.

"Enormous! Oh, look. You can see the queen's port."

They disembarked at the small port and Ling picked up the two bundles she had brought. When Anna asked her what was in them, she said the small bundle was a fish dish for the queen, and the large bundle, all the clothing belonging to the two girls, adding that the smelly article had been washed.

"Why did you bring our clothes?"

"In case the queen knows how to send you back home."

For some odd reason, Anna was not very happy to hear that, nor was Alison when she told her.

"Maybe we could ask her if we can stay for a few days," said Alison, like someone on vacation asking the hotel if she can have her room a little longer.

"It's better if we don't say anything," said Anna as they climbed the stairs leading from the port to the fortifications. "Staying might mean forever; if there's a chance, it's better for us to leave. Besides, you can imagine how our parents must feel."

"Maybe yours. I don't think mine give a damn."

"Don't say things like that."

There was a huge esplanade at the top of the stairs. At one end stood a very high tower, like a lighthouse. At the other end was a beautiful house. Like every other house in Mai, it was rounded in shape and had a cupola. But on top of the cupola sat a large sculpture of a black bird, like a gigantic crow. There was a low wall running along the esplanade on the ocean side. The girls wanted to go over and look, but Ling pushed them toward an arch leading to the entrance of the house.

"It's the queen's house. Take off your hats," said Ling and went through the arch which gave onto a courtyard filled with plants and flowers.

"We aren't dressed to go and see a queen," said Alison to Anna.

"We're dressed like Ling," said Anna. "Besides, in this world things must be different."

"What do you mean, in this world! In this country, you mean, in this hidden country - what's that?"

Sitting on the ground were two rag dolls, each one as big as either of the girls. One, with green curly hair, held a flute and the other, with straight black hair, a sort of small guitar. They had very wide feet with four toes and were barefooted, even though they were wearing trousers and multi-coloured shirts. Their faces had been painted with great expression.

"They are the queen's musicians," said Ling when she saw that the girls were looking at them. Having said that, she snapped her fingers and the dolls began to move, the one placing the flute to its painted mouth and the other plucking the guitar with its cloth fingers. Almost at once the courtyard was filled with lively music.

"Come on, we can't stay here, the queen is waiting for us," said Ling to the girls, who were watching the cloth musicians open-mouthed. She snapped her fingers and the dolls stopped playing.

"How do they do that? The music. How do they move?" asked Anna.

"By snapping your fingers."

"I don't believe it," said Alison when she heard Anna's translation and went closer to the doll holding the guitar to see it better. "It has to have a hidden mechanism in it."

Suddenly the doll smiled at her and she fell back with a cry. Then Anna went over and the doll reached out a cloth hand. Anna gave it hers and noticed that, although the doll's hand had the feel of cloth, it was an actual warm hand. She looked at its face which was still smiling and saw eyes that, although they were painted, had the depth of human eyes. Alison came back and gave her hand to the doll. Anna saw the startled expression on the other girl's face.

"It speaks English!" exclaimed Alison. "It asked me my name!"

"That's nonsense," said Anna. "It hasn't said anything."

"It communicates mind-to-mind," said a soft, strange voice, also in English.

Behind the girls there stood a tiny woman, as round as a ball. She seemed very old, but her eyes were brilliant and the colour of honey. Like everyone else, she wore trousers, a shirt and sandals. Her white hair was tied back in a plait.

"The Queen of Mai," announced Ling to the girls.

"And this is the girl with the unknown language?" said the queen in her soft voice, now in Catalan, as she pointed to Alison. "It's not so. She speaks the language of Calai. But the girls don't appear to be from there."

The heat was already beginning to dissipate and the sky visible through the circular window had lost the luminous quality it had a few hours before. The girls, the witch Ling, and the guitar-playing doll who knew English were with the little round Queen of Mai in a salon filled with manuscripts, sitting on piles of cushions on the floor. The cloth doll was at Alison's side interpreting silently to her what the queen, Ling and Anna were saying. From time to time the doll translated something that Alison said for Ling. The queen told them that the musical dolls communicated through telepathy, even though Alison told Anna she couldn't believe it. She still thought they must have a hidden mechanism somewhere.

In the salon with them was a brightly coloured bird that resembled a parrot. From time to time it repeated what someone was saying in a strong and sonorous voice. To Anna's amusement, it sat on her shoulder, nibbling softly at her ears.

The queen explained more than she questioned, perhaps because she realized that the girls' curiosity had been aroused. So she told them that she and Ling had created the dolls, using great patience and following a series of formulas that had been worked out centuries before by a witch ancestor of Ling and a Potian immigrant ancestor of the queen.

"My ancestor," the queen said, "knew a great deal about making music. She had learned it from her great-great-grandmother who, although she had ruled the country of Pot, was more interested in playing music. My ancestor and her great-great-grandmother and I were all called Lula, because all the descendants of the first Lula are called by that name. It is a Potian tradition that the Maians have preserved. To make it short, my ancestor from Pot and Ling's witch ancestor decided to make the dolls, but in those times, which were when we had an army, this business of making dolls didn't seem important to those who governed and our ancestors had to give it up.

"But we were able to do it!" added Ling, filled with animation.

"We have dolls too, of all kinds," said Alison rather irrelevantly. "They work with batteries."

"They aren't like these, Alison. Are you stupid or what?." interrupted Anna. "They're nowhere near like these."

"Come now, girls, don't fight," said the queen in English. Her English, however, sounded a little strange.

"How come you know English?" Anna asked the queen.

"How come I know what?"

"Oh. Alison's language."

"Because I learned the language of Calai. Ever since a queen from long ago, named Ico, went there and learned it, all the queens here in Mai have known it."

And she explained that Calai, as the people who live there call the place, or Gelgel as other people call it, is a very cold country located at the north of the known world.

"You see," said Alison to Anna. "Probably they are talking about Canada, so it is our world. I already told you that."

"So you are from Calai. I would not have thought it. You must belong to a distant group," said the queen, and looking at Alison, she added, "But I did not know that there were any people in Calai with yellow hair and blue eyes."

But Anna did not believe that Canada was Calai or Gelgel or whatever the place was called. And besides, in Canada people also speak French, especially in Quebec, and the queen didn't know anything about that, even though she knew a great deal about her world. As the queen explained in her gentle voice, more than a thousand years ago, many languages were spoken in the world, but because of certain happenings, the Common Language, Catalan, became established everywhere except in Calai/Gelgel.

"As far as I can figure out," added the queen, "the Common Language originated in Maiera and the Great Traveller spread it throughout the world."

"Who was the Great Traveller?" asked Anna.

"A man from Maiera. But it's a long story."

Each time that someone said Maiera it seemed to Anna that she had heard that name before. But where?

"Perhaps we should eat," said Ling, taking the little bundle that she was carrying. "I'm very hungry."

"What is it?" asked the queen with an excited look on her round face.

"A fish dish made by my sisters."

"Oh, how nice. They always do that so well."

"Then - oh no! I must have made a mistake," said Ling, opening the bundle and looking at a pile of dried herbs. "This is for a potion for toothache."

"Ling," said the queen, angry now, "when are you going to start paying attention to what you are doing? The last time you brought an orange instead of a potion for earache, and after you went away all cheerful with one of my dolls thinking that it was a plant."

"Yes. What a surprise I had when, right in the middle of the sea, I snapped my fingers absent-mindedly and realized that the plant was playing the flute," said Ling with a little laugh. The doll with the guitar looked at her as angrily as the queen.

"I hope you don't do such stupid things during sessions of the government. Well, it doesn't matter. We have some cakes in the kitchen. Do you mind bringing them? And don't get it wrong. They are beside Roc's food."

"Roc!" cried the brightly coloured bird.

"It's his name," said the queen, pointing at the bird and getting up. She went toward the kitchen as well, saying, "I'd better see what Ling is doing. She is the best witch we've ever had in Mai, but her head is always in the clouds."

The girls were left alone in the salon. Alison was staring at the doll moving her lips. Probably she was asking it where the battery was hidden, thought Anna while she petted the bird and concentrated on the name, Maiera. She wanted to know where she had heard the name before. She kept repeating it out loud until, suddenly, the bird cried, "Maieera!"

And Anna remembered a solitary valley where the wind rustled the stalks of grass, and hills through which an army of warriors came down shouting. "Maiera!" shouted Anna and everyone jumped, startled: the queen and Ling who were coming into the salon with the cakes, Alison, and even the cloth doll.

Chapter Eleven

THE MANUSCRIPT

Stammering over the words, Anna described the dream she had had and how afterwards she had seen the 'bruixot' in Toronto. The queen and Ling turned to her in surprise and the doll, with a look of concentration, seemed to be translating it all for Alison.

"You didn't tell me!" said Alison. Her cheeks were scarlet with anger. "And you knew where the 'bruixot' came from."

"The 'bruixot'!" repeated Roc.

"He isn't a 'bruixot'," said the queen in her soft voice, very calmly. "He's the Lord of Rocdur, a truly evil tyrant who has oppressed the people of Rocdur for many years, ruling with a fist of iron. As well, he is responsible for a great deal of suffering in other countries. Years ago he quarrelled with Maiera, because he wanted to join it to Rocdur; in fact, he claims that Maiera is part of Rocdur. I have no doubt that what you saw, Anna, was a battle between the Rocdurian and Maieran armies. You say that when the Lord of Rocdur entered the wood he said something?"

"Yes. I think that he said it to another warrior, but I don't remember what it was."

The queen left the cakes on a cushion and began to move

manuscripts around. "Keep going. Tell me what else happened and how you arrived in Ling's cellar," said the queen while scattering manuscripts all over. Clearly it was now time for work. "Ling, please, write down everything she tells us."

The witch took a sort of yellow paper and, with an old-fashioned pen and a pot of ink, got ready to write down everything the girl said. Anna went on describing it as well as she could, although it was difficult to explain some things relating to their world, especially the references to computers. But the queen seemed intelligent enough to grasp the idea. Anna finished her tale with her arrival in Mai.

"I'll never forgive you," said Alison, still furious and eating cakes. "You never said anything about the dream."

"At last," said the queen, pulling a manuscript out of a pile. She looked at it while everyone waited. "Ling, come and look at this. Remember I once spoke to you about 'The Manuscript of the Interference?' It's this one."

Ling read it with concentration. The girls said nothing.

"We don't know that what it says here is true," said the witch when she finished reading.

"No," the queen agreed. "But there is a good probability that it is."

"You mean that Anna..." Ling looked at the girl. "She is so young. And there's the other part."

"Yes, and we must not forget that the Lord of Rocdur has been ruling for more than two hundred years, so we can't know when the other happened..."

Anna had no idea what they were talking about, but one thing drew her attention. "The Lord of Rocdur is two hundred years old?" she asked.

"Yes," said the queen vaguely. "We must clarify a point, Anna. What did the Lord of Rocdur say to the other warrior as he came into the wood?"

"I can't remember."

"Can you remember if he said 'Arnom'?"

"Yes! Now I remember! Yes, that's it, for sure, he said 'Arnom.'"

The queen and Ling looked at each other and then at Anna. They were very serious. "Anna," said the queen to her with an air of great gravity. "Listen carefully. There is an ancient manuscript we call the "The Manuscript of the Interference," that seems to explain what happened to you in your dream."

"Yeah, right!" said Alison, who seemed on the point of exploding with rage and never stopping eating little cakes.

"Yeah, right!" repeated Roc.

"We don't know if it is true or not," added Ling, paying no attention to the girl or the bird. "And it's quite confusing. But there are too many coincidences to reject it."

"And... what's it about?" asked Anna, feeling very strange.

"It's here in the manuscript," said the queen, and showed it to Anna. But it was written in characters she did not recognize. They meant nothing to her. "In a moment in time, someone from another world will arrive in Maiera, in the Valley of Can, during a battle with Rocdur. One of the armies will be led by the Lord of Rocdur and the other by a man named Arnom. The person from the other world and the Lord of Rocdur will look at each other and will produce an interference between the two worlds."

"What we did not know until now," said Ling, "was that the person from the other world would be dreaming about it and that she would be a girl. Anyway, it's evident that you and Alison are not from Gelgel but from another world."

"Right!" said Alison, who had eaten almost all the cakes. The colourful bird said it too; the doll with the guitar looked solemn.

"And does this manuscript say anything else?" asked Anna, who was feeling stranger and stranger and had a knot in her stomach.

"Oh, yes," said the soft voice of the queen. "And put all together it is rather incomprehensible. Or it was until now. We've already cleared up one part, even if the rest is still obscure. It says that the person from the other world who has seen the eyes of the Lord of Rocdur will have to find, well, someone..." The queen sighed. "Otherwise our world will disappear."

"And who is this someone?" asked Anna in a tiny voice.

"We don't know," said the queen. "The manuscript says that someone else from the other world also went to Maiera and saw the Lord of Rocdur - who knows when in the last two hundred years. But it seems that there wasn't any interference. So then, it's a question of the person of the interference finding the other person. The only thing that seems clear is that the other person speaks the Maieran language, that is, the Common Language."

"And that isn't all," added the witch. "The rest is even more tangled up. It says, literally:

This race cannot be won
Unless the Potian first shun
Other Trails;
And with the Cat, pursue his quest
Turning steadfast to the west.

You see how odd the thing is. Which Potian? What Trail? Besides, there aren't any cats at all in Pot."

"Yes," continued the queen, "if the Potian doesn't take the Trail, nothing will be achieved."

"It is all that we know," said Ling. "And the manuscript says nothing about the voice that spoke to you in the dream. But what seems certain is that you, Anna, are the person in the interference."

"I'm leaving!" said Alison. She had finished the cakes and was turning toward the door.

"I'm leaving!" repeated Roc.

"Alison!" said the witch. "Don't be stupid!"

"Stupid!" repeated the bird.

But Alison was already outside running from the salon toward the courtyard. The doll followed her with cloth footsteps and Anna, half confused and dizzy, ran behind with Roc flying above her head. "It's my fault," she said to the queen and Ling as she ran. They didn't seem to understand what it was all about.

Anna entered the courtyard at top speed just as Alison was leaving it. The doll with the flute had its head turned to watch her leave and now turned it to follow Anna; the doll with the guitar who knew English stayed where it was with Roc on its shoulder, evidently not knowing what to do. Ling and the queen came into the courtyard.

"Help!" said Ling to the dolls and snapped her fingers. The dolls started playing music.

"Help!" repeated Roc in the middle of the music.

"Ling, please. That's really all we needed right now," said the queen, snapping her fingers and stopping the music.

"Sorry. My mistake," said Ling, clapping her hands twice; the dolls followed with the bird.

When Anna came out onto the esplanade, Alison was still running toward the tower at the other end. The sun had almost set and the sky was all the colour of blood, with traces of thin cloud slipping quickly by, pushed by the wind. "Alison! Wait! I want to talk to you!" shouted Anna, still running in pursuit of the other girl, but Alison was already climbing the stairs that circled the outside of the tower.

The queen, like a little ball with feet, Ling, the dolls and Roc came out on the esplanade as Anna started up the tower.

"Girls! Come back. It's dangerous!" cried Ling and the bird while Anna was already catching up to Alison at the top.

The top of the tower was just a flat surface; from it you could hear the wind whistling and far below, the loud crash of ocean waves. Alison had nowhere else to go. Anna had never seen her so angry, or with her hair so wild or with so much rage burning in her eyes.

"Listen to me Alison, I wanted to tell you, but..."

"Shut up! I don't want to listen!"

Anna didn't know what to do. She didn't like being there, with that horrible ocean right there below, nor with her hair slapping her face at every burst of wind. "Let's get down from here," she said.

"Go down then if you want to. Go on, leave. I don't want you here. Leave me alone."

But Anna didn't move and both girls stayed, one in front of the other, tense, on top of the tower, under a blood-coloured sky.

"I don't believe anything those two nutty women said," said Alison at last, angrily. "Interference! It's crazy!"

"You don't believe it because the manuscript doesn't talk about you." Anna was sick and tired of Alison's fits of anger and turned to leave.

"Stupid!" shouted Alison, giving her a shove.

Anna fell to her knees on the floor and felt a sharp pain that climbed up to her stomach. She took a deep breath, got up and, turning toward Alison, slapped her without warning and headed for the staircase. Her knees were hurting. But Alison charged toward her, grabbing her by the hair. There was a moment of struggle. Anna pulled back to free herself from Alison's grip but in doing so, went even further backward.

The last thing she saw was the expression of panic on Alison's face before realizing that she was falling into emptiness. Anna's body took a turn through the air and plunged toward the ocean. She heard Alison's sharp squeal at the same time as she saw an immense form with a fin under the water.

"No, no," she said as she fell, "no, please."

From the water an enormous shark's head rose up with its mouth open, scarlet and full of teeth.

"Mum! Mum! Daddy!" she screamed and closed her eyes.

She felt her stomach being squeezed in. The monstrous shark was eating her. She could feel its teeth clamping down on her stomach. She screamed and moved her arms like a crazy thing, feeling nothing but air.

She opened her eyes. She was flying over the ocean toward the esplanade. She put her hands on her stomach and felt something hard and thick grasping her around the waist. From up there, she saw Alison who had just run down the stairs from the tower, and the queen, in front of her house, making little jumps like a ball with the colourful bird on her shoulder and a doll on each side of her. The hard and thick thing that was holding her opened, setting her gently down on the ground of the esplanade. With an effort, Anna sat up - and shrieked at the sight of gigantic claws under a black bird the size of a small plane. Then Ling climbed down from the bird and crouched beside the girl.

"Easy, there, Anna," she said. "She's Blackie, my bird. She's very tame, even if she is rather lazy. If she'd taken a little more time getting down from the cupola where she was sleeping, the monster would have eaten you."

At that, everything disappeared, darkness enveloped her and Anna fainted.

When she opened her eyes Anna found herself lying on the cushions in the queen's salon. Little lights were flickering everywhere, from small candles set in ceramic candlesticks and inside colourful shells. Anna was so tired and felt so comfortable where she was that she could have stayed there forever. On the other side of the salon she could see the queen and Ling, their long shadows stretched out on the wall in the candlelight. They seemed to be concentrating on reading manuscripts. Close to Anna was Alison, with the guitar-playing doll, looking out the round window at a black sky embedded with stars.

"Alison," said Anna in a weak voice. She had to make an effort even to speak.

"Hey - you're awake at last," said Alison. "I thought you were going to sleep forever."

The queen and the witch raised their heads from their manuscripts. "Ling, bring the potion," said the queen as she went over toward Anna, still moving like a ball with feet. "How are you, Anna?"

"What happened?" asked Anna, sitting up. On top of being tired, she hurt.

"You don't remember?" said Alison, sitting down on the cushions as well. "Blackie, Ling's bird, saved you."

Anna shivered as she remember the gigantic bird, and more than that, the enormous mouth of the monstrous shark. But there, in the queen's salon, the terror of everything that had happened was easing off slowly.

"Alison has something to say to you," said the queen; Anna looked at the other girl.

"I'm really sorry, Anna. It was all my fault. But I never wanted you to fall into the ocean. Honestly." In the light of the candles her eyes gleamed.

"It wasn't anyone's fault," added the queen. "An accident can happen any time and that is why you should avoid anger and keep your head clear."

"I am so tired," said Anna, who felt that her head wasn't at all clear. "I hurt all over."

The witch brought a steaming bowl in from the kitchen. "Drink this, Anna. It will make you feel better. With a good night's sleep, tomorrow you will be fine."

The hot drink tasted like fish soup with a strong flavour of herbs. Anna swallowed it slowly and began to feel better.

"Now go to sleep. You too, Alison, come on, to bed," said Ling while she was arranging the cushions in the shape of mattresses. The queen covered them with soft embroidered cloths.

"Go keep Tian company," said the queen to the doll with the guitar. "And watch that you don't wake up Roc. That bird is so excitable."

"Tian is here?" asked Alison.

"He's below, in the port. He'll spend the night in his boat."

Anna yawned, a huge yawn that seemed never to end, and curled up under the embroidered cloth. The queen and the witch Ling had gone back to the manuscripts.

"We'll be friends forever, won't we?" whispered Alison, stretched out on the cushions and covering herself up completely with the embroidered cloth.

"Yes," said Anna smiling and half-asleep. Now she had a friend. There is nothing like falling into the Ocean of Monsters, she thought.

The soft sound of waves from the Sea of Mai, along with distant guitar and flute music and the voice of a man singing reached them through the open window. Anna closed her eyes and fell asleep at once.

The next morning the girls ate a breakfast of 'orecs', sweet fruits and little almond cakes that the witch Ling prepared for them. The queen was up in the top of the house, in her room under the cupola, recovering from working all night, Ling explained. Apparently she had not slept at all. After they had breakfast, the witch put the straw hats on them and pushed them toward the door with the two dolls and Roc. "The queen and I have a lot of work to do. We are trying to find some way of returning you to your world, so you will spend the day with Tian."

And what a day it was! Tian took them in his sailboat towards the west where the girls had seen low mountains from the tower of the lions; and in the estuary of a stream he moored the vessel at a little dock. Near there he went off to look for some herbs that the witch Ling had asked him to find.

The girls took off their hats, their sandals and their shirts, rolled up their trousers and ran into the water. They were in the sea swimming and diving while Roc flew over them and screamed when they splashed him. The cloth dolls, bored, watched them from the beach.

"If we can go back home," said Anna later, when they were sitting on the sandy beach drying themselves in the sun, "what will we say?"

"We'll have to dream something up," said Alison, taking out her comb.

"But Boulder saw me go through the mirror. How do we explain that?"

"Easy. Blackmail." She batted her eyes. "You do know what that is?"

"Yes, of course I do. But how?"

"Come on, stupid. Don't you remember what you said about her and Skinner? We tell her that if she doesn't keep quiet about the mirror thing we'll tell what we know about what's going on between them."

"In that case we'll have to talk to Skinner. It seems to me that Boulder doesn't give a damn what anyone knows."

"Then we deal with Skinner. He can say she's crazy. If they don't already think that. If she said that you left through the mirror..."

Anna wasn't convinced. Even though Boulder irritated her, she didn't want to make her seem crazy. Anyway, all that about blackmail bothered her. It seemed a dirty thing to do. She was considering it when Tian came back with a basket full of herbs.

"It seems to me that you are doing better than this pair," he said with a smile, nodding at the dolls who were looking sadly at him. "I don't think they like being here in the sun very much without being able to go swimming."

"They can't go swimming?" asked Anna, while Alison, combing her hair, followed the conversation in the mind of the doll with the guitar.

"Oh no! Certainly not. They would get soaking wet and sink."

"How awful!" said Anna, seeing the look of distress on the faces of the dolls.

"How awful!" repeated Roc.

"Maybe we should go somewhere else," suggested Anna. The dolls looked a little livelier. "What do you think, Alison?"

"Whatever," she said, as if she didn't care, and frowned, finding a knot in her hair.

"The witch Ling said we have to spend the whole day out here," said Tian, "so we have time for everything. Do you want to walk up the river? I know a beautiful place where it won't be so hot."

No sooner said than done. Tian left the herbs in the boat, grabbed the bag with the fish cakes, and together they walked up the river on a narrow path that threaded its way through the hills along the riverbank. The rocky landscape was dotted with small groves of trees that filled the air with a dry odour, and birds that Roc frightened by crying, "How awful! Maiera! Ha, ha, ha!", and made the girls break up with laughter while it provoked a confusion of flights and bird cries. Now and then, when Roc was quiet, they could hear insects humming in the still air.

The dolls walked slowly, watching carefully where they put their cloth feet. They weren't gasping for breath because no sound came out of their cloth bodies, but it seemed that their gasps stayed inside, leaving them oppressed, their eyes dazed. Anna gave a hand to the doll with the flute and the green hair to help it, and seeing that, Alison did the same with the one with the guitar, who smiled gratefully at her.

"Hey, look. It's the witch Ling with Blackie!" exclaimed Tian, looking down to the estuary to where the little sailboat was rocking back and forth.

Ling had just gotten out of the boat with the basket of herbs and was already climbing up on the huge black bird. It was waiting for her, balancing itself on the dock.

"Ling! Ling!" called the girls and Roc, but the witch didn't seem to hear and with a beating of its immense wings, Blackie flew up and took Ling over the sea.

"This is how Ling flies then, isn't it?" Anna asked Tian. "On Blackie."

"Yes. She herself can only rise up from the ground. Sometimes even high up, but when she has to travel she does it by bird."

"And does she go to very many places?" Anna wanted to know. They had already gone back to walking up the river.

"She makes a lot of short trips through Mai, even sometimes flying to the desert. Also over the ocean toward Pot, always close to the coast and generally at night so the Potians cannot see her."

"Do all the Potians have green hair?" asked Anna, using this opportunity to get as much information about this world as she could.

"So they say. Green and curly. And they say that they are small people with eyes the colour of honey, like our queen."

Anna saw that her friend was saying nothing, even if probably the doll was translating what they were saying. Would she still be doubting that they were in another world? Would she still think that the green hair was dyed and that everything had a scientific explanation? All she could guess about Alison was that she was very hot.

"Here we are," said Tian, leaving the bag on the ground and drying off his forehead.

They were at a bend in the river filled with rocks and shaded by large trees. Here the river ran in a series of waterfalls, and on the shore a very small child was playing. Seeing the group that was approaching, he stood up at once and opened his eyes wide.

"Mummy!" he called. "There's a big girl with eyes made of water and hair of pee-pee."

"Hair of pee-pee!" repeated Roc, settling himself on a branch. The child stared at him, startled.

Anna and Tian began to laugh, but Alison, to whom the doll must have translated what the child had said, seemed very offended. It was evident that no one had ever told her that her golden hair was the colour of pee-pee. The child left as fast as its little legs could carry it.

"Mummy! Mummy!" he called. And Roc on his branch repeated it. "There's a bird who talks and dolls that said 'hello' to me inside my head."

Further on was a spring where a woman was filling jars with water. The child held on to her trousers and looked at the group from between his mother's legs. Nearby a 'mouse' was grazing.

"The dolls and the bird belong to the queen," explained Tian, while approaching the spring. "The girls come from a group far-off in Gelgel and they are with the queen and the witch Ling.

Anna thought that this, then, was the version that Ling had given of their place of origin. The woman smiled.

"Don't be afraid," she said to her little boy. "They are the queen's people."

With this she finished filling her jars, tied them to the 'mouse' and, climbing up with the boy, waved good-bye and left. The boy kept on watching them, amazed, until the 'mouse' turned behind some rocks.

Tian took off his sandals and shirt and slipped into the river. He was a rather old man, thin, with hair that was almost white. Even so, he swam like a fish. Clearly he felt at home in the water, thought Anna, who also loved to swim. What must it be like, she wondered, as she watched the movement of Tian's arms through the water, to have lived in Mai all your life. To know only one country, isolated from the rest of the world, where there was a government full of women and where everything went well; where there were amiable witches and a queen who was tiny and intelligent and yet unpretentious. Where you could see gigantic birds and lions that shone like gold and dolls that played music and communicated by telepathy. And sailing up and down a beautiful sea that is closed off by a wall that separates it from monsters. Anna shivered. Then she frowned. Were the only monsters the giant sharks from the ocean? What was there farther away, beyond the desert? What people lived there? What was this other world like? This world which could disappear if she didn't find that person who had been to Maiera.

Chapter Twelve

THE COMPASS

Tian came out of the water and stretched out on a rock to dry himself off. Alison, sitting beside Anna, seemed to be lost in thought as well. "Do you like dancing?" she said out of nowhere and stood up.

She went toward the dolls who were under a tree and snapped her fingers. At once they poured out lively music. Alison began to dance, leaping and moving her arms like a ballerina. "Hey, Anna, come and dance."

Anna stayed at the riverbank without responding, but watching her enviously out of the corner of her eye. At last, as if it she didn't care one way or the other, she moved closer to Alison and stayed half-way there without moving. Alison caught her by the hand to make her dance. Anna began to follow the melody a little stiffly at first until she relaxed; suddenly she decided that she was very happy. Tian, with his shoes and shirt on, left them dancing and went off to prepare their meal.

Later, while they were eating, Anna asked him if he had children. Tian sighed and told them that he had had one boy, but that he had drowned during a storm.

"In the Sea of Mai?" asked Anna. Alison had stopped eating.

"Yes. It was a bad day. We don't have many like that. The waves were high and ferocious. He should not have taken the boat..." He remained silent, looking toward the river and Anna asked him no more questions.

After they had eaten, Tian settled himself to take a 'little drift' - a nap - under a tree with a doll on each side of him. Roc had flown over to a wood to screech at the birds and the girls were sitting on a rock in the river, soaking their feet in the water.

"I don't like that blackmail idea you had, Alison."

"So maybe you have a better idea?"

"No. And... where will we say we've been?"

"Why worry? We won't ever get back, probably. As far as I'm concerned, it's all the same. Only I would like to find conditioner for my hair."

Anna looked at the waterfall, iridescent as the water caught the light of the sun. The kingdom of Mai was very beautiful and probably you could live very happily in it, but she was beginning to feel uneasy. Her parents must be going crazy looking for her, and even her grandparents in Catalonia, if they knew about it, must be very worried. And watching the water leap from the rocks she thought that she could never be happy here. Besides, she missed Puff.

"I want to go back," she said, looking at Alison.

"Okay then, go back if you can. In fact I'd like to go back too if I could. I think that here I'd get tired of eating fish and oranges and hardly anything else all the time. And I doubt if I'd ever find anything different to wear...or any conditioner."

Anna sighed. Would Alison ever change? The only thing she worried about was her damned conditioner. "Okay, then," Anna went on, "Let's say the queen and Ling can get us back. What story do we give everyone? It's got to be good, because we'll probably have to talk to the police and it's not going to be all that easy."

"We could say that we hid in the library where your mother works. It's totally huge, isn't it?"

"In Robarts! You're crazy. Probably they already searched

for us there. We couldn't say we were in a park, either. Not in January. It's too cold. No one would believe it."

They sat there saying nothing, thinking. Anna looked over to the trees where Tian was sleeping still and taking off her shirt, dove into the water from the rock. She felt good in the water, even if the soaking didn't give her any ideas for when they went back home. She swam over to the waterfall thinking about what Tian had said. The kingdom of Mai was not perfect, she thought. There were tragedies like everywhere else. The only difference seemed to be that death here was not caused by other people.

Hours later, they arrived back at the queen's port. The girls were so tired they could hardly climb the stairs; even Roc, settled on Anna's shoulder, had calmed down a little and only made little noises in her ear. The dolls seemed exhausted and dragged their cloth feet through the esplanade toward the house. On top of the cupola, Blackie sat immobile. It was impossible to tell if she was asleep. Anna looked nervously at the wall overlooking the Ocean of Monsters and entered the courtyard with Alison.

The queen's salon was a mess of manuscripts, bowls filled with herbs, artefacts, and jars. "Ah - here you are," said the queen, her voice softer than ever.

Seated on a cushion, she seemed to be trying to regulate a sphere, a little more than a hand's span in width, on which were drawings and an arrow that turned. Anna realized that the queen had dark shadows under her honey-coloured eyes and her long plait of hair was half undone. "Ling! The girls have come back! Ling! Ling!"

"Ling!" screamed Roc from Anna's shoulder. "Ling! Ha! Ha!"

"Anna, please," said the queen. "Take Roc out to the courtyard. That bird never shuts up and he simply cannot stay here now."

"And the dolls?"

"They can stay. They don't make any noise. But no one is to snap their fingers!"

When Anna came back from the courtyard, the witch Ling was in the salon. She looked very tired and her clothes, face and hair were covered in dust. She was standing upright in front of the queen with a pillowcase in her hands and the queen was looking furious. "Am I permitted to know what you want to make out of an old pillowcase, Ling? I asked you for the tool bag."

Ling went out with a distracted look in the direction of the kitchen.

"Why is she covered with dust?" asked Anna.

"She spent the whole afternoon examining the basement... That's enough conversation for now," and she went back to concentrating on her object.

Hours passed, and through the round window they could see the sky darkening. Ling prepared a potion for herself and the queen which gave them energy. Then with great rapidity they moved objects, consulted manuscripts, whispered, mixed liquids from the jars in bowls that gave off fumes and, as well, scraped the dirt from the soles of the girls' boots onto a cloth. Maybe, Anna thought, they believe that boots are marvellous things? Or were they such a clean people that even the soles of boots had to be scrubbed?

Ling carried some lighted candles and Anna remembered that her bag had the firelighter in it. She wanted to give it to the queen and Ling, but now didn't seem a good time. Maybe later. The witch noticed the girls, sitting quietly under the window with the dolls. She went back to the kitchen and brought them 'orecs' and little cakes. The girls looked at the food without much appetite but ate anyway out of pure boredom.

"When I go back home," said Anna softly, "I am going to have a huge plate of pasta with a lot of cheese and tomato sauce."

"And I'm having an enormous steak with French fries. And Belgian chocolate," said Alison, batting her eyes.

They woke up at nightfall, having fallen asleep on the cushions without realizing it.

"Come on, get up," Ling said to them; she looked very tired in the candlelight.

The salon seemed different. The mess of manuscripts, jars and objects had disappeared. In the centre of the room was a low of candles forming a circle and in the middle of the circle rested the sphere that the queen had been working on.

Ling took them to the bathroom where she rinsed their hair thoroughly with water until she was sure it was very clean. Then she combed it for them, and rubbed their skin with lotion.

"What's that?" asked Anna.

"It's to lighten your skin. If you go back home with a suntan they will ask you more questions than you might want to answer. That's why it's best if your hair is very clean too or they will be able to tell that you have been swimming in the sea," answered the witch. And Anna decided that although Ling was rather absent-minded, she did think of everything.

Then she made them put on the clothes they had been wearing when they arrived, and since Alison had come without a jacket, Anna let her have her heavy sweater and wool hat.

"So, are you ready to send us home?" asked Anna as she entered the salon.

"Yes. I think so," said Ling.

"But you're not sure?"

"Not entirely. It's about taking you to another world and so - well, it's difficult to be sure what will happen." Seeing the expression of alarm on the faces of the girls, she added, "Relax. I think the worst thing that could happen is that you'd just stay here."

Anna put on her winter jacket and felt very hot. When Ling gave her the bag she took out the firelighter and the flashlight. Holding one in each hand, she lit them. There was a silence in which the queen, Ling, and even the dolls, looked at them open-mouthed.

"You can keep them," said Anna smiling, "although I have to tell you that they won't work for long."

"If you didn't have to go quickly, I would ask you how they were made," said the queen. "Thank you for offering them to us, but we will just keep the stick with the fire. It's better if you have the one that sends out light. You might need it." And Anna put it in the pocket of her jacket.

"Anna," said the queen, looking into her eyes. "Have you thought what you want to do about the Manuscript of the Interference? I mean, will you look for the other person in the manuscript?"

"Well... How?"

"I don't know, Anna. I've never been in your world."

"An awful lot of people live there. There are even millions who speak your Common Language."

"I understand the problem."

"And if I don't find him, this world will disappear?"

"So the manuscript says, so it is possible that it is true. Nevertheless, you have to decide if you want to find him. It is your decision. Besides, there is the other part of the manuscript about the Potian and the cat and the Trail to the west, so it's possible that finding the person isn't all of it."

"And if I find this person, how do I let you know?"

"If you can return to your world, you can come back to Mai."

Anna looked at Alison who said nothing, but Anna knew how she must feel finding herself completely shut out from the manuscript. And she considered everything that the queen had said as well; the possible consequences for this world if she did not find the person. It would be very difficult, but... She took a deep breath as she always did when she wanted to give herself courage.

"I will do it," she said in a clear voice, her dark eyes bright. "I will find the person, I will look for him or her all the time and I will come back to Mai. And Alison will do it with me. We will save this world together."

Alison looked at her as if she could not believe what she was hearing.

"Of course I will do it," she said when she found her voice again.

Anna seized her by the wrist as she had seen them do in movies and looked straight in her eyes.

"We will look for the person," she said.

"We will look for him," said Alison, smiling.

"We will save this world."

"We will save it."

"Perhaps you will have to spend years looking for him," interrupted the queen.

"We will find him!" said both of them.

"We will find him!" The distant voice of Roc was heard from the courtyard. The girls burst into laughter.

"I think the moment has come," said the witch, who had been following the doll's translation from English into Catalan and seemed very impressed. "Listen carefully, girls. The queen and I will explain what you have to do. Put on the sandals that climb up your leg and we'll go into the centre of the circle."

The girls put on their boots and all together, with the doll with the guitar, they went into the circle of candles. As soon as they were inside, the queen took the round object with the arrow and the pictures.

"This is a compass," she explained.

"Ah," said Anna. "It points to the north."

"No. I don't know why it should point north," said the queen and Anna decided that this was not the moment to argue about a compass. "With the compass it is possible to cross space. The arrow points to the place where you wish to go. When I was young I used it to go to Fosca in disguise... Well, we have no time now for stories. Concentrate hard on the picture of the walled city with a lot of detail. That is Mai. Do you see that picture inside the city? This house? Good. It's Ling's house. If you put the arrow exactly on that house you will stop there. And here, this other picture in the form of a pot, that is Pot. The sketch with the mountains and a castle in the middle is Rocdur. No matter what happens, avoid it. This other, very large with lakes, is Sura. And the one that is painted white with mountains on one side is Gelgel. Will you remember all that?"

The girls nodded yes and the queen continued. "The picture of the peninsula with many villages and a city beside the sea is Fosca. And, finally, this picture, which has sea and little mountains and valleys, is of Maiera."

Anna sighed and looked intently at the picture. Where would the Valley of Can be?

"So everything is very easy," said Alison. "We set the arrow to point to one of these places and there we'll be."

"No, Alison," said the queen. "It is not easy at all. For Mai, or maybe even Fosca, yes, it is, if you are in this world. For Pot, there is the problem that we are not sure what it's like inside, and as for the other countries, we don't even know their exact dimensions; there could be errors. Besides, the biggest problem is travelling from one world to the other. So, use the compass only to come to Mai. Now then, the compass alone is not enough. To travel you have to light a 'wax'."

"A what?" said Anna.

"This," said Ling, pointing to a candle. "You have to light one, or more if you wish, but you can't have any other light. When you have set the arrow to the place where you want to go, seize the compass very tightly and put out the 'wax'."

The girls were completely drenched in sweat, but it was hard to tell whether from anxiety or from the winter clothing they had on. Ling put a little copper chain from which hung a small container of yellow liquid around each one's neck.

"Is that also to get us home?" asked Anna.

"No. It is extract of sea monster and has great power. It will protect you from the Lord of Rocdur," said Ling, opening a cloth in which there was some dust. She took a little of it, put it on an empty space on the compass, and moved the arrow to the space with the dust on it. "This is dust from the sandals that you were wearing when you arrived. We're hoping that with this dust the compass will bring you to your world."

A little light went on in Anna's head. "Now I've got it! I understand now! The Lord of Rocdur and his people... The mud on the palm of the hand must have been from his boots...from sandals that climb up the Lord's leg."

"Very clever," said the queen. "Ling and I thought the same thing when we read your story of what happened. It gave us the idea for how to send you back. In fact, the mud that you saw on the palm in the mirror was, without a doubt, from the sandals of the Lord of Rocdur, from when he had been in your world. The business of the mirror we still don't understand, though."

"And the blood?" asked Alison. "The blood on the palm?"

"We don't know that either, although my opinion is that they must use blood in the same way. It must be blood from a particular person. But we are not sure how it works because we don't understand the role of the mirror or of the object for writing that you told us about."

"The computer?" said Anna.

"Yes, that," said the queen. "But enough talking and back home for the pair of you."

They gave them a little bag of earth from Mai. When they wanted to come back, they were to put some grains of it on the picture of Mai on the compass for greater security. Then they told them to hold the compass very tightly in both their hands. They were not to let go of it for any reason. And the queen, the witch Ling and the doll left the circle, leaving the girls alone in the middle clutching the compass.

"Now you won't have a compass," said Anna.

"It doesn't matter," said Ling. "With patience we can always make another."

Outside the circle Ling rose up in the air and opened her arms. All the candles in the circle rose up as well, forming a spiral that began to move, turning, slowly closing the circle where the girls were.

"The doll with the guitar said good-bye to me," Alison told Anna.

"Yes, and the one with the flute said good-bye to me."

The candles turned so quickly now that the girls could only see a spiral of little flames forming a smaller and smaller circle.

"Good luck, girls." It was Ling's voice. "You'll always be welcome in Mai."

"Until we meet again," said the soft voice of queen.

"See you soon!" shouted Anna. She was beginning to feel a sensation as if she were there and not there.

"See you soon!" screeched the far-off voice of Roc from the courtyard.

Suddenly the candles went out and everything was dark.

Anna strained her eyes to see. There were diminishing yellowish lights and some red lights; farther beyond she saw what looked like an exit with bright lights. There wasn't enough light to see clearly, but it seemed that she was in some sort of tunnel. She noticed that she was still clutching the compass and she saw Alison's silhouette.

"Alison?"

"Yes. Where are we?"

"I think it's a tunnel. Don't move. I'll turn on the flashlight."

They were in a broad tunnel. She moved the light down to their feet and they both felt their stomachs lurch. On each side of them were tracks. "Don't move, Alison. If it's the subway and we touch the tracks, I think we could get electrocuted."

"And what do we do, then? There's no place to go if a train comes!"

"Have you got a good grip on the compass?"

"Yes."

"See that light beyond us there?"

"Yes."

"Run! Toward the light! Don't touch the rails!"

They began to sprint between the rails by the light of the flashlight, jumping over the occasional red lights along the line. "That light has to be a station," yelled Anna, panting for breath. "We have to get there before..." A distant roar filled the tunnel and Anna turned for a second; a light, still far away, was closing up behind them. "Run, Alison! Run! The train is coming!"

The roar got louder and louder, the train's headlight began to light up the tunnel, and they hadn't reached the station. Anna had never run so fast. Her chest hurt. The sound of the train was deafening, but the station was opening up just ahead of them. They were almost there. Anna scrambled onto a little walkway just before the platform started and helped Alison up.

"Quick!" said Anna, getting onto the platform. "Beside that trash container."

"Why?"

Anna pulled her and both of them crouched down beside a large trash container. Their hearts were pounding and Anna felt dizzy. The place looked familiar; on the wall of the other platform she read the name of the station: "Spadina."

"We're home," said Anna, closing her eyes; the train entered the station with the noise of a giant monster. "We mustn't let anyone see us. We have to hide the compass."

Chapter Thirteen

SECRETS

Tam is at the market, finishing up a little story he is telling the butcher and her friend, the woman who owns the fruit and vegetable stand, both sturdy Rocdurians.

"And then the soldier was seized with fear, because the woman looked angrier and angrier and had a huge celery in her hand. He kneeled down, asking forgiveness from the shopkeeper for having tried to take the apples without paying. And the woman said to him, 'you may have fought in many battles, you presumptuous soldier, but look at you, shaking with fear! Go on, off to the barracks before I smash your nose with this celery!' And the soldier let go of the apples and ran off as fast as he could, as frightened as if the woman had been the Lord of Rocdur himself."

The two woman break into laughter when they hear the end of the story. The butcher gives him a little package with a small piece of lamb in it which Tam quickly puts into the bag under his tunic. The other woman offers him a handful of little fruits from Pot.

"You always think up a good one, Tam," she says to him.

Tam thanks them and catches up with Sua, who has brought him shopping with her.

"I don't know how you do it," laughs Sua as she accepts one red and one yellow fruit from the boy's hand. She closes her eyes as she tastes their sweetness. "Oh, my, but they're good!"

In a few months Tam has turned into someone significant among the shopkeepers at the market. He tells them brief stories that make them laugh and one gives him little fruits, another a handful of nuts, a third a small piece of meat. They have even, sometimes, given him sweet ginger imported from Sura. Products that no Potian would ever be able to get.

The boy takes one of the baskets that Sua is carrying and, together, they go up the street to the large house with flowers in the windows. The house of the Chief of the Army.

It is a beautiful day in early spring and the Town seems to smile under an intensely blue sky. Even the Castle up on the mountain has a less menacing appearance than usual. Besides, today Tam is very happy. Until yesterday, he has had no news of his family. Although he knows they have arrived in Pot without problems and are living on a plantation owned by Rocdurians where his parents are working, Tam has been anxious. But just yesterday he received news from Pot that his parents and his grandmother are well, even though Tam knows they must have had a hard time of it.

Now Tam is living at the Chief's house helping Ep and Sua, the Potian servants, and as always, is the Chief's storyteller. This arrangement has been the work of Tariana, who cleverly convinced her father that Tam should be taken on as one of their servants. She was also the one who arranged everything for his parents' and grandmother's journey to Pot. As Tariana knew, her father did not always agree with the orders from the Castle - he was a warrior, not a murderer of old people. But even so, the Chief had objected. Not only was he accustomed to giving orders but also to following them without question. Negotiating the trip for Tam's family, especially in such a short time, turned into a tug of war between the Chief and his daughter. The boy staying to live with them almost had the Chief cheering; but handing over horses and two wagons to the boy's family to go to Pot was something else.

"Didn't you say that Tam's grandmother works in the fields?" the Chief asked Tariana.

"Yes, but she just fell sick and since she is a little old...

"She just happened to fall sick right today, eh?" said the Chief, as if he found it hard to believe.

The Chief finally gave up. Tam's family arrived in Pot the morning of the tenth day after the notice had been put up concerning the executions of Potians too old to work. Not only did his family get there, but they brought with them two more families with very old grandparents. The Chief, though, knew nothing about the other two families, nor did he know that Tariana had written a letter to the owners of the plantation, under the Chief's seal, in which she recommended the travellers for jobs there.

Tam often remembered standing on the road under a sad winter sky and Tariana giving him her hand. He watched as the two wagons, packed tight, moved farther away down the road to the south, toward the country he had never known, a place of desert, jungles, and small lakes and marshes. Would he be able to go there some day? Would he see his family again? To whom would his grandmother tell stories of Pot now? Grandma Lula, descendent of the women who had changed the destiny of the Potians, and now, old and shrunken, moving away in the cart to escape a terrible death, returning to a place from where she had escaped another terrible death: starvation. Tam inflated his nostrils, suddenly feeling an immense and unfamiliar anger.

Because Tam had always been optimistic and, thanks to his imagination, able to survive, he had never worried too much about the conditions they lived under. Now, for the first time, he noticed them and the injustice of it all.

The wagons were already only little specks in the distance. Tariana must have noticed the tension in the boy's hand.

"Tam?"

He looked at her. His honey-coloured eyes were full of hate. "It is all the Lord's fault," said Tam, the words coming out very slowly.

"Yes, Tam, you're right. It is." The girl grabbed his shoulder. "But never say that to any other Rocdurian. Come on, let's go or my father will send soldiers to find me."

The Castle had not found a single useless old person in the miserable villages around the Town, and families with old people, even if they still worked, had already begun to travel toward Pot just in case. It was said, though, that they had killed old people in other districts of Rocdur. The shopkeepers talked about it in low voices in the market, with a certain anxiety in their voices. It was about Potians, inferior people, but to execute the old? Near the Town there had been other executions. For several days they cut off the heads of any illegals they caught. Although executions of illegals weren't something new, there didn't used to be so many all at once. Clearly they had entered a period of harshness. And not for the first time.

The days passed and everything returned, it seemed, to normal. At first there was a little confusion since some of the Potians who had left were needed in the fields and the mines.

"Those poor unfortunate illegals," said Sua one day while having supper with her husband, Ep, and Tam. "They have lost their lives, and all for what? When it comes down to it, they've had to bring people in from Pot because there aren't enough Potians to do the work."

"Don't you get mixed up in all that," said Ep, scraping his plate clean with his spoon. "We are doing well in this house and we don't want problems."

"Oh, yes? And do you want to tell me, you fool, what will happen the day we get old?"

Ep said nothing, kept on scraping his plate, this time with his finger, without raising his eyes. Tam, lost in thought, drank a glass of goat's milk.

Now Tam leads a rather quiet life. The Chief has not been called up to fight any battles and between a period of calm and Tam in the house telling stories, he sleeps better and is in good humour. As well, every day in the middle of the morning, Tam goes out, accompanying Tariana on her ride - her on horseback, him walking behind. When they get to the forest, Tariana gallops off and Tam is free until they find each other again in the same place to go back to the house for lunch. Tam takes the opportunity to go to the cave in the river under the waterfall, where he keeps his cat. He always manages to catch a rabbit in the hidden traps that he sets here and there - Potians are not allowed to hunt - and when he can he brings a little meat from the market. The cat is already as big as the boy, who thinks that it must be the food he gives him that is making him grow so much. The entrance to the cave is behind some rocks beside the waterfall and, with branches and ropes he brought from the house, Tam has made a sort of door to keep the cat from going out when he's there alone. Tam knows perfectly well that they will kill him if they see him.

Sometimes Tam sits down on a rock watching the cat play nearby. If he has been drinking water and a ray of sunshine falls on him, his fur is so yellow and shiny he really seems made of gold. Tam has called him Groc.[2] And while he sees him there on the riverbank, playful and rolling over on the ground completely happy, Tam wonders where he came from. How did he get to Rocdur where he found him tiny and crying in a thicket? Where did he come from? Where was his mother?

Today, early in the morning, just as he gets back from the market and with the sweetness of the little fruits still in his mouth, Tam finds Tariana ready to go out. The girl looks extremely pretty in her green dress with her red hair tied back with a black ribbon. When they reach the forest Tariana, as she always does, adjusts the saddle, tucks up her skirts and mounts the horse astride, like a man, with one leg on each side.

"We're free, Tam. Go and enjoy yourself," says the girl, smiling, spurs her horse and disappears between the trees.

Tam runs down the hill toward the river, thinking that Groc will be happy he is so early. Arriving near the waterfall, though, he stops, silent, behind some bushes; he has heard hoofbeats. It could be a hunter, although they don't usually come by here. Farther on he sees a green spot that moves between the trees. When it enters

---

2   Groc means yellow in the Common Language (Catalan).

a clearing the sun lights up red hair and the profile of a girl. It is Tariana.

Tam moves toward the waterfall very carefully, because not even Tariana should know of the cat's existence. Hiding between the bushes, he arrives at the entrance to the cave. And the cat is so happy to see Tam! He puts his paws on the boy's shoulders and almost knocks him over.

"Hey, easy there, Groc. Here, I brought you some meat," he says, opening the package and putting the meat on a stone.

Groc eats it in flash, licks the stone clean so that not a scrap of it remains and goes off to drink from a pool that is filled from the spray from the waterfall. Tam frowns; Groc needs to eat more and today he won't be able to check the traps for rabbits if Tariana is wandering around here. What's to be done, he wonders. He'll use the time to do a little cleaning.

First he washes the bag that he carries under his tunic and puts it to dry in the sun. And then he lights the candle he has hidden here, since the light that seeps in through the waterfall is not strong enough to see well, and he examines the cave. He notices that Groc has been scratching the ground at the back of the cave, under a pile of rocks, probably trying to find a way out. The cat gets at it now, scratching like crazy and covering Tam with dirt. Some rocks are displaced and almost fall on the cat.

"Stop that, Groc, you'll hurt yourself!" Then Tam sees a hole between the rocks. There seems to be a space behind it.

Groc slips through the hole. Tam sticks the arm holding the candle into it and then he slips through into another cave on the far side. Groc is in a corner and when Tam holds up the light he sees a figure, seated, with a skull for a head. Frightened, Tam steps back, trips over a stone and falls, letting go of the candle. Now the cave is almost pitch black. But the candle is still burning. He picks it up again, and trembling, brings the flame closer to the seated figure. It is, in fact, the skeleton of a man in a tunic that has been reduced to rags. What is he doing here? From his neck hangs a chain with a medallion on it. Tam takes it off with great care, but even so, he knocks the skull off. It falls, rolls on the ground and stops at the boy's feet, staring up at him with eyes that are holes filled with darkness. Groc pounces on the skull, playing with it until Tam gets angry and the cat stops.

It is a large and heavy medallion, made of gold; four angles project from the circle, one of them drilled so a chain can go through it; in the middle of the medallion is a picture of two crossed swords and a castle that looks like the Castle of Rocdur. Tam moves the candle to the skeleton again, and near it he sees a little book with leather binding and a number of yellowish pages covered with writing. Near it are a writing stick and a dried-up pot of leaf ink. Tam explores the rest of the cave with the candle and finds a ceramic bowl and the remains of an ancient fire. He takes the book.

"Let's get out of here, Groc, in case more rocks fall and trap us inside... That's how this man must have died," he says, while making the cat leave by the hole and going out himself right after him.

Tam spends all morning filling the hole with rocks and branches so that Groc can't go in and get trapped in the other cave. When he finishes he puts out the candle and sits down to look at the dead man's book. He doesn't know how to read and because of that he can't tell what it says, but in the book there are also pictures that surprise Tam. One is of a dragon flying over mountains and villages; it is a frightening creature with a look of pure evil. Another picture is of a castle very like the Castle of Rocdur; but with windows. Three horsemen are riding away from the castle, each with a banner. Tam moves closer to the waterfall to see better, because he notices that one of the riders is holding a banner depicting two crossed swords over a castle, just like the picture on the medallion. There is a tree on the second banner and the last portrays a village or town. Tam goes past the written pages and finds another picture. This one is also of the three riders with the banners, although now they are on foot without their horses and with their swords raised in front of a cave. Tam keeps going through the pages, but they are all covered with writing, without pictures. If only he could understand what the letters say...

A leaf falls out from inside the end cover. It is a map, although very different from the one the Chief has over his fireplace. Tam can't make sense of it. There is the Castle of Rocdur, with windows, the way it is on the banner, and a series of roads leading to it which have nothing to do with the roads that Tam knows. As well, the medallion that the skeleton was wearing is drawn in two places on the map.

The boy comes out of the cave and checks the position of the sun. It is almost time to be at the wood where he is to meet Tariana, even though he is sorry he has to leave Groc after paying so little attention to him. He puts the small book and the medallion in the bag under his tunic, well hidden, gives Groc a little kiss and leaves. As he is going through the wood he sees Tariana's horse drinking water from the river, but not alone. There is another horse; both without riders. Maybe the girl has been injured? But who does the other horse belong to? Tam stands in the bushes, not knowing what to do, when he sees Tariana coming out between the trees. Tam rubs his eyes, unable to believe his eyes. Tariana is holding the hand of a Suran.

The Suran is a young man, slender like all those of his race and as tall as Tariana. The girl and the Suran kiss and at once mount their horses. She slips once more into the forest and he goes up the river. As he passes close to Tam's hiding place, the boy gets a good look at his face. Who is the man? How is it possible that the daughter of the Chief of the Army of Rocdur would embrace a Suran?

When Tam thinks that the Suran is far enough away, he starts to race toward the place where he always meets Tariana. When he arrives, the girl is already there.

"Tam! Where were you? It's very late and you know how angry my father gets when he does not know where I am."

"I got here a little while ago," says Tam, lying, "and since you weren't here, I went to see if I could find you."

"Well, don't do that again." The girl spurs her horse who begins walking with Tam behind him. "If I'm not here, wait, but don't look for me."

"Where were you?" the boy dares to ask.

"What?" The girl stops and looks indignantly at Tam. Her cheeks are red. "It's none of your business where I was!"

"I thought you might be hurt," he says hesitantly. It is the first time that Tariana has been angry at him.

"I'm sorry I shouted at you, Tam." The girl seems more relaxed and they continue on their way. "But don't look for me. I don't need anyone and I have enough of that already with my father checking on me."

Tam hasn't the heart to say anything more. He feels saddened, though; it worries him that Tariana is hiding something from him so unthinkable as the scene he saw by the river and that he is hiding from her what he carries in his pocket. But he must keep it well hidden if he doesn't want trouble for Groc.

That same evening soldiers from the Castle come looking for a Suran at the stables and take him to the Castle. The wise men cover his eyes and lead him to the Hall of Mirrors where they have brought him more than once before. He kneels. Waiting in the room are the Secretary and the Lord of Rocdur.

"Tajun," says the young wise man with the big nose and the untrustworthy air, "you already know what you have to do. Listen carefully and tell us everything that the Gelgelians say."

Another wise man, the one with the eyes like storm clouds, is kneeling in front of a mirror. He appears thin to the point of emaciation. The Lord whispers in his ear, "You had better do it right this time. Another mistake like the one you made with the girls from the unknown world and it won't be a few months in prison but your head rolling on the ground."

The wise man, drenched in sweat, closes his eyes and puts his palm, stained with Calpor's blood, on the mirror.

The Lord clenches his fists, recalling the time they found the girls using the mud from the unknown world from his boots; something they had never been able to do before. They found them in an extraordinary place containing a series of white chairs in very small rooms. And they seemed to have the blond girl at least, with the whirlwind produced within the mirror, but she disappeared and not another trace of either of them could they find. He sets aside his thoughts when seven ferocious-looking men seated in a circle around a fire appear in the mirror.

"Why not do it? Rocdur knows nothing and we will be victorious," one of the men is saying, one who is dressed entirely in black leather and wears a fur hat, also black.

"Raven, you always were reckless," says one of the others to him. He wears a fur hat as well and has hardened features with eyes that glitter, metallic and cruel.

"Me! Isn't it you, Calpor, who wanted to mount an offensive against Rocdur with all the clans? And now you want to drop it, without any justification?"

Hearing the name 'Calpor', Tajun stops a moment before continuing to translate what the Gelgelians are saying.

"Oh, no. It's not the same, Raven," says Calpor, his hardened features illuminated by the fire. "I wish victory for all Calai. You want it only for the *RedSword*, for your clan. You know very well that not all the clans have agreed to launch an offensive against Rocdur."

"It is certain that not all the clans agree with it, but what you say about Calai is not true. You also want victory for your people, for the *OldLand*. And there's no need to say what we all know, that you of the *OldLand* are assimilating all the clans.

"Perhaps." Calpor, expressionless up to this moment, smiles maliciously. "Before me, all together you were just a collection of incompetents."

The men around the fire begin protesting. Calpor stands up and looks at them. They fall silent, except for Raven. "We *RedSword* can mount an offensive all alone. You, Calpor, can do what you like with your bloody *OldLand*," says Raven boldly.

All at once Calpor leaps at Raven and slices his cheek open with a knife. "You will do what I tell you to do, Raven," says Calpor to him, licking the bloodied knife. "There will be no offensive against Rocdur."

Calpor leaves, slipping into the night, and the other men follow him. Only Raven has remained beside the fire, trembling, his eyes streaming tears of pain and his hand pressing down on the rough wound on his cheek. Another man appears in the light of the fire; he is carrying a cloth that Raven puts on his wound. The image in the mirror is beginning to be erased now that Calpor has gone, although Raven's voice, directed at the other man, can still be clearly heard.

"We will follow our plan. We, the *RedSword,* are ready to inflict considerable pain on Rocdur. If they don't know we are preparing to attack, we can conquer the whole north of their country and win huge booty. All our *RedSword* groups will meet on Abledeer Plain in twenty days and will attack Rocdur at once. Not one Rocdurian in the villages of the north is to be left alive."

Voice and image of Raven and the other man disappear completely from the mirror and the image of Calpor mounting a horse becomes clear.

"You. Clot," says the Lord to the wise man with the eyes like storm clouds, who still has his hand on the mirror. "What - do you want us to hang around contemplating how Calpor rides?"

Tajun tenses. Perhaps he guesses the commanding voice is the Lord's. But he is led away at once. The Lord and the Secretary climb immediately to the room at the top of the tower.

"Do we have enough soldiers in the north to stop Raven?" the Lord asks the Secretary.

"To know what is being prepared can help a great deal, Lord."

"You haven't answered my question!" he says, smashing his fist on the table. "Do we have enough soldiers in the north? Yes or no?"

"No, I don't believe so, if Raven actually attacks with all the *RedSword* at once. But the Chief of the Army can give you a better estimate of the situation."

The Lord claps his hands and two Potians come in. "Let the Chief of the Army be summoned." The two Potians leave at once. "Now, this Suran, Tajun," says the Lord. "We don't need him any more in the Hall of Mirrors now we know Calpor is not intending to attack Rocdur."

"Lord, to have someone who speaks the language of Gelgel can be very useful to us."

"I have said we do not need him. The only reason we had for bringing him to the mirrors was Calpor's attack. Now that he has decided not to attack Rocdur, we don't need the Suran."

"And if Calpor changes his mind, Lord?"

"It's always the same! You, placing obstacles in front of everything!" He seizes the cup of wine and drinks it all in one go. "But as for that, yes. The Suran Tajun will be very useful to us against Raven. So, let us follow the same plan as before. That he dies in battle and if he survives, we execute him."

"Yes, Lord."

"Have the emissaries that we sent to Fosca returned?"

"Just before we saw the Gelgelians in the mirror, Lord."

"And? What did the Foscans say?"

"They will permit only two persons of rank from Rocdur to enter the country, with no more than four soldiers and two servants, Lord."

"Do we frighten them that much? Excellent. Then the Chief must go to get an idea of their military capacity and to bring back all the information he can on their defences."

Later, at the Chief's house, once he is back from the Castle, everyone hears the news. A few days from now he will have to go with a delegation to Fosca, made up of the Secretary, as the Lord's ambassador, two soldiers from the Castle and one of his Potian servants. The Chief will be accompanied by two of his soldiers and one servant. The Chief has decided to take Tam.

Tam does not know what to think of all this. On the one hand he is delighted. To see another country! A country that Tariana has told him is very rich and has a sea and different people whose skins are a darker colour. On the other hand he is very worried. How will Groc get anything to eat?

That night Tam sleeps badly in his little room beside the kitchen. Early in the morning he is awakened by the persistent beating of the drums in the soldiers' barracks. He sits on his straw mattress, very tired. What are all those drums? He has no time to think because Tariana comes into his room.

"Get a move on, Tam, if you want to come with me to see the soldiers march to Gelgel. Everyone must be out on the road already."

In no time at all Tam and Tariana are on their way. Just as the girl had said, there are a lot of people from the Town waiting to see the soldiers. It is a real event each time the army marches off to battle. Most enjoy the spectacle, even though some mothers cry secretly, all of them shopkeepers in the big Town market, who know their sons may not return. There are so many horses and riders, soldiers beating drums, and other soldiers leading ferocious dogs. And there are wagons and a lot of foot soldiers, some so young they look like children; and further behind, just ahead of the catapults as high as towers, the Suran cavalry pass by with their lances and their faces painted with horizontal lines in the colour of their clan.

But one Suran is not riding at the rear with the others. He is at the side of the commanding officer. The Rocdurians on the road remark on it, wondering who this Suran can be. But Tam recognizes him at once; he is the Suran who was by the river with Tariana. Out of the corner of his eye the boy looks at the girl; she never takes her eyes off the Suran, even though he shows no sign of noticing her; his dark eyes with the two blue stripes under them are looking straight ahead. And shortly after he cannot be seen any more through all the dust stirred up by the horses.

"Do you know who the Suran is who's riding at the head of the troops?" Tam asks the girl as they are going back home.

"Me?" She turns bright red. "How should I know?"

"Because you go to the stables a lot."

"Ah - yes. Now that I think of it, it seems to me that his name is Tajun or something like that. He looks after my horse sometimes."

"Why is he riding at the head of the troops?"

"I don't know," she says, frowning.

Tariana walks slower than usual and seems lost in thought; Tam asks her no more questions. When they return home the girl shuts herself in her room saying that she is tired.

Chapter Fourteen

THE HISTORY OF THE DRAGON

Tam has finished all the work Ep and Sua gave him. The morning passes and Tariana has not come out of her room; in a moment or so it will be time for lunch. The boy has spent the whole morning thinking about his cat; he has to find some way of going to see him today, but who will look after him during the trip to Fosca worries him more.

The only possible solution is to ask Tariana for help. How much worse can it get if he does? Although when it's about cats you can never tell what will happen. Not only are they forbidden, but Rocdurians are terrified of them. When there's a report of a cat entering Rocdur - usually from Fosca or Maiera - no matter how small the animal is a troop of soldiers is sent out to kill it. Sometimes they are forced to cut down a tree because the cat has climbed up it. Not even soldiers armed with swords dare to climb after it. More than once Tam has seen this happen while he was hidden in the woods, but it has always puzzled him. It's true that cats can scratch, but the Rocdurians seem to go a bit far.

After lunch, Tam is really worried. He has to go to see Groc, Tariana is not leaving her room, and he's not allowed out alone.

He makes up his mind and climbs up to the second floor. He knocks softly on the girl's door and Tariana opens.

"What do you want?" she says in a cold voice.

"I have to talk to you."

"Come in if you want to that badly." She doesn't seem pleased to see him.

Tam realizes that the girl's eyes are red from crying, but pretends that he doesn't notice. Tariana sits in an armchair and Tam kneels.

"Cut out the dramatic stuff, Tam. Sit in the other chair. There's no one else here. So, what do you want to say to me?"

Tam is thinking that maybe this is not a good moment; Tariana does not seem to be in the mood for anything, but it is now or never. Three days from now he will be on the road to Fosca. "Tariana, I have a problem."

"And who doesn't?"

"Yes, that's true. But this is urgent."

"For you, problems are always urgent. Now what's going on?"

As well as he can, Tam explains the existence of Groc in the cave. Tariana turns pale and says nothing. She simply looks at Tam, appalled.

"A cat!" she says, finding her voice at last. "Have you lost your mind! This is really serious, Tam!"

"Will you help me?"

"Help you? With what?"

"Look after Groc - my cat is called Groc - until I come back from Fosca."

The colour has come back in the girl's face, stronger than before, but this time from indignation. "What are you thinking of? Risk my life for a cursed cat!"

"Groc is very gentle, Tariana, and besides, no one would see you. No one has ever seen me."

"Tam, it's one thing to risk my life to save your family and another, very different, to do it for a cat." Tariana is really angry. Tam's eyes fill with tears. "Do you know that they will cut off your head for a thing like that? You know perfectly well that cats are forbidden in Rocdur."

"Will you tell?" asks Tam, very sorry he said anything to the girl.

"Don't be stupid. Do you think I'm capable of telling, you idiot? Of course I won't tell, but I'd cheerfully spank you for it. And there's no way I will look after that cat."

"Can we just go there today? To feed him?" The boy's face is covered with tears.

Tariana has never seen him cry before. "How can you get like this over a cat?" she says, mopping his face with a handkerchief.

"I love him very, very, very much. He is... he is like a little brother."

"You're really weird, Tam." Tariana sighs. "All right. We'll go and see your cat and take him something to eat. No, don't smile. I haven't said that I will look after him, only that we'll go and see him."

"Thank you, Tariana," he says, thinking that maybe he should mention the cat's size. What will happen when she sees him? In the end, he says nothing.

Tam opens the door to the cave and slips inside. Tariana, always so brave, waits a little distance away, looking completely intimidated. Tam is holding a really big parcel of meat that Tariana got from the cellar. As usual, he sets it on the stone and Groc devours it all at once. Today, at least, he seems to have had enough to eat. While the cat drinks from the pool Tam opens the door wider and waves at Tariana to come in, but the girl gets a look at the animal and backs away, wide-eyed. Tam goes out, closing the door.

"Tha...that is a monster," the girl exclaims without taking her eyes from the door. "He can't come out, can he?"

"No. But don't be frightened. He's a very gentle kitten."

"You're crazy!" Tariana looks at the boy, still wide-eyed. "That can't be a cat!"

"He's a big sort of cat."

"I'm going back. I don't want to know anything more about that thing you have in the cave." She turns to leave.

"Tariana," says Tam, looking serious, "I'm staying with Groc. I'm staying here until they find both of us and kill us."

Tariana tries to grab the boy, but Tam is already at the door, opening it. Groc sticks out his head and looks at Tariana. She screams.

"Quiet, Groc. This girl is Tariana, and you frighten her. Come on, let's go inside. From now on, I'm going to live with you." And he slips into the cave with the cat, closing the door.

Tariana stays where she is a moment without moving, and then very slowly she draws near the cave. "Tam, don't be stupid. You can't stay here." As there was no response, she continued, "You told me that you used to let Gross - uh - Groc out. Why don't we let him go out now and I'll look at him from a distance?"

Tam and Tariana have been sitting down near the waterfall, watching Groc splashing about on the bank of the river and then stretching out on a rock to dry off. He stays there for a good while, dozing. The sun is already very low and the sky is turning bright red, yellowish pink, and ochre stained with copper. In the light of the setting sun, all the colours of the sky paint the gleaming yellow fur of the cat stretched on the rock. Groc yawns, stretching his front paws, arches his back and sits up on his haunches, majestic and unreal under the light of evening.

"Isn't he pretty!" says Tam, smiling. He is very proud of his cat.

"Yes. Truly beautiful," says the girl without taking her eyes from the cat.

As soon as she speaks, Groc jumps down from the rock and moves toward them with a spring in his steps. Tariana clutches Tam's arm. She's clearly afraid, but doesn't move, letting Groc come close to her. The cat's huge head is so close to the girl that it almost touches her. She can see the white lines under his eyes, the dark point of his nose, and the fur of his muzzle of a yellow so pale that it looks white. Tam strokes him and murmurs things at him; Tariana holds her breath. Groc places a paw on the girl's knee and yawns; he already has eye teeth big enough to instil terror. Very carefully she strokes his paw with her finger. The cat licks her hand and raises his head again. He and the girl look at each other; Tariana's dark blue eyes are reflected in the amber eyes of the cat.

Suddenly Groc lies down on his back at the girl's feet; his belly and neck are the same shade of pale yellow as his muzzle.

"He wants you to scratch his belly," says Tam, showing her how to do it. "Like this."

Tariana imitates him. Groc is so happy he keeps making little noises and licking her hands. The girl laughs and Tam thinks that maybe all will go well.

Two days have gone by since the afternoon Tariana met Groc. Yesterday as well they went to see him, and today is the farewell between Tam and Groc because tomorrow the boy leaves for Fosca. Tariana now seems relaxed when she is with the cat and he is happy to see her. Today she decides to go into the cave so the cat can get used to her being there.

"I still don't understand where he comes from," says Tariana. "I have never seen a cat like this one in Rocdur. I know there are wild cats in Sura and in the south of Gelgel, larger than the cats in Fosca and Maiera, but they aren't like him. Groc doesn't resemble any cat in the known world."

"Maybe he comes from the unknown world."

"How? Crossing the oceans?" says the girl, walking up and down in the cave. She stops in front of the wall at the back. "Why have you put branches in here?"

Tam realizes the moment has come. He would rather have waited until returning from Fosca before telling her about his discovery. There has already been enough trouble over the cat. But when he thinks about it, he decides it's better to get it over with, so Tariana won't poke around in the wall when he is gone. "Tariana," he says, looking at her.

"What? Oh, no, Tam. When you say Tariana in that voice it always means problems."

"Not a problem, exactly. But there's something else I should have told you about."

"Not another cat!"

"No. The book and medallion that belonged to the dead man in the next cave."

Tam and Tariana are sitting outside the cave looking at the little book. Tariana has already said she does not know what the pictures on the medallion mean, although clearly it's the Castle of Rocdur. Tam shows her the pictures in the book, but she does not know what they are about either. What she does know is that many centuries ago there were dragons in Rocdur. The map with roads going to the castle and pictures of the medallion makes no sense to her. So, she begins to read aloud what the book says:

These were dark times in the kingdom of Rocdur. The plague had cut short the lives of thousands of Rocdurians, even many youths filled with health and strength. After some years no trace of the illness remained, but in the kingdom of Rocdur men and resources were lacking, for almost no one was working in the fields or the mines, nor was it ready to defend itself from a possible attack from a neighbouring country. Even the king and all his children were dead. Rocdur was being ruled by those nobles who had escaped death, the majority of them more ambitious than capable of restoring the kingdom. In fact, without a king, Rocdur was not a kingdom any more.

No one knows exactly how it happened, but one day, from a cave hidden in the mountains to the north, a dragon appeared. It is known that in far-off times, dragons lived in Rocdur, but that was many centuries ago. They said that perhaps a dragon's egg had been left behind in the dark of the cave from remote times, and now that the nobles had ordered all the trees from those regions to be cut down, who knows if the sun might not have entered the cave and warmed the egg that the dragon broke out of.

Whatever might have been the cause, the fact is that some woodcutters saw a gigantic form emerging from the cave. Their blood ran cold in their veins. They left their tools and ran down the mountain, except for one who, filled with fear, hid himself behind a tree trunk to watch.

When it came out of the cave, the dragon stretched out its wings. It was immense, completely black except for its horn, under its wings, and its eyes, which were bright red. It opened its mouth and out from it poured huge flames that it cast at the men who were still running. It ate them, nicely roasted. Only the one who was hidden behind the tree trunk was saved, for, his meal finished, the dragon went back into his cave and the man was able to run to a village where he told what had happened.

They sent messengers to other villages, and just as soon as they had left there, the people who were gathered in the square heard a terrible scream up in the sky. It was the dragon coming down toward the village and screaming in that terrifying way. It had become even bigger and was wild and appalling. Everyone ran home to his house, but even so some ended up roasted and eaten by the dragon.

Time passed and every day the dragon flew over Rocdur and ate more people. The nobles, who hid in the royal castle when they heard that the dragon was coming, decided that someone was going to have to kill it. Three men were chosen for their skill in arms: Farró of the Town; Carian of the Forest; and I myself, Gilan of the Castle, nephew of the dead king.

One day, when the dragon had finished his meal near the castle, we began the journey toward his cave. All three of us were mounted on horseback with banners, swords and, as far as I was concerned, a heart filled with fear. It took us many days to get there, riding along the forest paths, always hidden between the trees, never lighting a fire, keeping watch by day and by night, until we were close to the cave. We left the horses in the wood, so that no sound would disturb the dragon, and we went toward his cave on foot.

Farró, who went in front, turned, hurrying us with his look. Farró was a very tall man, even for a Rocdurian, and big and daring. He made as if to enter the cave, but Carian pointed to above the entrance where there was a rock that jutted out. We climbed up without a sound. When we were there, Carian threw a rock into the woods, making a great racket. We waited. The dragon must have heard it; it came out of its cave shrieking. The cry was so intense and terrifying that I could not move. But Farró jumped on it from above and with one blow drove his sword into the back of its neck. Carian jumped to the ground and thrust his sword into its belly. One and the other drove their swords into it with great violence; the shrieks of the dragon deafened me and I could not move. The dragon fell dead with a huge crash. And it was then that the misfortune happened, for all at once Farró and Carian,

*soaked in the blood of the dragon, threw themselves at the horn. It was
to be expected, since it has always been said that the horn of a dragon
killed with a weapon made by human hands gives great powers to the
one who possesses it.*

*They cut off the horn with their swords like a pair mad with rage and,
having done it, fell to quarrelling over keeping it. From above the cave, I
watched with my heart stopped from the terror of the sight. Farró gave
Carian a blow, leaving him half stunned on the ground, and at once,
with the dragon's horn..."*

"What?" says Tam.

"I don't know. There is nothing more written."

"How can that be?"

"Perhaps when he was writing that, the rocks fell and left him
in the dark and he could not continue."

"And you don't know what he's talking about?"

"No. I've never heard the story of the dragon. And it's very
strange that no one has written a history of Rocdur for all that
long period of time. As if nothing has changed since who knows
when."

"And the books that you have, what do they say?"

"Well - the permitted books only say the same old things:
that the Lord and the Castle rule in Rocdur, that we are the
most important country in the world and our army is the most
powerful that has ever been. The ones my mother gave me before
she died are very old books that speak of remote antiquity and,
according to what they say, Rocdur became a kingdom... This is
also what this little book says, that it was a kingdom, and now
we know why it left off being one."

"And we also know why the Potians do so much work in
Rocdur."

"Why?"

"It says that many people died of the plague and there weren't
enough people to work and, besides, there were those who died
afterwards, eaten by the dragon."

"You're right! And that also explains why there are so many
Surans - to fill up the army! And because of that, there aren't a

lot of Rocdurians... Tam, we are beginning to understand many things."

"But we don't know what all that business of the three horsemen and the dragon was about."

"No. That's true. It seems to me that there are many hidden things in this country. One thing that I have never understood is how it can be that the Lord has ruled for such a long time. My mother told me that when my grandparents were young the Lord already ruled in Rocdur, and the Secretary was also there. Can you imagine how many years ago that was? And they don't look old at all."

"That's right. But they look really weird. What's wrong, Groc? Are you bored?" says Tam when the cat rubbed against the boy's legs. "Poor thing, he wants to be petted... Tariana, why are cats prohibited in Rocdur?"

"I don't know. Maybe because they're not of any use? But still, I'm not sure. In fact, I never thought about it. It seems incredible that up to now I always accepted the prohibition against cats as if it were nothing, and right now it occurs to me that it makes no sense. It must be one of the Castle things, like everything else."

"Is there something else they keep hidden?"

"Who knows? As far as I can tell, there are a lot of them. Probably they have the answers at the Castle to all the questions we ask ourselves, and without a doubt they must even know the story of the dragon and the three horsemen. Someone has to know it and they'll have kept it hidden for reasons of their own. Sometimes I think I'd like to see the inside of the Castle, just to see what's there," she added. "Come on, Tam. Don't give me that terrified look. I'm not thinking of going, even if it would be interesting to know what they are hiding in there."

"Maybe while I'm in Fosca you'll have a chance to find out something about the dragon. Couldn't you take a look in those books of yours?"

"Right. With my father not around, I'll be able to spend a lot of time going through them really carefully."

"And, Tariana, what will you do about meat for Groc? You don't know how to hunt rabbits."

"Oh, that. I didn't tell you that I've come up with a plan for getting meat. There is a group of Rocdurian ladies in the Town - hopelessly old-fashioned - who organize things for the army. They send food for the dogs and brushes to comb the horses with and things like that. I'm going to worm my way into the group, and that way I can order huge amounts of meat at the market, saying it's for the dogs of war that have gone to the north. I'll keep enough of it to feed Groc."

Chapter Fifteen
DELEGATION TO FOSCA

The birds are singing and Tam wakes up. It is the day they are leaving for Fosca. He gets dressed at once and puts on the boots the shopkeeper at the fruit stall gave him yesterday when he was at the market with Sua.

"Here, Tam," the woman said to him. "These boots aren't any use to me. My son was very young when he wore them and now he's completely grown up. He's one of the soldiers on the road to Gelgel." Her voice trembled a little as she said it.

"I hope everything goes well for you in Fosca," said the woman from the next stall, the butcher.

Because everybody knows that Tam is going to Fosca with the delegation. Everyone, that is, meaning all the stall-keepers in the market of the Town; there aren't any other Rocdurians, except for the Chief and Tariana, that Tam has any contact with.

The boots are comfortable. With them on his feet, he doesn't feel the cold of the tiles at all. He smiles happily and brushes his hair to make himself really neat and tidy. Going with a delegation to Fosca doesn't happen every day. He gets the leather bag Tariana has given him and in it he puts the brush and his little cape with a hood; it can be cold in the mountains. Ready now, he goes to the kitchen.

Sua gives him a small package of cheese and boiled potatoes and scrubs his face with a damp cloth. Then she gives him a big kiss. "Come on, get moving, the Chief is already outside."

"Be good and do everything they tell you," says Ep, giving him a hug. "Good luck, kid."

And Tariana is there in the doorway, whispering in his ear, "Don't worry. I'll take good care of Groc."

And there in the street is the Chief with two of his soldiers. The sun is already warming up the chilly morning. Down the road from the Castle come the Secretary, two soldiers from the Castle and a wagon driven by a Potian - he is the Secretary's servant. Tam climbs up on the wagon as soon as they arrive, but the Potian, a sick-looking young man, says nothing. All together they set out on the journey. From the top of the Castle tower, the burning red eyes of the Lord keep close watch on them through the window.

The days pass and the delegation to Fosca crosses Rocdur toward the southeast, through wild lonely mountains where from time to time they find a Potian with a flock of goats or sheep, kneeling by the road when he sees them pass by. At night they set up large tents for the Chief and the Secretary and small ones for the soldiers. The servants sleep out in the open with a blanket for cover. Tam, perfectly healthy, sleeps like a log, but he notices that the Secretary's servant is looking worse every day. He is a slender young man, with beautiful eyes; all that Tam has been able to find out about him is that his name is Map. Tam and Map prepare the meals, although apparently the Chief and the Secretary are in too great a hurry to wait around, so that often all they eat is boiled potatoes, cheese, and a handful of nuts. No one speaks during the entire journey. The Chief never asks Tam to tell a story and he is relieved, because he would not want to tell one with the Secretary there; he seems a sinister man. It occurs to Tam that the Chief and the Secretary don't like each other. The journey is full of silence.

One evening a storm threatens and they pass the night in a castle over a valley. The Master of the castle is a Rocdurian in charge of a field of gold deposits. As they go through the valley, they see a rocky river where a lot of Potians are working with sieves panning for gold. There they stand, with their feet and legs in the frigid water all day; they are all sickly-looking. It seems as if even their gaze is frozen by the icy water of the river, and all that for miserable pay, thinks Tam. He knows very well how little Potians are paid to do any kind of work. The Master of the castle wears huge earrings and rings of gold; all his teeth, even, are made of gold and when he talks to the Chief or the Secretary, welcoming them at his door, to Tam it looks as if the Master has to make an effort every time he opens his mouth, as if his jaws weigh him down.

Since there is a storm, the servants sleep in the stable and during the night the thunder wakes Tam up. He hears the Secretary's servant groaning and saying: "Nop, Nop."

"What's the matter?"

"Nothing. Don't say anything. Sleep." Then a flash of lightning reveals the look of terror on Map's face.

The next morning travelling along the muddy road is difficult, especially for the wagon. Tam worries about Map; he keeps closing his eyes and sighing as if he has no heart left to carry on.

One day the mountains aren't as steep or as wild, and toward afternoon they arrive at a plain where a broad river glides, much broader than the one near the Town. Each bank of the river is lined by a row of apple trees. The river flows south, directly toward Pot, thinks Tam with a sigh, and they cross it at a bridge where some Potians are making repairs. They kneel as soon as they see them, except for one who doesn't notice. A soldier from the Castle points him out to the Secretary.

"Arrest him!" says the Secretary. "And hang him from the bridge."

And so they do without paying attention to the cries and entreaties of the Potian. Tam's stomach turns and he looks at the

Chief. The eyes of the man find those of the boy and there is an instant of understanding between the two. Tam guesses that the Chief does not like that execution.

They have left the apple trees, the river and the bridge with the hanged Potian behind. They are crossing a large expanse where the fields are planted with vines and after that come barren wastes instead, with a wretched tree here and there and lots of tiny flowers. It takes them more than a day to cross it, and at the evening of the second day they arrive at the border with Fosca, where there are two military guard towers and soldiers everywhere. The soldiers kneel in front of the Chief and the Secretary, and Tam realizes, from the expression on their faces, that they are pleased to see the Chief; he seems to be a great figure among the warriors. On the other hand, they look at the Secretary with fear and mistrust. Tam watches everything. He will have a lot of things to tell Tariana when he returns.

The Chief and the Secretary enter one of the towers with the chief of the Frontier Army. Not for the first time, Tam observes that the Secretary, blind as he is, walks confidently as if he guesses what is ahead of him. The soldiers and the servants are waiting outside when one of the Castle soldiers approaches the wagon and Tam's heart skips a beat.

"You over there, useless!" he says to Map. "What are you doing planted here in front?"

Map, trembling, says nothing.

"Move the wagon out of my sight. Wait! Get down first." While Map is getting down, shaking even more, the soldier looks at Tam. "You, take the wagon out of here."

Tam takes the reins and moves the wagon to the side of the tower. Out of the corner of his eye he sees the soldier striking Map in the stomach with his fist and knocking him to the ground. The soldier leaves him there rolling around and turns to his companion. The two fall over themselves laughing. The Chief's soldiers and the soldiers on the frontier stand expressionless, saying nothing.

Tam is used to seeing Rocdurians mistreat Potians, but generally they have a reason for it, even if it is a terribly unjust one. He does not remember ever having seen an assault committed for something to laugh at. He is going to have to tread warily while he is around the soldiers from the Castle, especially if the Chief isn't nearby. He helps Map climb up to the wagon, because the man can hardly stand upright, and without saying anything, they wait.

Crossing Fosca is astonishing. When they enter the country, a dozen Foscan soldiers are waiting in front of their barracks for them. They are to escort them to the chief town. At first Tam cannot take his eyes off them. They have dark skin, even darker than the Potians when they tan in the summer sun, and they are tall, although not as tall as the Rocdurians. Some have very curly hair, so it almost looks like a hat made of hair; some have hair only as curly as the Potians, but black, and others have only a slight curl in their hair. All the soldiers ride elegant horses and their clothing is very attractive, softer than the clothing in Rocdur and more colourful; more than that, they seem terribly clean. Tam smiles, thinking that, for all that Rocdur says it is the most important country in the world, compared to the Foscans, the Rocdurians look like miserable wretches.

They cross through the middle of the peninsula of Fosca on wide smooth roads. During the journey they see a lot of people working in the fields; people wearing tunics of white or yellow or red or blue, or with patterns or stripes of all colours that are a joy to look at there between the tender stalks and the trees covered with flowers. And from time to time they see a Potian. This was something that Tam had not expected. And what surprises him most about those Potians is that they don't kneel when the Rocdurians go by.

Frequently they see villages as well with white houses that look very pretty, although they never go into them. They still sleep in tents, with Tam and Map in the open air - a great pleasure for Tam, now that there is good weather with warm gentle breezes.

Sometimes they stop to eat in a sort of small castle that as far as he can tell was built just for that - eating in. Tam and

Map, sitting in a corner, enjoy magnificent meals. Among other excellent things, there are red fruits that they call 'tomatoes', some very good grains called 'rice', and lamb. They certainly know what that is, even if Map has never eaten it before.

Just before they arrive at the chief town, which the Foscans call a 'city', and which is named La Bonica, riders meet them with the news that the city is in mourning. The Counsellor, the ruler of the country, has just died. Tam hears them talking from where he sits in the wagon, because they speak out loud and not in the hidden murmurs that Rocdurians use when there are Potians nearby. It appears that the Counsellor's death means they will have to stay in La Bonica longer than they had foreseen. They must speak to the Counsellor and right now there isn't one.

"How many days?" asks the Secretary in that voice that seems to drag out each word.

"There will be two days of mourning," says one of the recent arrivals. "And after that, the Foscans will have to choose a new Counsellor. Four days more. You will be able to see the new Counsellor seven days from now."

Tam does not understand it. What does 'the Foscans have to choose the one who rules them' mean? Then he remembers what his grandmother told him. In Pot, in the old days, after the death of Lula, the Potians chose the cleverest person to take Lula's place and this they went on doing until Pot became very poor, the land turned into desert, and the Potians began to emigrate to Rocdur in large numbers. Maybe in Fosca they do things the same way. But, even so, how could a country this big and with so many people in it do it in four days?

Before Tam can figure it out, the delegation, escorted by the Foscan soldiers and now the riders from the city as well, goes straight to La Bonica. And truly the city is as beautiful as its name. And big! Tam would need more eyes to look at it all. It has wide streets with a raised area where people walk, and streets paved with flat stones, not like the ones in the Town of Rocdur that are made of earth and turn to mud when it rains. And the houses are big and tall and almost all of them have windows and balconies filled with flowers, like the Chief's house. Here all are like that, and each one is right next to the other, except when there is a road, and all of it is filled with streets and with public squares, not like the ones in the Potian villages in Rocdur, which are cramped and dirty, nor like those in the Town that have nothing in them but a big stone pedestal in the middle holding the flag of Rocdur. In La Bonica, the squares have trees and fountains with water that rises up out of the top and then falls in arcs that sparkle in the sun, and the drops that fall make little pools where birds drink. And how many birds they have! And cats, too, slipping around a corner. Little cats, like the ones they kill in Rocdur. Do the Rocdurian soldiers and the Chief see them? Surely they are suffering great anxiety if they do.

Tam notices that Map is holding his head up and that he seems to smile just a little. A fleeting smile, that is gone as soon as it appears, but then another turns up, especially when he sees some pretty Foscan girl watching them go by.

Now they are going along the broadest street he has seen yet and, far down, he spies water. It must be the sea, thinks Tam, but he puts those thoughts aside when they all stop in the middle of the street, in front of another very wide street where a troop of mounted Foscan soldiers have just appeared, all wearing white tunics and blue capes that almost touch the ground. Each one is carrying the blue and white banner of Fosca.

A crowd of people follow behind the soldiers. Some mounted, others on foot, all in silence. And then a carriage appears painted all in blue and drawn by twelve horses. On top of the carriage is a long box, also blue, and many flowers, strange flowers and in all colours. The procession passes in silence, turns down the street and enters into a very large house with columns. When it has passed, the Foscan riders tell them it is the Counsellor's funeral and indicate that they, too, are to go down that street. With them go numerous Foscans who have been gathering nearby. Before realizing it they are surrounded by people and can barely move.

The horsemen and the Foscan soldiers dismount; they walk, leading their horses by the bridle. The Rocdurians are uneasy. They have arrived at the large house that the funeral procession entered and people are beginning to complain about the delegation being on horseback. The Chief tells his men to dismount and continue on foot, even Tam and Map, who will have to lead the cart horses by the bridle.

They move slowly through the crowd and when they pass in front of the big house with the columns, the horsemen from La Bonica and the Foscan soldiers stop, forcing the whole delegation to stop. From the big house they can hear voices singing. In Rocdur, Tam has only ever heard little songs sung by a Potian under his breath; now he thinks he has never heard anything so beautiful. Listening there in the street, everything surrounding him disappears and the voices remind him of the river near the Town. Some voices are deep and strong, and others clear and delicate, like the river that is dark and powerful in some places and in others clear and gentle as it flows. And the voices seem to pursue each other, as the water of the river does, until they all blend into a single song, as the river does under the waterfall. And then they glide, fused into one, broad and powerful, which draws out and out and leaves, like the water of the river which goes far beyond and does not return.

There is a great silence. Tam feels a brutal blow on his back.

"You, chunk of filth there, get moving," says one of the soldiers from the Castle.

The delegation pushes its way back down the street to a castle with many columns that the Foscans call a "palace."

It's been a while since they arrived. Tam is looking out the window at the intensely blue water, its waves breaking on the shore, and at ships coming and going. The palace is right beside the sea. He takes a deep breath of air with its unfamiliar smell and smiles. He is in his own room in the palace. It has a pitcher of water and a washbasin on a marble table and there is a mirror and a little table at the side of the bed, a real bed, with another pitcher and a glass as well. But Map isn't with him.

The "chief steward", the man who received them at the palace a little while ago, realized at once that Map was ill and had to see a "physician." Tam didn't know what a physician was until someone explained it to them, since none of the Rocdurians understood it either. The Secretary was opposed to it, saying that his servant was fine and no one had to see him. Besides, he wanted him locked in a room next to his.

"Secretary," said the chief steward, "you will lack nothing while the delegation from Rocdur is in Fosca. But here we do not lock servants up and we care for the sick, so you will have to adjust yourselves to Foscan customs."

There was an uproar and another man, very important, whom they called, "Senator," came and it all ended up as the Foscans wished. But, for Tam, the best of all is that they have given him a room far, far from the Rocdurians.

And now, while Tam is looking through the window, the door opens and a boy comes in. He has a very clever look about him and is apparently a servant in the palace.

"Hello. My name is Sapid and the chief steward tells me that I am to fill your water pitchers and take you to the kitchen to eat. You can go to many parts of the palace, but you can't leave it without permission from your people and it seems to me that they won't give it to you." He smiles and winks. "Although there are ways of going out without being seen. What's your name?"

"Tam," he answers cautiously. He is unsettled by everything.

"Are you hungry?" he asks him, and before Tam answers Sapid adds, "Obviously you must be. Let's go to the kitchen."

The palace kitchen is enormous and filled with servants hard at work. Tam doesn't understand why they make him wash his hands before sitting down at a table beside Sapid, but he does what they tell him and wolfs down the roasted bird they give him, and which they call "chicken." Tam is starting to think as he licks his fingers that the best thing about Fosca is the food.

Five days have passed since the delegation arrived and the Rocdurians are desperate to see the new Counsellor. Tomorrow he will be chosen and the day after the Rocdurians will have their meeting. Tam has spent all five of the days in the palace eating, sleeping, looking out the window and playing with a black and white cat that Sapid keeps in the kitchen. Still he hasn't had a chance to visit La Bonica, even though the Foscan boy has promised him that he will see it before going back to

Rocdur. The Rocdurians have left him in peace and he has only had to go to the Chief's room once, today, to tell him a story. The boy thinks up one about a battle between the Rocdurians and the Gelgelians. Since Tam has no idea what the Gelgelians are like, he imagines them as monsters with a single eye in the middle of their foreheads and moving in jumps like goats. The story ends with victory for the Rocdurians. The Chief applauds, pleased. Suddenly he turns serious and says to him, "Tam, pay no attention to anything you see in Fosca. Everything looks as if it's going well here, but Rocdur is a much more important country. The most important in the world! You know that, don't you?"

"Yes, Chief. And the one that has the most powerful army."

"Very good, Tam, very good. That pleases me. Come on, you can go."

On leaving the room Tam moves quickly; he knows that the Secretary's room is around here and doesn't want to run into him. But before he goes down the stairs, a door opens. The tall thin blind man comes out.

"Who is there?" the Secretary calls out loudly.

"The Chief's servant, Secretary," he says, thinking that it is better not to try to get away.

"Come here at once!"

When Tam draws near the man and is about to kneel, the Secretary seizes him by the arm and twists it until it hurts.

"What are you doing here, you cursed Potian!"

With the pain in his arm, Tam hasn't the breath to answer, but the Chief, who certainly has heard the voices, is already there. "What's going on?" he says.

"Your servant was spying on us." He twists Tam's arm and the boy cries out.

"I beg your pardon, Secretary, but you are mistaken," says the Chief. "The boy was with me."

The Secretary lets go of Tam, who is looking at the Chief with eyes filled with tears. The look on the Chief's face - just as it did when they hanged the Potian from the bridge - expresses how powerful his dislike is for the Secretary's actions.

In the palace kitchen Sapid's mother, one of the Foscan servants, is massaging Tam's arm. Sapid, who is with them, cannot believe what happened. All the servants are baffled and amazed, and make him a particularly tempting fruit drink. As usual, Tam has captivated everyone with his stories, especially the night before during supper when he told them the story of Nana, the green dragon and the Potians' hair.

"What sort of people are the Rocdurians?" asks Sapid's mother as she massages his arm. "How can they be so brutal? That's all we need if there's to be a war with Rocdur!"

Tam opens his eyes wide. War between Rocdur and Fosca? How can that be?

Sapid notices the boy's surprised expression. "Didn't you know that there could be war, Tam?" he asks. "Why do you think the delegation from Rocdur came to Fosca? Probably they're looking for some excuse or other to invade us. Everyone's been talking about it for ages in Fosca, even though we don't know exactly what is going on. People with family in the army say that the troops are preparing for an invasion. Besides, they are recruiting soldiers from everywhere. I wanted to be soldier to defend Fosca, but you have to be seventeen and I just turned sixteen. I don't know why they don't let younger men enlist."

"That's all we need!" says his mother who has finished massaging and sets two plates of fish and rice down on the table for Tam and Sapid. "As if you weren't still in school just the other day."

"What is 'school'?" asks Tam with his mouth full.

"Where children learn to read and write and a heap of other things!" exclaims Sapid. "Don't you have it in Rocdur?"

Tam shakes his head.

"Well, I'll be! What a country you live in!"

"Sapid," says his mother, "don't bother Tam about things that are not his fault. Besides, you didn't really like going to school."

"I liked the stories they taught us. True stories, and some of them were almost as good as Tam's, although not as amusing. There's one that I always liked, about the Great Traveller. Do you know it, Tam?"

"No," says the boy, as he scrapes the last of the fish from the bones.

"Strike me silly! I can't believe it. Well - it's a story about a lot of countries because the Great Traveller is the one who gave us the Common Language, which actually is the language of Maiera. Obviously, given the relations between Rocdur and Maiera it isn't strange that they haven't told it to you."

"And what did he do to give us the language?"

"He just went around everywhere, which is why they call him the Great Traveller. He wanted to learn all the languages in the world, because in those times, centuries and centuries ago, there were a lot of them. And according to what they say, he learned them really well. But the Great Traveller was like you, Tam, because he told a lot of really good stories, but it was hard work for him to tell them in languages not his own. And so, to cut it short, people ended up learning his language in order to hear more and more stories, and slowly the language of Maiera ended up being the one everyone used."

"So you see, Tam," says Sapid's mother, "maybe you have never gone to school, but by telling good stories you can come to be very important. Come, now that you've finished your meal why not go to see Map?"

"How is he?" asks Tam, getting up and going out of the kitchen with Sapid.

"Much better than when he got here. The poor man was starving. Now he is eating well, although he still seems to be frightened. The slightest noise makes him jump. He is in his room and Mansueta, my sister, who is the assistant to the palace physician, spends a lot of time keeping him company."

When Tam enters the room, Map is standing in front of the window beside a Foscan girl, taller than he is. He looks very pleased to see Tam and he has changed a bit. His cheeks have more colour, he is clean and tidy, and his beautiful honey-coloured eyes have a new brilliance. The greatest change, though, is that now he talks.

"When we go back to Rocdur," Map is saying, "the Secretary will make me pay for all this."

"Don't think about that now," says Mansueta to him "It will all work out well, you'll see."

" The Secretary came near to breaking Tam's arm a little while ago," says Sapid.

"When we were coming to Fosca," says Tam, "the Secretary had a Potian hanged because he didn't kneel. And my family had to go as fast as they could to Pot; they wanted to execute my old grandmother."

Mansueta looks at them in amazement and takes Map's arm. He looks at the floor. One of those sighs filled with sorrow that Tam has heard many times escapes him.

"Yes. And I..." He sighs again.

"What, Map?" asks Mansueta. "What do you want to say to us?"

"I had a brother... He was called Nop," he says with a sigh that seems to come from the bottom of his heart. "We were orphans and still children when we went to stay at the Castle as servants to the Secretary. Life there was terrible, but at least we were together. One day, when we were bringing the Secretary his supper, my brother, who was carrying a very heavy pitcher of wine, tripped right in the Secretary's room. The pitcher broke and all the wine spilled onto the floor..."

Map sighs again, one of those sighs that seems to affect everyone around. Now, instead of looking at the floor, he fixes his eyes on the wall in front of him. Mansueta puts her hand on his shoulder. "Go on, Map," she says. "It will do you good to talk about it."

"Like a bolt of lightning, the Secretary threw himself forward to where Nop was, because even though he's blind, the man seems able to guess where everything is. He began to beat Nop and when he had him on the floor he kicked him until his legs were tired. I tried to stop him, but he grabbed me by the back of the neck with a hand of iron and I couldn't move. I had to watch him kicking Nop. And the most terrifying thing about it was that he was doing all this with no expression at all on his face. I spent the whole night looking after Nop, although I could do little for him. The Secretary had ruptured his insides."

Everyone in the room shivers. Map carries on with his eyes filled with tears. "In the early morning my brother was dead."

Map remains silent. The tension has gone from his face as if explaining to them what happened has lifted a weight from him. All at once Mansueta bends over and kisses him on the cheek. Map turns as red as one of the fruits they call tomatoes, thinks Tam.

Chapter Sixteen

THE SENATE CHAMBER

The next day Sapid leads Tam out of the palace through a hidden passage. The Rocdurians have all gone out - Secretary, Chief and soldiers. The Foscans have taken them sailing in a small boat, probably to get rid of them and while they're at it, to make them seasick, Sapid says to him, laughing, because apparently that is what usually happens to people who aren't used to sailing. Today the Foscans choose the new Counsellor and the Rocdurians are in the way.

"How do you choose a new Counsellor?" Tam asks him while walking toward the port.

"The senators choose him," says the boy, taking some little fried fish out of the bag he's carrying and offering some to Tam.

"I thought that all you Foscans choose him."

"Well, yes, we do. The assemblies of the Foscan peoples choose the senators to represent them and the senators choose the Counsellor. Do you understand that?"

"Yes, I think so," he says doubtfully. His head has already been crammed with too many new things at once.

At the moment, Tam is thinking about going back to Rocdur and how everything will return to being as it was. But he will never be the same again. He has seen too many things and learned more. And right now, arriving at the port with Sapid, he sees more things still. Ships that, seen up close, turn out to be very big and hung with ropes everywhere, thousands of ropes; and a lot of men carrying boxes and packages.

"What is all that?" he asked the Foscan.

"Merchandise for Maiera."

"Do you have dealings with Maiera?"

"Of course!"

They stand there a while watching the noisy bustle of the port. Some men land from a ship that put into port a little while before. They appear relieved to have arrived. On shore, they embrace their families, telling them that they have just escaped being attacked by pirates.

"What are pirates?" asks Tam.

"You don't know that either? Boy, you don't seem to know anything. Pirates are people from the Islands who live from robbery. Sometimes they attack Fosca and Maiera, too, and they attack our ships a lot. Come on, let's go to La Bonica."

Sapid takes him to see the craftsmen's shops - something that Tam has never seen in his life. In Rocdur, ceramic, glass and leather goods are made to order by Potians working in square, ugly buildings, not like these beautiful shops where people come in and hand over money and carry away a bowl or some shoes or a flask. There are also shops that have cheeses or clothing or books. Tam looks at one of those books and sees that it is written in letters quite different from those in the little book that the man who died in the cave had. Sapid explains that although everyone uses the Common Language for speaking as well as for writing, the written characters are very old, from before the Great Traveller, when there were many languages, and each country has kept the kind of letters they used in those days.

Tam would like to take something to Tariana, who is looking after the cat for him, and also to Sua and Ep. In a shop he sees a chain with a beautiful little white ball on it and points it out to Sapid.

"Good heavens, boy, who do you think you are? That is a pearl and it's worth a lot."

At last he buys a package of rice for Ep and Sua and a green bow for Tariana. He spends all the salary that they have given him since he started working at the Chief's house: a gold coin that is almost invisible it is so small and that has a hole in the middle.

Sapid also takes him to see the public baths, one for men and one for women. They are buildings made of marble with columns and inside there are huge tubs filled with cold and hot water. Tam understands now why Foscans are always so clean. Sapid tells him that he had thought that Tam should bathe there, but he has a better idea. They go to a little beach above the port and bathe in the sea with other Foscan children. The salty tang of the water tastes pleasant in his mouth, but it stings his eyes.

Later, while they are stretched out on the sand listening to a group of boys beating drums, Tam wants to know how it is that there are Potians in Fosca and how they came there.

"Well, in fact, the majority are Foscans of Potian origin," says Sapid, and Tam remembers something that Tariana told him a long time ago, that Tam was Rocdurian because he had been born in Rocdur. "Every once in a long while, some Potian arrives across the Ocean of the Monsters. That's how they all came here."

"Why don't they go by way of Rocdur? There is a piece of Rocdur between Pot and Fosca. I've seen it on the map that the Chief has over his fireplace."

"And do you think that the Rocdurians will allow them to pass? Their only choice is to go by the ocean. Only one little stretch is difficult and, if they get past that, the rest is over shallow water where there are no monsters because they are too big to swim in it. It is also like that to the east of the Foscan and Maieran Sea toward the pirate islands. There isn't any land but there's not much water between the ocean and the sea. That's the reason we don't have monsters in the sea. Well, except for very little ones." Tam looks toward the water. "And they don't come very close to the coast."

Suddenly a boy arrives running as fast as he can and yelling, "We have a new Counsellor!"

That night Tam has trouble sleeping. There is an uproar in the streets of La Bonica and, as well, what Sapid has told him after supper makes him wakeful. In the first place they have not chosen a man as counsellor but a woman; her name is Vela and until now she has been a senator. According to Sapid, it is the first time they have chosen a woman, and it seems that the majority of Foscans are very pleased, even though some are grumbling. Tam is thinking about of Nana and Lula. Just imagine. Now in Fosca too it will be a woman who rules; he wonders if this new Counsellor is going to be as clever as his ancestors.

Even so, what keeps Tam awake the most is that Sapid has told him that tomorrow, during the interview between the Rocdurians and Counsellor Vela, Map and Mansueta are to be married in secret. Then no one will be able to take him away from Fosca.

"Here, Potians marry Foscans?" Tam asked him, still surprised by the news.

"It's not very common, but it isn't forbidden. What happens is that Potians or people of Potian origin are often poor, not all of them, but in general, and so there are Foscans who think people of Potian origin are inferior to them. For this reason, those of Potian origin who don't live in the country live in the outskirts of La Bonica in poorer districts. But things are changing, because there are more and more people who believe we are all equal. The law already makes no difference between Foscans, no matter what their origins, so now it's a question of the people not making those differences either."

And now Tam, stretched out on his bed, thinks about Tariana and the Suran Tajun. Maybe with them it's like Map and Mansueta; maybe to be from another race means nothing.... Or shouldn't mean anything.

Tam knows the next morning will be the last day he spends in the palace at La Bonica, since the Rocdurians want to leave right after the interview with the Counsellor. The boy doesn't feel like going back to Rocdur even though he misses Groc. While he is putting his things in his bag Sapid arrives, and giving him a wink, tells him he wants to take him to see the negotiations between Rocdur and Fosca.

"Are they letting us go?" asks Tam, surprised.

"No. But there are ways of doing it."

Sapid and Tam go through a series of narrow hidden passages that the Foscan boy knows very well, and that take them underground to the castle beside the palace. It is not exactly a castle, but more a very grand building, bigger than the palace, and also with columns. Finally they slip through a door and climb a staircase to the top, where there is a little room with a low ceiling and a hole in the wall. Through it they can see and hear what happens in the Senate Chamber below.

Down below Tam sees a lot of senators, men and women, seated on a series of long, curved benches that form semicircular steps in front of a sort of large chair, blue in colour. All remain silent when a woman wearing a long white tunic enters through a side door and sits down in the blue chair with serene confidence. Everyone stands until she sits down.

"She's the new Counsellor," says Sapid. "Last night she had the ceremony of taking over possession of her new position, and today is her first time acting as Counsellor. It's difficult, starting out by dealing with the Rocdurians."

Tam is thinking that woman seems so sure of herself that maybe she'll survive the encounter, and wonders if Nana could have been like this Foscan woman. Also he thinks that even though the Lord of Rocdur has a lot of power, Counsellor Vela seems to have more still, of another kind. That woman doesn't make people afraid, but she inspires great respect.

A voice in the chamber draws him from his thoughts. "The delegation from Rocdur!"

There is a murmur of expectation. The Secretary and the Chief enter by a door in the back of the Chamber and cross down a corridor that passes through the middle of the senators' benches, right to the centre of the semicircle where the Counsellor Vela is.

The boots of the Rocdurians resonate on the white marble. Some senators discretely pinch their noses and Sapid giggles.

"What's going on?" asks Tam.

"The Rocdurians smell."

When the Secretary and the Chief arrive in front of the Counsellor, they stop. The Secretary remains immobile, without saying anything, without doing anything, planted there like a stick, thinks Tam. The Chief, however, seems impatient and keeps looking now at the ceiling, now at the floor, turns a little to look at the senators; it's clear that all that magnificence is making him uneasy.

"Welcome to the Senate of Fosca," says Counsellor Vela in a clear voice, but without much emotion.

"We wish to speak with the Counsellor of Fosca," says the Secretary abruptly.

From the benches there arise indignant voices and Sapid laughs again. "I guess no one has told them that the new Counsellor is a woman."

Counsellor Vela, perhaps thinking that the Secretary, being blind and unable to see her, doesn't understand that she is the Counsellor, speaks again. "I am the Counsellor, Secretary."

"And I didn't come here to talk to a woman," he says, dragging out the words; on the benches the senators protest.

"In that case, Secretary, you can return to Rocdur," she says once more in a clear voice without intonation.

There is a heavy silence. The Chief says something to the Secretary.

"Well, then, Counsellor," says the blind man, dragging out the word, 'Counsellor.' "The message from the Lord is this. Rocdur is offering to eliminate the pirates. With Foscan ships."

A murmur of surprised voices can be heard from the benches of the senators. The Counsellor raises an eyebrow and smiles, but says nothing. Tam and Sapid, crouched in the little room, watch it all without losing a single detail.

"We know very well that you are often attacked by the pirates," continues the Secretary. "We offer you an end to this problem." He pauses. "Without a doubt you are wondering what our motive is for wishing to help you. Let me clear that up for you. If we exterminate the pirates Rocdur can attack Maiera from the sea."

Abruptly the Counsellor stands up; in an instant there is silence from the benches of the senators.

"And what makes you think that we will allow you to attack Maiera?" asks the Counsellor in a voice that resonates throughout the Chamber. "Maiera is a friend to Fosca. Or did you not know?"

The two Rocdurians remain silent, with expressionless faces, even the Chief. It seems clear that they did not know. After some moments the Secretary speaks again. "If that is so, now is the moment to choose your alliances well. Do you wish an alliance with Rocdur or with Maiera?"

"Perhaps I ought to put that question to the senate," says the Counsellor. "Senate, which one will be our ally?"

Members of the senate speak to each other, until one of them passes through the benches noting something down on a sheet of paper. Finally he seems to be counting.

"Our alliance is with Maiera," says the one who was counting.

"There you have your answer," the Counsellor says, sitting down again, and adds, "I am sorry that you have made such a long journey for nothing, but there is no appeal against our decision."

"You don't know what you are doing," the Secretary continues without moving and his face as inscrutable as always. "The Lord of Rocdur is not going to be at all pleased with your answer."

"It is a matter of indifference to me if he likes it or not," she says in a perfectly calm voice.

"Rocdur has the most powerful army in the world!" exclaims the Chief, who up until now has said nothing and no doubt wishes to put in his two cents worth.

"Oh, yes?" says the Counsellor. "And what do you mean by that? Is it a threat?"

"You have only two options," interrupts the Secretary. "Either you are with us or against us."

There is complete silence, an uncomfortable, oppressive

silence, until all at once the Counsellor shatters it by bursting into laughter. Her laughing fills the Senate Chamber, as much as if it were full of little bells, or at least so it seems to Tam.

"And who do you think you are, giving us these absurd options? The interview is over," says the Counsellor, as she gets up once more and begins to leave; she turns and Tam thinks he sees a mocking smile. "I wish you a good journey."

Counsellor Vela leaves the chamber by the same door through which she entered, and the senators stand up and start going out. Sapid grabs Tam's arm. "Let's get back to the palace! Fast! The Rocdurians will probably want to go at once."

"Will there be a war, Sapid?" asks Tam, following the boy down the stairs to the hidden passageways.

"It looks like it to me." He stops for a moment. "Do you want to stay? We can hide you in Fosca and no one will ever find you."

"No," he says with a sigh. "My cat is waiting for me."

The departure of the delegation runs into a problem. Map is nowhere to be found. Finally someone tells them that Map is staying in Fosca. He has just married a Foscan woman and according to Foscan law, cannot be made to leave.

Tam is ready to go. He is in the Chief's room helping him pack when the Secretary comes in and, without a reason, strikes him, knocking him onto the floor. "Cursed Potian," he says to him, his face without expression as always and as if he could see the boy with his two scars. "You have helped my servant run away."

"No, Secretary. I knew nothing about it," says Tam, kneeling as best he can.

The Secretary raises his hand to strike him again, but the Chief seizes the arm forcefully. "Secretary, my servant has done nothing. The proof is that he has remained with us. He has not fled."

"How dare you?" says the blind man, freeing himself from the strong hand of the Chief and leaving the room.

The Chief frowns and looks at Tam's red and swollen cheek. "It's nothing, Tam. Worse things happen in wars. But... During the return journey stay as close to me as you can, always."

Chapter Seventeen
Anna's Diary

As it always did, winter left the city slowly and unwillingly. It was already March, the days were growing longer, but the cold persisted. Gusty winds and unexpected snowfalls alternated with rain or the sun shining down on sad, leafless trees.

Anna was still working on her diary, still kept hidden under the loose board in her closet. Since she and Alison had returned, she had written a lot about her journey to the other world. She wanted to remember every detail of what had happened and get it all down, but for weeks she could never move past the point where she was falling into the Ocean of Monsters. Every time she saw the mouth of the gigantic shark, a lump formed in her throat and, drenched in sweat, she stopped writing.

Then, suddenly one day, she got it down on paper and kept going, able to write about everything else that happened.

The witch Ling, Queen Lula, Tian, the dolls, and the bird, Roc, seemed very close when she described them from her room on the third floor of the house in Toronto. And Anna worried, thinking that if she did not find the person who went to Maiera, all of them and the entire other world could disappear forever.

But how was she supposed to find a particular person when all she knew about him was that he spoke Catalan? And how to do it with Alison and go back to Mai with her as she had promised? Ever since they got back, Alison wasn't even allowed to go to Anna's house.

The return home that night in January had been easy. Because it was after dark on a Sunday no one saw them. When they came out of the Spadina station, the ticket collector was half-asleep and the street was empty. They decided to say that they had hidden in Hart House, a building at the University of Toronto filled with hiding places that Anna had explored every inch of when she was a little girl. They would say that they had hidden because they wanted to write a mystery novel set in Hart House and they had to do research on it.

"My father, when he has to write an article, says that first he has to do the research," said Anna that night as she walked through the deserted streets with Alison.

"And what do we say we've been eating?" Alison asked her.

"That we bought things... and we brought them with us."

"And how come I went there first during school hours? And without my jacket?"

"Well, it's all part of the novel that we want to write," said Anna confidently, sure of her creative powers.

"And what about Boulder? The mirror and all that?"

Anna stopped a moment, frowning. Alison waited, wrapping her arms around her sweater; coming from the hot weather in Mai, the cold of a Canadian January really made itself felt.

"I know!" said Anna. "Hypnotism. We'll say that I hypnotized her."

"Yeah, right! No one will believe it."

They went first to Anna's garage in the back of the garden and, without a sound, they hid the compass, the bag with dirt from Mai in it and the little bottles of extract of monster.

"If we don't wear the little bottles on us," said Alison, "we won't have protection from the Lord of Rocdur."

"And what do you want? To have them find them and ask us millions of questions, and the police analyse them and all that? We'll be able to carry them afterward, when everything has calmed down. For now, stay far away from computers and mirrors.

The look on Alison's face made Anna think how terrible it might be for her friend to stay far away from mirrors.

When the two of them appeared at Anna's house, Nuria ran to hug them both and Anna noticed the dark rings under her eyes and how haggard she looked. Her heart ached to think of her mother's anguish during those two days of not knowing where she was.

Nuria called Anna's father at once and Alison's family. But before calling the police to say that the girls had turned up, she asked them, "And Miss Boulder? Where is she?"

Apparently Miss Boulder had disappeared the same night as Anna. Mr. Skinner had said that the teacher was with him preparing examinations, when she went to the bathroom and he never saw her again. The girls were quite surprised at this development. What had happened to Boulder? She can't have been in Mai. Someone would have seen her. Where was she?

Now they had a new teacher, pleasant and clever, called Clara. The students all loved Miss Clara but Mr. Skinner seemed to loathe her. Whenever he had a chance to make her life miserable, he would say something like, "Miss Boulder would have done this differently. Shall I explain?" But Miss Clara would smile sweetly and keep doing things her way.

Days passed. Everyone was angry with the girls, although it seemed they had gotten away with the 'novel at Hart House' story and it didn't occur to anyone that the disappearance of Miss Boulder had anything to do with them. The worst thing about it was that Alison's parents would not allow her to go back to Anna's. Even so, Anna succeeded in moving the compass and the little bag of earth from Mai out of the garage and hiding them in the basement. She added to them another little bag, one with Toronto earth from the garden of her house, and two little candles with a lighter. She gave the little bottle of extract of monster to Alison at school, secretly, so that her friend could return to spending hours doing her hair in front of the mirror.

The most difficult thing was for Alison to get her own way and learn Catalan. Anna agreed that she had to learn it. How else could she help find the other person of the Manuscript? And the one who really helped them with that problem was Miss Clara. One day they stayed after class with her at lunchtime and explained that Alison wanted to learn Catalan. Miss Clara said she would help them if they promised her to study hard and not go back to hiding in Hart House or any other place. They promised it with all their hearts, since they would not be hiding. Going to Mai wasn't hiding or anything like it.

The two girls set themselves to work hard. Miss Clara managed to talk to Alison's parents and convince them to allow her to take classes in Catalan, although not as a regular student. She went to the Glendon campus of York University where Jordi Roig taught it in the evenings. The chauffeur drove her there, not only on the days when there were classes, but on other days as well, when Anna's father gave her private lessons in his office. Since she was already good at French, Alison caught on to Catalan quite quickly, practising it at school with Anna.

All this astonished Alison's friends, who were furious that she wasn't paying any attention to them. Anna knew now that Alison was no longer interested at all in any of them; the only thing that interested her was finding that other person and going to Mai. Just like Anna.

Anna's Diary, March, 1998
Dear Diary,

Today Alison came to the house. It was the first time they've let her come since we got back from Mai in January. Still, Alison's chauffeur had to drive us, and he waited in the car for her in front of the house. Alison and I have decided to make a short visit to Mai, since we want to test the compass. We will leave from the basement at home.

As we were driving home, at the corner I saw the homeless woman I've seen before, including the night of the cracked mirror. Well, I had an idea. Without the chauffeur seeing me and without explaining to Alison what I was going to do, I went out to the street through the garage to where the homeless woman was standing. Alison stayed in the kitchen grumbling that if we didn't get a move on we wouldn't be able to go to Mai.

I gave the woman in the street some money and she gave me a toothless smile. I had gone out to talk to her to find out something important. It was hard for her to talk - I don't know if it was because she doesn't have any front teeth or because a whole winter on the street has left her mind a little touched, but she told me what I wanted to know and also that her name is Rose. I told her to follow me to the house and she did, dragging her blanket with her.

When Alison saw her, she jumped and I whispered in her ear why I had brought the woman in. "You're crazy!" said Alison and didn't want us to do it, besides saying that Rose was no rose, that she smelled and that she was already making her feel sick. The woman paid no attention and stood in the hall talking to Puff.

When we finished arguing, Alison and I went down to the basement with the woman dragging the blanket behind her. She seemed sort of frightened and didn't take her eyes off us, maybe thinking we were planning to hurt her. I closed the door, leaving Puff upstairs, and I took out the compass, the two little bags of earth, the candles and the lighter; one candle I set on a stool and the other I put in my pocket with the lighter and the earth from the garden. We lit the candle and turned out the light. The woman looked at the door and then at us, moving her head up and down as if she wanted to escape and didn't know how.

"Now we're going to a very beautiful place," I said to the woman. To calm her down I added, "If you don't like where we're going, we will bring you back."

I don't know if that calmed her down at all, though; she must have thought that we were crazier than her. Alison and I did everything that the Queen and Ling told us to: some grains of earth from Mai on the picture of the country, the arrow pointing to Ling's house and the candle lighting the compass. Then we sat on the floor and we took the compass with both hands, or Alison and I did because the woman only took it in one hand. With the other hand she held on to her blanket. I blew out the candle.

In a second we were in a cellar with shelves filled with bottles of all sizes and small packages of herbs. A little light entered through a small window near the ceiling. The woman looked at us with amazement in her eyes and her mouth hanging open. Alison climbed up the stairs yelling, "Ling! Ling!" In no time at all one of her sisters came. She embraced us and seemed very happy to see us. Suddenly she said, "What a smell! Who is that woman?"

I told her the woman's name was Rose. She had no home, or friends or family either, because she told me that in the street. In Mai they could give her a place to live and if she didn't like it we would take her away another day. And before Ling's sister could say anything, I climbed up the stairs to the second floor, leading the woman by the hand, still dragging the blanket behind her. I put Rose in front of a window from which she could see the city and the sea and I asked her, "Do you like it?" She didn't say anything, just looked out the window. Then she stroked my hair and smiled.

Well, diary, everything has been very quick because Alison and I wanted to get back to the house before my mother came home and at Ling's house there was only that one sister. I told her the woman does not speak the Common Language, but she speaks the language of Calai or Gelgel, and maybe the Queen or the doll with the guitar would be able to understand her if she wasn't happy in Mai. Also we asked her if they had seen Boulder in Mai, but they hadn't seen anyone like her. Alison said a few things in Catalan, feeling very pleased with herself, and we returned to the basement at my house. Puff was going crazy scratching at the door.

No one found us missing and no one knows anything about what we did. Except when Mum came home she said, "What is that smell?"

Anna's Diary, March, 1998
Dear Diary,
Today Alison told me that everything has gone crazy at her place. She says last night her father came home from the office and locked himself up with her mother in a room - who can tell which one, they have so many - and they heard shrieks coming from it. Apparently they've fired two of the maids because they have to save money. Alison knows

nothing more about it, except she thinks there have been problems in her
father's company for some time.

I have nothing else to say. All I do is study. It is amazing, all the
things I'm learning, but I'd rather go to Mai and learn something about
that world. Still, we don't know when we'll be able to go without anyone
finding out about it.

Anna's Diary, March, 1998
Dear Diary,

Apparently Tony, Alison's cousin who gave us so much help, called
her secretly. He wants to know when I'm going to give him the boxes of
Lego I promised him. And it isn't that I don't want to buy them, but I
don't know how to get them to him without anyone knowing. I'll have
to figure out something.

Alison says that all their money problems at home are still going
on. Yesterday her parents were talking about selling a really valuable
painting they own.

Nothing more.

Anna's Diary, March, 1998
Dear Diary,

Today it's supposed to be spring and it's been awful. I thought the
wind would blow me away it was so strong. And today of all days,
Alison came to school on the subway. They don't have a chauffeur any
more. She didn't come alone, though. One of the maids came with her,
that young, really nice girl that I met at her house. Alison told me her
father had to be at the office really early in the morning and didn't have
time to take her to school, and her mother had to go to the club and
didn't have time either. They won't let her go alone.

Alison arrived at school with her hair in a mess and one eye bright red
because she had gotten something in it and scratched it. She's wearing
really dark sunglasses and spent the whole day bumping into things
and everyone's been laughing at her. What's worse, the kids in her old
crowd seem to know what is going on at her place. The father of that
really stupid guy, Charles Garland, does business with Alison's father
and since he knows what is happening, he's told everyone else. But from

what Alison has said to me, I know the worst thing for her was realizing how little attention her parents pay to her; she really notices it now.

It's been a terrible day for Alison. During the break I found her in the washroom crying, right there in the middle of the room in front of the mirror - still cracked - that she went through to the Kingdom of Mai not that long ago. Alison looked at it, crying, as if she'd like the crack in the mirror to swallow her up again and she could wake up in Ling's house and hear the sound of the waves and see Ling's sisters come in, bringing her oranges... I know she thought all those things while the tears were rolling down her cheeks. I grabbed her by the shoulder and told her that soon we would be going to the other world. And then Angela, the Jamaican girl that Alison used to laugh at so much before, came into the washroom. I told her that Alison didn't feel very well and Angela said to her, "Don't worry if they laugh at you, Alison. It's not worth it. There are bigger things to worry about than that." And Alison looked at her and sort of smiled.

Anna's Diary, April, 1998
Dear Diary,
Alison and I are studying a lot and she is continuing with Catalan too and knows more every day. Now the maid takes her to the university. Her parents wanted her to quit and Miss Clara had to get her back in again. Between one thing and another we don't have time to get ready for any journeys to the other world, so we're just hoping to find a good opportunity.

Anna's Diary, April, 1998
Dear Diary,
Alison's parents have cancelled their trip to Mexico. And apparently they want to get Alison out of the way for a while. They have to move and they're looking for a smaller house with six bedrooms, because where they live now has ten. It all has to be smaller, but I don't know what they mean by small. They also have to get rid of a cottage they have by a lake and of the apartment in Paris. In any case, they seem to think that with Alison around it's harder for them to make all these changes and my mother, when I told her, had a fabulous idea. It occurred to her that maybe, when school is over, Alison could go with me to Catalonia

and stay with my grandparents on my mum's side at their farmhouse in Montvell. The whole summer! At least two months! I hope Alison's parents say yes. In Catalonia it will be easier to find the person in the Manuscript.

Anna's Diary, April, 1998
Dear Diary,
I have a lot of homework to do, but before anything else I have to tell you that Alison will be spending the summer with me at my grandparents' house. First we go Barcelona for a few days and stay with Grandmother Montse, my dad's mother, and then to Montvell. It's all settled! We will both be able to look for the person of the Manuscript.

Anna's Diary, April, 1998
Dear Diary,
Everything's ready for a short visit to the other world. Tomorrow will be the day. It is Alison's thirteenth birthday and she's having a party. Afterwards I'll sleep over at her house and during the night we'll go to the other world, but not to Mai. Even though Queen Lula told us we were only to use the compass to go to Mai, Alison and I thought that we should take a look at Maiera because, who knows, we might find some clue there that would help us find the person we're looking for. Besides, even if the distances aren't accurate with the compass, what does it matter if it takes us to one place or another in Maiera? I am so nervous I don't know if I'll be able to sleep tonight.
Oh - I bought a stack of boxes of Lego for Tony, now that Alison has invited him to the party and I will be able to give it to him. I told Mum that the Lego was for Alison, and she was absolutely amazed to find out that Alison liked to play with Lego.
I have the compass and everything ready inside the bag I'm taking tomorrow. I hope we're lucky. I'll explain later.

Those who used to be Alison's friends weren't at the birthday party. She didn't invite them; but she couldn't get rid of Charles Garland because her mother had invited him. Anyway, he left early; he must have felt uncomfortable with the crowd at the party. There were Angela and Ryan and other kids from school, and Tony Walnut was there too. The girls gave Tony the boxes of Lego that Anna had bought for him and all of Alison's Lego as well.

"You keep it all, Tony," she said. "I don't think they'll move it to the new house, so it's better for you to have it."

Tony looked so amazed, with his blue eyes shining behind his glasses and an almost blissful smile, that the girls could hardly keep themselves from laughing. And he was so overwhelmed with all the presents that it didn't occur to him to ask what had happened with the shirt and the mirror.

"Your cousin really lives in another world," said Anna to Alison.

When all the guests had left, the girls put everything to go to Maiera under Alison's bed. Not only did they have the compass, candles, earth from Toronto and the firelighter, but they went prepared for whatever kind of weather it turned out to be: a winter jacket and a summer shirt. A bedroom had been prepared for Anna, but the girls asked the young maid to let them stay in Alison's room so they could write their novel. The girl protested a little, saying that the book they were writing had already brought enough problems, but Alison talked her into it, saying it was her birthday. When she left, they locked the door. They changed, set the lighted candle on the chest of drawers, put out the light and caught tight hold of the compass with the arrow pointing to Maiera. Alison blew out the candle.

Chapter Eighteen

BATTLE BY NIGHT

They heard a whistling sound, powerful in intensity, and a huge fireball fell with a deafening roar beyond where the girls were standing. They had no idea where they were and they didn't have the courage to move or speak; wide-eyed, they kept a tight grip on the compass. They were up on a height, and directly below them, close to where the fireball had landed, they heard screams and deep, angry voices, and saw here and there what appeared to be a mass of tents burning. Through the smoke and flames they could see outlines of people running and maddened horses. More fireballs passed through the starry sky and fell, crushing tents, men and horses. Among the roar of the fireballs and the general clamour they heard the galloping of many more horses.

"Get down!" said a nearby voice.

The girls jumped and turned in the direction of the voice, but all they could make out was the shape of a thick bush.

"Get down! They can see you!" said the bush, moving a little closer.

They crouched down at once and Anna had the sense to put

the compass in the bag. She crawled on all fours toward the bush with Alison behind her.

"What are you doing here?" the bush asked them in a boy's voice. A head appeared.

The girls, too busy trying to see who was talking to them, said nothing.

"Who are you?" asked the head.

For a moment, a fireball lit up the head of the boy talking to them. He had long dark hair and a face so dirty that all the girls could see were his bright dark eyes. The fireball fell on the makeshift camp below and they were left almost in the dark.

"Who are you?" the boy asked again.

"Who are you?" said Anna, feeling real panic, but making an effort to seem calm.

"I'm Ival, from Maiera like you. Now hide." The girls dived behind the bush with the boy. "Let's hope they don't see us now that there are three of us."

"That who can see us?" asked Anna, sitting close to Ival and noting that the boy hadn't washed in some time.

"The Gelgelians or the Rocdurians! It'll be just as bad if one sees us as the other."

"But..." said Anna. "Aren't we in Maiera?"

"Are you crazy or what? And you still haven't said who you are or what you're doing here."

Alison already knew quite a lot of Catalan, but still felt insecure about using the language. She asked Anna if she had understood what the boy was saying. Hearing her speak English, the boy stepped back.

"Do you speak Gelgelian?" In the light from a fireball, the boy looked surprised. "But you're from Maiera, right?"

"Yes," said Anna so as not to confuse things any more. "Um... we know Gelgelian and sometimes we speak it for practice."

Ival remained silent for a few moments. The fireballs were no longer falling, but the galloping of horses was very close.

"Let's get out of here," said the boy at last, grasping the bush and beginning to move slowly; Alison gasped in surprise.

"What happened?" said Anna and Ival at the same time; Alison touched one of the boy's legs.

"It's a wooden leg," said Ival calmly, moving ahead again and leaving Anna sickened at the thought.

"Where are we heading?" she asked.

"Right now, toward the catapults, and after that I want to climb to a rocky hill near here."

Ival stopped. The horses were right there and they heard dogs as well. "Don't move. Hide in the bush."

They watched through the foliage almost without breathing. Further down from them, on the plain, an entire army on horseback advanced toward the area where the fireballs had landed. Some of the riders carried torches, lighting up others who rode with swords raised and helmets covering their faces, giving them a terrifying look. They were all dressed in scarlet. Ferocious-looking dogs ran alongside the army.

"They're the Rocdurians, right?" said Anna, who had already seen them in the Valley of Can.

"Yes, of course."

From the side where the camp had been came a large number of horsemen galloping toward the Rocdurian army. Their horses wove back and forth erratically as they galloped and the bloodthirsty screams of their riders filled the air. In spite of the light from the stars and the torches of the Rocdurians, the girls could not see them in detail, except that they seemed to be dressed in animal skins.

"Who are they?" said Anna in a tiny voice.

"Who do you think they are? They're Gelgelians, and if they haven't been crushed by the missiles from the catapults, there are a lot more of them."

A group of dogs, panting and growling, passed very close to the girls and Ival. Anna felt herself trembling all over, but the dogs passed by without stopping.

Ival grabbed the bush again, advanced a bit, and stopped to look at the plain. The Rocdurian army was almost in front of the rise where the bush was. The Gelgelian riders clashed against them; some from the front and others on their flank. In

the light of the Rocdurian torches the girls and Ival could see
the Gelgelians striking blows to left and right with their short
swords and axes. They moved in and out of the ranks of the
Rocdurians; their horses reared up, plunged forward, drew back,
turned rapidly, galloped a short distance and charged once more
straight at the Rocdurians, who seemed to lack their high level
of skill in horsemanship. If there were many Gelgelians on the
ground it was because the Rocdurians attacked in a disciplined
way and in great numbers. It was obvious that the Rocdurians
were holding the Gelgelians down. Suddenly, out from the fires
in the camp came a large army of Gelgelian horsemen to join the
battle - so many that the Rocdurians were almost encircled by
Gelgelians.

They heard the beating of many drums coming from the same
direction as the Rocdurian army. The noise they made was so
loud it drowned out the blows and yells of those fighting. The
drummers were getting closer, but before they arrived, a compact
group of other riders joined the battle. They carried lances, were
naked from the waist up and had long black hair. And if the
Gelgelian horsemen had seemed a lot better than the Rocdurians,
those joining the battle now outshone the Gelgelians.

"Surans!" exclaimed Ival.

The acrobatic manoeuvres those horsemen performed with
their mounts were unmatchable. Some rode kneeling on their
horses, and there were even a few who stood on their backs,
from where they struck Gelgelians with their lances, jumped to
the ground to recover their weapons and in a leap once more
mounted their horses, which had not stopped for a moment.

The drums were already very close, and with them came
the Rocdurian army of foot soldiers also carrying torches. They
joined the combat. The ranks of foot soldiers were falling under
the attack of the Gelgelian cavalry, but even so, there were always
more. The entire battleground was now a confusion of riders of
every kind, foot soldiers and dogs, since the Rocdurians dogs
had joined in and were attacking the Gelgelian horses.

Ival, who had kept on moving with the bush, stopped
suddenly.

A Rocdurian foot soldier was running toward them A Gelgelian - on foot no doubt because his horse had been killed - was following him, a raised axe in his hand. They didn't have clear view, but they could see that the two fighters were heading straight for their bush. It looked as if the Gelgelian had almost caught the foot soldier when a Suran rider appeared at a gallop behind them. The Rocdurian soldier had almost reached their hiding place when the Gelgelian who was following him fell face down with a lance through his back. The Suran jumped off his horse, pulled out his lance and went toward the Rocdurian, who had fallen on his knees, crying, clutching his arm.

"Are you hurt? Let's see," said the Suran, looking at the arm. "How old are you?"

"Fourteen," said the boy in a small voice.

"You have a good wound there, boy," he said, tying a bandage around the arm. "That will keep it from bleeding. Don't you have a sword?"

"I lost it."

"Head for the rearguard following this elevation, and watch that no officer sees you. The battle can't last long. The Gelgelians are losing."

The two girls and Ival, crouched behind the bush, were almost afraid to breathe. Even though they couldn't see their faces, the Suran and the Rocdurian were just a couple of yards away from the bush.

The Suran mounted his horse with a leap and went back to the fight, while the Rocdurian hurried off in the direction suggested by the Suran. The bush waited until the soldier was far away and began to move again, this time faster.

They came to a place where they were in the shadow of a small hill and stopped. Ival left the bush and climbed up through the rocks; the girls went after him, hanging on as best they could. As Anna was following Ival, listening to his wooden leg hitting the rock, she thought how agile he must be to climb like that with only one leg. Distracted for a moment, lost in her reflections, she grabbed onto a piece of rock so sharp that it cut her hand. Luckily her feet were well placed and her other hand had a good grip, because she almost let go entirely, nearly falling on Alison. Ival caught her by her wounded hand, pulling her up to a flat piece of rock he was on, and Anna cried out.

"What's wrong?"

"I cut myself. It's nothing."

All three of them kept on walking along the narrow flat ledge up to a shallow cave with rocks in front of it, set far enough apart so they could see what was happening on the plain. Under the stars they saw nothing but the little lights of the Rocdurian torches and a series of moving forms. The blows and yells continued, even though the drums had stopped.

"Right now no one will find us here," said Ival. "They are too tied up in the battle."

"How did you know that this place was here?" asked Anna.

"I saw it a few days ago."

"Ival," said Anna. "Where are we exactly? We're lost."

"Lost? Where were you before getting lost?" His tone expressed a certain suspicion. "And you still haven't said who you are or..."

"She is Anna and I am Alison," said Alison, interrupting them unexpectedly.

"I've never heard those names before. And why are you wearing such strange clothes?" The girls said nothing. "You don't want to tell me, eh? Well, you have to be from Maiera so I won't ask anything else, right? And since you say you don't know where you are, I can tell you that. We are in Gelgel, on Abledeer Plain. In the middle of a battle between the Rocdurians and the Gelgelians. Happy?"

When he finished saying it Alison grabbed Anna's arm. In a low voice she said to her in English, "We have to go home right away."

"No. Not yet. Besides, what do we do with the boy? And you must have realized that Maiera could be dangerous."

"Maiera, yes, but this isn't Maiera. And we're in the middle of a battle."

"Who are you?" said Ival abruptly, this time in English.

"Do you speak Eng... Gelgelian?"

"Yes, I know some, enough to understand what you're saying."

"And you, who are you? Eh? How come you know Gelgelian? And what are you doing here, too?" said Anna in a tumble of words.

"You like asking more than answering, don't you, girl? Fine. I have nothing to hide. I learned Gelgelian in Maiera, from an old man who knows it. And I'm here because I was a prisoner of the Gelgelians and I escaped during the fighting."

"And how did you get to be a prisoner of the Gelgelians?"

"I came to Gelgel on a mission for Arnom."

"Arnom!" said both the girls at once.

"Do you know Arnom?" Alison asked him in Catalan. "Where is he?"

"Yes, I know him. And where do you want him to be? He's in Maiera. Listen, why do you speak with such a funny accent?"

"Better for us to speak Gelgelian," said Anna. "Alison speaks it better than Cat - uh - the Common Language."

"How come?"

"It's a really long story."

"I'm all ears."

Anna sighed and began to consider. What could she tell this boy they didn't know at all? Could he understand that they came from another world? And supposing that he believed it, wouldn't it be rash to explain to someone they didn't know the whole history of how they came to be there? She had to find some sort of convincing explanation without exposing themselves too much. But, all at once, before Anna opened her mouth, Alison spoke: "We come from another world."

Anna could have hit her. Why must she say these things just to make herself noticed? But she limited herself to pinching her friend's arm. "Alison means that we have lived very far from other people."

"Oh, yes?" He didn't sound convinced. "Where did you live?"

"In the north of Maiera, near Gelgel."

"In the mountains?"

"Yes."

"And how did you get to Gelgel? You told me you were lost. How did you get lost?"

"It's a secret," said Anna, who was already sick of the whole thing, and besides, she didn't know the geography of this world and didn't want to get herself into deeper trouble.

"Why do you have a wooden leg?" asked Alison abruptly.

"I cut my leg in the fields harvesting wheat, and it got infected. They had to cut it off. This wooden one was fine for a little while, but now it's not working so well for me. When they made it I was fourteen and now I'm fifteen and I've grown and it's a little short for me. Sometimes when I'm walking my back hurts because I can't stand straight."

"Did you walk to Gelgel?"

"No. I couldn't walk that far! I rode until the RedSwords caught me."

"Who are the RedSwords?" asked Anna.

"You don't know? One of the Gelgelian clans, the ones who are fighting with the Rocdurians. Raven, a really ferocious captain, is their leader."

"And why did you come to Gelgel?" Anna asked again.

"I already told you. Arnom sent me."

"Why did he send you to Gelgel? Isn't it very dangerous?" Anna asked him once more.

"It was all complicated. I was supposed to go deep into the mountains of Calai-Onva, but I didn't want to have to climb over so many mountains. I figured I would go over to Gelgel, travel along the plain and then go back into the mountains further north. I'd go a little out of my way, but the path would be flatter. I thought I'd be able to get away from the Gelgelians easily because they're not used to mountainous country. Then suddenly I found myself in the middle of all the RedSwords at once. That was when they took me prisoner; right here where we are now, on top of these rocks."

"What is that place that you were talking about?" Alison asked him. "The what mountains?"

"Calai-Onva! You're not going to tell me that you don't known about them?"

The girls said nothing.

"Didn't you say you lived in the mountains in the north?"

"Yes," said Anna, making an effort to imagine the geography of the countries around. "But in the Maiera part."

"So, right next to Calai-Onva."

"We don't know a lot of things because we've always lived very isolated from others with our parents, both mine and Alison's, in two houses close to each other but far from anyone else."

"Mine is bigger," interrupted Alison.

"Why did you have to go to Calai-Onva?" Anna asked Ival, ignoring Alison.

"Since you don't seem to know anything at all, I'd better tell you that in Calai-Onva live the only Gelgelians who are not part of the great alliance. Or so we hear. And Arnom wants to know if he can count on the help of the people of Calai-Onva in the event that Rocdur succeeds in invading Maiera and they have to send people there to escape them. And since I can speak the language of Gelgel well and I'm clever, or so Arnom thinks, then he sent me as an emissary. I went alone because, as we know, in Calai-Onva they don't much like seeing foreigners in their mountains. And no one knew that the RedSwords would be gathered in Abledeer Plain. According to what I heard when I was a prisoner, their leader, Raven, wanted to attack Rocdur with his whole clan. Apparently he had quarrelled with Calpor."

"Who?" said both the girls.

"The leader of the Oldlanders, another of the Gelgelian clans - he's worse than Raven. They say that one morning, years ago, Calpor left his tent and yelled: "I will conquer the whole world!" In nothing flat he brought together all the Oldlanders and then the other clans and he's been attacking Sura and Rocdur for years... Hey, look! I think the Rocdurians won the battle for the plain."

It was beginning to get light. Slightly. Just a feeble light with a faint tint of blue and light grey clouds. They could see the plain more clearly, where bushes and some tents were still burning, the rest being only ashes and fragments. Over to the left now they couldn't see any warriors fighting, but there was a whole line of figures on foot or horseback. They couldn't see well enough to figure out what was going on. Far to the left were the catapult towers. A lot of figures were moving around in between them.

"Anna, did you know that your hand is covered with blood?" Alison said.

"I hurt myself climbing up here." She looked at the cut. It didn't seem to be much at all.

"You gave your hand to Ival, didn't you?" said Alison. "You could get infected." She took a little bottle of cologne from her pocket and put some on the wound.

"Ival," said Anna, biting her lip because the wound was smarting. "Is Calpor going to attack Maiera?"

"He can't. The only part of Gelgel that touches Maiera is the mountains of Calai-Onva and I just told you that those Gelgelians are different."

"And the others, the ones who follow Calpor, can't get through the mountains?" asked Alison.

"No. The mountains are very high, and the Gelgelians from the plain wouldn't be able to get through them."

"So Maiera is not in danger?" Anna asked again.

"It certainly is, but not from the Gelgelians. It has more than enough from the Rocdurians."

Dawn was already pink with streaks of blue. They were beginning to see everything clearly. Alison gave a enigmatic smile, batted her eyes and took a little object from her pocket. She showed it to Anna.

"Alison! What a good idea!" she exclaimed in surprise and looked doubtfully at Ival.

"What is it?" the boy asked, since the girls weren't letting him see it.

"Something the pirates had," said Anna, who had already come up with an explanation. "A long time ago, Alison's father lived on the coast and one day after a storm he saw a box floating near where a pirate ship had been wrecked. There were a lot of valuable things in it, and so Alison's father became very rich. Inside the box he also found this thing that Alison has. We call them binoculars. They're used to see distant things clearly."

Anna was not entirely sure that Ival had swallowed that story, but what else was she to say to him? Alison was already looking at the plain through the little binoculars.

"What animals!" she said. "There are dead men everywhere - they must be dead. They're all lying on the ground. Oh! Poor creatures. There are dead horses too."

"Let me see," said Anna. "Come on. Give them to me."

Alison gave her the binoculars. They were very small, but one could see a great distance through them and everything was fairly clear. Anna went over what had been the battle field and, in fact, saw a lot of bodies on the ground, men and horses. A ray of sunlight, still feeble, illuminated a place where there was a whole line of Surans. They were circling around one of the horsemen, who had a black object on the end of his lance. Anna could not see it clearly. "Ival, what are those Surans up to? Here, look through the binoculars."

Ival spent a little time figuring out how they worked, and looking very frustrated. Then he wouldn't give them up, gazing through them with his mouth open. "From what I can see, the Surans are happy. Look - that one has something on top of his lance. Yes. It's Raven's bearskin hat! That means Raven is dead!"

"Let me look!" said Alison, taking the binoculars. "Now I see. Oh, and it looks as if the Rocdurians have a lot of prisoners. The Gelgelians have black hair too, don't they?"

"Yes. In fact they really look like the Surans, especially the northern Surans, but they're bigger and have smaller eyes. Or so they say. Can I look?"

"Come on, Alison, let him have the binoculars. He knows better than we do what's going on."

Ival looked again. He kept moving the binoculars from one side of the plain to the other. "I think the Rocdurians defeated the *RedSwords*. The Rocdurians have a lot of prisoners; they won't last long. They will cut off their heads in no time at all." There was a gasp of horror from the girls. "Beyond, to the north, I can see Gelgelian horsemen fleeing. Not many, though. It will take them a long time to rebuild the clan, if they ever do it. The women and children they left alive are marching north too. It's funny they let them go; I guess they already have enough prisoners."

"What were the women and children doing in a battle?" asked Anna.

"They didn't bring them to fight. I already told you the *RedSword* led by Raven wanted to attack Rocdur and they brought everyone together here before starting an attack further south. What they didn't expect was that the Rocdurians would attack them in Gelgel, and at night. Somehow Rocdur must have found out what Raven was planning."

"Come on, it's my turn," said Alison. "Let me have the binoculars."

It was fast getting brighter and Anna was beginning to think that they should return to Toronto, but what could they do with Ival? They couldn't leave him here. A cry from Alison brought her back to reality.

"Anna, look! It's impossible," she said, frightened but still looking through the binoculars.

"What's happening? What did you see?"

"Look over there where the women and children are leaving," said Alison in a low voice while giving her the binoculars.

Anna looked without being sure what she was to look for. All she saw was a group of women, some with small children in their arms, and older children following them. The whole group was heading north to where the few escaping *RedSword* horsemen had gone. The women and the children were on foot, advancing with difficulty over the uneven terrain. Anna went back over that group, up and down, trying to find what had upset Alison. One of the women turned, probably wanting to see where the enemy soldiers were. For a few moments her face stayed in focus in the binoculars. Anna opened her mouth in astonishment.

"It's Boulder!" she screamed, not able to contain herself and without taking her eyes off her. "Boulder!"

Miss Boulder went back to walking with the others, in fact she advanced faster than anyone and in no time at all was at the front of the group walking rapidly toward the north.

Anna stopped looking with the binoculars. "What is she doing here?" she said to herself. She drew near to Alison, whispering in her ear, "Do you think she went through the mirror with me and we went on to stop in different places?"

"What else could it be?"

"What's going on?" asked Ival. "Who have you seen?"

Anna explained to him that they had seen a woman they had known some time ago in Maiera. Ival looked with the binoculars and saw her walking at the head of the group.

"Ah. I know who she is. I saw her in the camp when I was a prisoner of the *RedSwords*. I thought that she was Gelgelian, although she seemed different, fatter and with pale skin. I never looked at her close up, though, only at a distance, and always giving orders to other people. That's why I remember her. I wouldn't be at all surprised if she ended up leader of the escaping *RedSwords*."

"What are we going to do?" said Anna. "We can't leave her here."

"Really?" said Alison. "And what do you want to do? Go down there to look for her and let the Rocdurians see us and cut off our heads? What we have to do is return home right now."

They heard voices not far away. Ival crawled over and looked between the rocks. "Rocdurians! They're climbing up here. We have to go. Follow me, quick!" And already he was crawling behind the rocks on his hands and knee.

"Come on, Anna," said Alison. "Put the jacket over your head so there won't be light. Quick, we have to go back!"

Anna took out the jacket and gave the compass, the candle, the firelighter and the dirt from Toronto to Alison. "Get it all ready. I'm going to see how Ival is."

"Are you crazy? Come here!"

But Anna was already outside, standing up. She saw Ival hiding between the rocks, getting away, and two Rocdurian soldiers climbing up to the heights. Anna didn't want them to see Ival. She wanted them to look at her so the boy could get away. "Good morning, you pair of idiots!" she yelled at the soldiers, and slipped into the cave putting the jacket on her head as Alison had done. She already had the candle lit and the compass clutched in her hand. They blew the candle out.

Chapter Nineteen

THE MIRRORS

It has been more than a month since Tam came back from Fosca and spring has already gone, leaving the mountains and the forests green and filled with wild flowers. It is summer and Tam and Tariana go out in the morning as they have always done, she to go riding and the boy to visit his cat, although now they meet later at the cave behind the waterfall. Tariana always wears the green ribbon he brought her from Fosca to tie back her hair.

Tam found Groc very lively when he got back from Fosca, and bigger than ever. Now, with the good weather, there are a lot of rabbits. Not only does Tam trap them, but the cat is learning to catch them himself. When they aren't hunting, the boy and the cat swim in the shallower parts of the river. Tam thinks he might be as clean as the Foscans now, and it seems to him that it makes him feel better.

When Tariana arrives at the waterfall, she and Tam stay there talking for a good while, until they have to go back for lunch. Tam has told her a number of stories about Fosca: what happened to the delegation and everything else he can remember about the country. Tariana listens to him entranced, always eager to hear more. But she has little to tell him. During Tam's absence, in addition to looking after Groc and going to a few meetings of the Rocdurian ladies' group that send things for the animals in the army, she read and re-read the books she has, but found nothing that spoke of the dragon and the three riders.

Tam guesses that Tajun, the Suran, has not come back from Gelgel, or Tariana would not be spending so much time with him every day. He knows the army that went north returned to the Town some time ago; not only did everyone see them come back, but the owner of the fruit and vegetable stall at the market told him that her son was home because he had been wounded. At the beginning, the woman was extremely worried, since the boy was feverish and she feared that he would die. But one day the boy got much better and then recovered. The woman was so happy she filled Tam's hands with fruit without knowing what she was doing. What Tam cannot understand, though, is that Tariana doesn't seem at all worried. That ought to mean, thinks Tam, that Tajun's absence is not because he has been killed in battle; there has to be an explanation that he hasn't heard yet. One day the boy can't contain his curiosity any longer and he asks the girl, as if it meant nothing: "Tariana, do you remember that Suran who rode north beside the commanding officer? You told me that sometimes he looked after your horse."

"Yes. What about him?" she says, rather stiffly.

"Nothing. I thought he should be back from Gelgel."

"Since when were you interested in Surans?"

"It's not that. But that Suran seemed special."

"He might be special, but he hasn't come back. The Surans at the stable say he killed the leader of that clan of Gelgelians. They were talking about it for several days."

"Why hasn't he come back?"

"They say he is working with the army in the north, and is very important right now. He won't be coming back to the Town until later."

"And what will they give him when he comes back?"

"That I don't know," says Tariana, laughing. "I don't think the Castle would give many honours to a Suran."

Tam doesn't ask anything else because now he understands.

Today, while Tam hunts rabbits with Groc, he hears the trot of a horse and hides with the cat. But then he sees that it's Tariana; she has come to find him earlier than usual.

"We're here, Tariana!" the boy calls, waving his arms.

The girl goes toward them and Tam notices that she has a distant look on her face and doesn't smile when she sees them.

"Let's go to the cave," is all she says.

Moments later, they are seated in the cave and Tariana says nothing, just looks at the waterfall. It seems to Tam that she may be looking at it, but she doesn't see it. Probably she only sees what is going on in her head. The boy amuses himself by scratching Groc's belly while he waits for Tariana to say something. Suddenly the girl breaks into tears - a storm of crying, with deep sobs. Tam doesn't know what to do. At last he decides and strokes her hand with his finger, just as Tariana, all that time ago, stroked Groc's paw.

"What's wrong, Tariana?"

The girl dries her face with her sleeve and tries to calm down. She tilts her head and looks at the boy, her eyes red from weeping. "I have to tell you a secret, Tam. And you must never tell anyone. Agreed?"

"Yes, Tariana."

"It's about the Suran, Tajun."

That is what Tam was expecting.

"He has come back from the north, but he isn't at the stables, he's in the Castle; he has been there for days now. Some Surans told me they came back from the north with him and they say the Rocdurians soldiers brought him back in chains. They arrived at night and took him straight into the Castle."

"Why?"

"No one knows, but what they do know is that they were going to lock him in the dungeon." Tariana breaks into tears again.

"Didn't you tell me that he had done great things in Gelgel?"

Tariana says "yes" in between sobs.

"Then why have they done that?"

"And when has the Castle done anything that makes sense?" says the girl, drying her face with her sleeve again. "Maybe..."

"What?"

"Maybe because Tajun knows about things that are hidden in the Castle, or for some reason only those in the Castle know. Tam..." Tariana looks at the boy. "I have to tell you something else... Do you remember what you told me about the Secretary's servant and the Foscan girl? That they married? Well - it's like that between Tajun and me. Do you understand?"

"Yes, Tariana."

"Really?"

"Yes. Of course I understand." The girl seems surprised at the way Tam takes the news, as if it's nothing... "Tariana, how is it that Tajun knows things about the Castle?"

"Because they have taken him there lots of times to listen to the Gelgelians."

Now Tam really is confused. He looks at the girl, opening and closing his eyes as if he cannot believe it.

"How can that be?" he says, astonished at what he has just heard.

"I don't know, but they can listen to them, and since Tajun knows the language of Gelgel, they take him to the Castle so he can translate what the Gelgelians say into the Common Language. They take him blindfolded, so he can't tell what they do to listen to the Gelgelians, but he says he thinks they can see them as well, because of things he notices while he's there and because they blindfold him."

"And do the other Surans know this?"

"No! Not at all! No one knows it, except Tajun, me, the Castle people, and now you. I don't believe that my father knows about it, either, although I'm not sure of that. Tajun says that there are men dressed like the Secretary at the castle who are the ones who blindfold him, men that he has never seen anywhere else, and they must live in the Castle and never go out."

"And what will they do to Tajun?"

"I don't know," says the girl with anguish in her voice. She sighs.

"Can we do something to get Tajun out of the Castle? We could try to help him flee."

Tariana holds Tam by the shoulder and smiles weakly. "Thank you, Tam, but no one can enter the Castle."

That evening, after supper, Tam has to tell a story for the Chief and when he finishes he says he is very sleepy and goes to his little room. Stretched on his straw pallet, he thinks and thinks. He tries to remember everything he learned in Fosca to see if that gives him an idea, but nothing he remembers seems to be of any use. He sets himself to call into his mind, minute by minute, everything that happened and, little by little he gets sleepy and his eyes start to close.

Tam dreams that he is in the Senate Chamber of Fosca. He is there alone with the Secretary, who says to him: "You are with us or against us," and grabs his arm and twists it and then he hears the laughter of Counsellor Vela that rings through the empty hall and the Secretary lets go of Tam and covers his ears while he howls like a madman. Tam flees, climbing up the wall of the Chamber like a lizard and comes in through a hole into the little room where Sapid is. He says, "Run, Tam, through the passages, through the hidden passages!" Tam runs with Sapid, hearing the howls of the Secretary, who is running behind them. In the passage there is a door that has a small carved piece set in the wood, rounded in form. The door won't open. The howls of the Secretary turn into owl-like hoots and are getting closer. Sapid puts a tomato on the carved piece, turns it and the door opens.

Tam wakes up in his little room. There is complete silence in the Chief's house; outside an owl hoots. He sits up for a moment thinking about what he has just dreamed. As happens with most dreams, he can't find any sense in it and lies down once more, closing his eyes. He is already falling asleep when he opens his eyes wide. He sits up, thinks, gets dressed and leaves the room, climbing the stairs to the second floor, groping his way. Arriving in front of the Chief's door, he listens for a moment; he is snoring. He goes to Tariana's bedroom and slips in without announcing himself. Just as he thought, the girl is awake; she is sitting in an armchair, crying. By the light of a candle, Tam notices the astonishment on the girl's face when she sees him there.

"I have the solution, Tariana," he says softly. "Where did you put the little book and the dead man's medallion?"

It is later. Tam and Tariana are in the basement of the house with a torch; each one has a bag. They pull aside the worm-eaten cupboard and slip into the hidden passage. Tam has a plan in place for going to the Castle, but first they must check whether he is right about one thing. When they arrive at the vertical piece of black marble on the wall, Tam takes the dead man's medallion and places it in the engraved picture; it is the exact size and shape. With great facility he turns the medallion and the stone moves on its own a good piece. Tariana pushes it and the stone opens wide as if it were a door. On the other side there is another passage smelling of long disuse. The girl and the boy look at each other and begin to laugh.

"Tam, you are a genius! If you've been right about that, there is no question that you're also right about the map. It's a map of the underground passages that go to the Castle."

"Now let's go and get Groc."

"Listen, Tam. I don't want you mixed up in all this."

"But..."

"It looks like this can get us into the Castle; but what about after? What will happen if they catch us?"

"They will cut off our heads."

"Exactly. The business with Tajun is mine. You've already done enough. You have done an enormous amount and I don't want anything to happen to you. Please. Go home, go to bed, and if they ask you, you don't know anything."

"No!"

"What do you mean, no?"

"No. I'm coming too."

Tariana begs and threatens. Neither is any use. She cannot convince Tam. There is nothing the girl can do but give up and follow the boy's plan: leave by the opening into the forest, collect

Groc, go back to the passage, go to the Castle, free Tajun and hide him in the cave under the waterfall with Groc. Going to the waterfall at night is difficult enough, but going back to the passage with Groc is even harder. The cat is so happy to see them that he all wants to do is play. At last he calms down and when they get back to the passage as far as the opened stone in the wall, he is quiet, doing what Tam tells him.

Now they are going through a passage on the other side of the stone. But there is not just one, there are many that keep dividing; they form a whole network of passages that match exactly the drawings in the map from the book. There are a lot of stairs and Tam begins having pains in his legs from so much climbing. Optimistic as he is, he thinks that everything will work out well, although when he thinks about what will happen if someone sees them, he begins to be seized with worry. But that was why they have brought Groc with them; he might be able to frighten the people from the Castle.

Tariana is ahead. She stops in front of a stone like the other one, with an engraved piece. According to the map, on the other side is the Castle.

Tam places the medallion in it and turns. They hear a slight sound and the stone moves just as the first one did. Tariana pushes it and goes over to the other side, holding the torch in front of her; Tam and Groc follow. There is no one on the other side, or at least, no one still alive. But they are in a huge space. The walls are carved out of the rock and there are a great many skeletons lying in pieces on the floor; others, fastened to the walls with metal rings, radiate an indescribable sense of grief and despair.

"Where are we, Tariana?" says Tam softly, holding onto the girl. "Groc! That's enough! Stop playing with those heads!"

"I don't know where we are, but it looks like the place where they left people to die. There's a staircase over there where light is coming in. We'd better leave the torch here."

They climb slowly toward the light and enter a room that is also carved out of rock. On one side there is another staircase going up, probably toward the main part of the Castle. On a wall there is a torch and a door reinforced with iron; beside it hangs a ring with a lot of keys on it. The girl grabs the torch and gives the keys to Tam.

"Try to find out which one opens this door. I think we're getting there."

Tam tries a very big key that turns easily in the lock. When he opens the door, they see a dark passage lined with doors with heavy bars. Behind them are tiny rooms, dark and dirty.

"Those have to be the prison cells," says Tariana. "Tajun! Tajun!"

Beyond they hear a noise and a voice. "Tariana?"

They run toward it. The Suran is clutching the bars of one of the doors.

"Tariana! What are you doing here? How did you get in?"

The girl gives the torch to Tam and embraces the Suran through the bars. "The keys, Tam," says Tariana, letting go of Tajun. "I'll explain later, Tajun. First I have to get you out of here."

They still haven't opened the door when Tajun sees Groc sitting quietly beside Tam. The Suran opens his eyes wide and seems completely stunned by the whole thing: Tariana, the Potian boy and a gigantic cat in the prisons of the Castle. He doesn't seem able to say anything.

"Now!" exclaims Tariana, opening the door and embracing the Suran again.

"Hey! Don't leave me here!" says a voice coming from a cell farther on; there are arms extended through the bars of the door.

Tam goes over with the torch and stops dead. In that cell is a boy who doesn't look like a Rocdurian, a Potian, a Suran or a Foscan. As well, he has a wooden leg.

"He's a boy from Maiera called Ival," explains Tajun, drawing near with Tariana. "The soldiers caught him in Gelgel and took him prisoner with me. Tomorrow they take him to the torture chamber because he has not told them what he was doing in Gelgel."

Tariana, who with that explanation has started trying keys, opens Ival's door. "Look at that! What a huge cat!" says the boy when he sees Groc.

"Come with us," says Tariana, heading toward the other room. "We can get out of the Castle the way we came in. Hurry!"

"Tariana," says Tajun, catching her by the shoulder. "We can't flee."

"Tam has found a hidden passage and..."

"No. They will find us. If they can listen to the Gelgelians, and maybe even see them, they could do the same with us. It's too risky. First we have to find the place where they took me and see what can be done. I think it will be easy for me to find. The rest of you must leave. I will do it alone."

"Oh, no, you don't! But Tam, yes, he has to leave."

"No! Groc can help us," says Tam, pointing at the cat.

"Where did that cat come from?" asks the Suran.

"It's a long story," says Tariana. "Right, then everyone up."

Before going up, Tajun takes an iron bar from a corner and goes toward the staircase.

"Where are we going?" asks Ival, who has no idea what they are talking about.

"To the Castle," says Tajun. "Then we will escape through the hidden passage. Where does it come out, Tariana?"

"In the forest. We won't have any trouble getting to the cave under the waterfall where you can hide."

"Not in the cave. The Castle will have them search every inch of earth to find us, Ival and me, and sooner or later they will find the cave. What we will do is go to the west. Will you come with me, Ival?"

"To the west?"

"Yes. To Sura. I know that Maiera is in the other direction, but I can't take you there."

"It's all the same to me," says Ival. "I'll come to Sura."

"And me, too," says Tariana, taking Tajun's hand.

"And us," adds Tam. "Groc and I will take the trail to the west as well."

They open the door at the top very cautiously and find

themselves in the enormous entrance hall of the Castle. Not a soul is around. Tam shivers in the pitiless cold and silence that envelops the place. In the middle of the entrance hall a broad staircase, black like everything else in there, climbs to the second floor.

"It's up there," whispers Tajun.

They climb slowly, making no noise. Ival has to be very careful that the wooden leg doesn't slam down on the steps.

They reach the top. "To the right," says the Suran, again in a low voice.

They turn down a passage where there are six doors, three on each side, and at the end of the passage, one more that Tajun points to. When they reach it they open it gently and slip into a large room where there are six mirrors and a big table covered with a great many bottles. Two burning torches on the back wall provide the room with dim light. They close the door.

"It has to be here," says Tajun, looking at everything around him, but evidently without knowing where to start.

"What are these bottles?" asks Ival as he pulls the stopper out of one. "Ugh! It's full of blood!"

Tariana turns to look as Ival runs his hand over one of the mirrors and, all at once, there forms in it the image of two girls dressed in very strange clothing. They seem to be sitting on beds, reading.

"Anna! Alison!" yells Ival. Tajun runs to put a hand over his mouth.

The girls in the mirror do not see them and continue reading while four pairs of eyes look at them from the room.

"Maierans," says Tajun softly, taking his hand from Ival's mouth. "Do you know them?"

"Yes. They were in Gelgel."

"In Gelgel? What did you do so you could see them?"

"I don't know. I only touched the mirror with my hand."

Tajun touches another mirror and nothing happens. He takes Ival's hand and examines the palm, but it is so dirty that all he can see is dirt.

"What is this blood?" the Suran asks, examining the sleeve of his shirt around the wrist. Did you hurt yourself?"

"No. I don't know what it can be. I've got it! It must be Anna's."

"Whose?"

"The girl in the mirror with the dark hair. She cut herself climbing that hill in Gelgel."

"Run your hand over another mirror."

Ival does it and the girls appear again. Now there are two mirrors in which they see the girls doing exactly the same thing in each one: reading in bed, completely unaware that they are being looked at.

"It's the blood," says Tajun. "That's what does it. That's why they made a cut in my arm the first time I came here."

"Yes," says Tariana who is looking at the bottles on the table. "Here's a little bottle with your name on it. Oh! There's one with my father's name, and this is the Lord's!"

At that moment, the door opens and a man with eyes like clouds in a stormy sky appears. If the group in the room freezes, the man at the door cannot be more surprised, thinks Tam, seeing there the Suran Tajun, the daughter of the Chief, a Potian boy, the Maieran prisoner and two mirrors with girls reading in bed on them. Before he reacts, Groc comes out from behind Tariana, snarling. The man does not even seem to have the strength to open his mouth or to ask for help. In one leap, Tajun has him by the hair and closes the door.

"One sound, and I break open your head with this iron bar," he says to him.

The man does not take his eyes off Groc who is making low-pitched growls full of menace. Tajun listens at the door and, not appearing to hear anything more, drags the man right into the centre of the room. Suddenly, a voice is heard from the mirrors.

"I hope Ival is all right," says the dark-haired girl in the two mirrors. "If the Rocdurians find him he'll be in a real mess. Do you think maybe we should have brought him with us?"

"He ought to be able to get himself out of it," says the other girl. "He looked like he knew exactly what he was doing."

They say nothing more, but continue reading. There is total silence in the hall. Everyone is standing, looking open-mouthed at the mirrors. All at once, Ival reacts and hurls himself, limping, toward one of the mirrors with the girls in it. "Anna, Alison," he says softly, running his hand over the mirror as if he wants to touch them.

The man with eyes like storm clouds profits from the general astonishment to get away from Tajun with a tug, although he leaves a handful of hair in the Suran's hand. "Help!" cries the man as loud as he can. "Soldiers!"

As soon as he does it, footsteps sound outside the room. The man with eyes like storm clouds is now on the floor, trembling, with one of Groc's paws on top of him, when the door flies open and five men dressed like the one on the floor come in, followed by two soldiers. The five men stand together at the door, but the soldiers come into the room. Tajun knocks them down at once with a blow from the iron bar, then turns and smashes a mirror in bits. The five men in the doorway exclaim, horrified, but staring at Groc, don't dare to come in. With another blow of the iron bar, Tajun knocks all the bottles from the table. They break, leaving a pool of blood on the floor. He breaks another mirror that falls in little pieces on the floor, and another and another. He gives a blow to one in which the girls are, breaking it into a thousand fragments. He moves Ival aside and is already about to destroy the last mirror, when more soldiers arrive and he hurls himself at them, yelling, "Tariana! The mirror! The mirror must be broken!"

Tariana is still holding the key-ring; she hurls it at the mirror, creating a pattern of cracks. Tajun does what he can with the soldiers, raining blows left and right, but there are a lot of them.

"Groc! At them!" says Tam.

The cat leaves the man with eyes like storm clouds and bounds toward the soldiers who back away, horrified. Ival has turned to the cracked mirror the girls are in and runs his hand up and down on it. "Anna! Alison!" he cries out. Little bits of mirror are falling onto the floor.

Tariana gets set to throw the keys at the mirror again, this time with greater force, and tells Ival to step aside, but the man with eyes like storm clouds pushes the girl, throwing her onto the floor and seizing the keys. Tam throws himself at him and bites his leg, moving back at once. Tariana gets up in a daze but even so, goes for the man and knees him in the stomach; the man, almost breathless, grabs her by her long hair, immobilizing her. Tam bites him again and the man screams, letting go of the girl and the keys. Now that the soldiers, terrified of the cat, are leaving, Tajun heads for his companions, but just then the Secretary arrives at the door.

"Who is here?" he yells.

"A cat," says Tam and Groc roars; the Secretary does not move.

"Ival, get away!" says Tariana, the keys in her hand.

"Anna! Alison!" says Ival to the mirror.

All at once the girls disappear and the mirror shatters. To the surprise of everyone except the Secretary, Ival is sucked into a little crack in the pieces of the mirror that have not fallen yet, but not before the man with eyes like storm clouds grabs him by the good leg. Both of them go through the little crack and the remains of the mirror come crashing down in countless fragments.

Tajun strikes the Secretary, knocking him down and yells, "Out of here! Tariana! Tam! Everyone out!"

They leave in a flash running through the passage. Everyone lets them go by because Groc is running behind them. When they arrive at the broad staircase going down to the entrance to the Castle, they are taken by surprise by the tall, broad figure of the Lord of the Castle. He is carrying a sword the size of Tam. His red eyes are watching them and all three shift their glance from those terrifying eyes. All at once, the Lord sees Groc and lets his sword fall to the ground with a clatter. Tam, Tariana, Tajun and Groc take advantage of his reaction to get down the stairs; they race to the next flight of stairs going down to the prison cells, and in no time at all are in the room with the skeletons. They grab the torch, pass through the stone that acts as a door and close it. For the moment now, they are away from danger in the hidden passages; no one can follow them here.

They walk and walk and walk. The passages and the forest are behind them, and now they are going down a mountain. They know the soldiers from the Castle must be looking for them, whether Groc frightens them or not.

"We will enter Sura by the south, near the desert," says Tajun. "They don't keep as close a watch there and besides, they know I entered Rocdur much further to the north. They might think I want to leave the way I came in, or I hope they will."

"Maybe they think we want to go to Pot or to Fosca," says Tariana.

"Maybe."

They keep going down the mountain. Tam is so tired he walks dragging his feet and with his eyes half shut. Groc also seems rather tired. He stops and sits down.

"Groc. Come on, walk," says Tam to him, but the cat doesn't move. "Groc can't walk any more! He isn't used to it."

"There is a house very close to here that I want to get to," says Tajun. "We need food, water, and horses. Only one more little effort."

All of them together get the cat moving, even though he keeps stopping and sitting down. In spite of the delay, they come close to a fairly big house and approach it in silence. Tam, Tajun and Groc wait in the shadows while Tariana knocks at the door. She is prepared for anything at all - to fight or to run. A woman with a candle, wearing a shawl over a nightgown, opens the door and is left open-mouthed looking at the daughter of the Chief of the Army. Tam comes up to the door. "Tam!" exclaims the woman of the fruit and vegetable stall at the market. "What's happening?"

Tajun also comes to the door and the woman cries out.

"What is all this? What are you doing here with a Suran?"

"All we want is food and water," says Tariana.

"And a pair of horses," adds Tajun.

"No," says the woman, beginning to close the door; obviously she has realized that they are fugitives.

"We won't harm you," says Tajun, putting his foot in the door so the woman can't close it. "We only want what we have asked for."

"No," the woman says again. She seems rather frightened; Tam looks into the shadows where Groc is sitting. He doesn't know whether to call him or not; if the woman sees him she could have a heart attack.

At that moment a boy appears behind the woman.

"What's happening, Mama?" says the boy and stops, absolutely amazed at seeing Tajun. "Mama! That's the Suran who saved my life in Gelgel when they wounded my arm!"

It's late at night and the fugitives are still climbing down the mountain. Now they have two horses dragging a sort of cart that Tajun fixed up. Instead of wheels, it has two thick poles bound together with a net of ropes making a sort of soft platform. The poles drag on the ground at one end only; the other end is tied to the horses. Both the horses' hoofs and the ends of the poles that touch the ground are covered in cloth packed with straw so they won't leave tracks. In addition, from time to time Tajun dismounts and sweeps the path they have ridden over with a broom they gave him at the house. They gave them everything: horses, poles and ropes, cloth, packages of food and bags of water. The market woman said that the life of her son was worth more than all that.

In the early hours of the morning they cross a valley and go down over another mountain. They move along little used tracks, although Tajun seems to be very sure about where they are going and is constantly on the watch.

They spend days going down mountains and crossing valleys and streams, heading south and west, until one day they leave the mountains behind and move onto a very dry plain they will have to cross all the way to Sura. They know very well that even if they were lucky enough not be seen up to now, they will not avoid the soldiers at the border.

Chapter Twenty

GRANDMOTHER MONTSE RECEIVES A VISIT

In Toronto spring flew past. In May there were still deceptive and unpredictable cold snaps, as usual, with intermittent rain and grey skies that refused to leave the city, so that no one quite realized that the trees were shaking off the rain with branches that were covered with foliage. Then all at once it was already summer: a splendid June filled with lilacs and sweet-smelling honeysuckle, and trees so leafy that the narrow streets were covered by green arches. The sun, finally, turned warm in a bright blue sky. And at school it was the time for finishing class projects, studying for exams and learning what should have been learned in April or February or maybe even October.

Anna and Alison, who had spent a good four months studying hard, didn't need to review much and could enjoy the good weather when they weren't in class. And could also take another trip to Mai from Anna's basement.

This time they got to see Ling. She told them that Rose, the homeless woman, was happy in Mai. The girls told her everything that had happened in Gelgel: how they had ended up there when they wanted to go to Maiera, how they had landed in the middle of a battle on Abledeer Plain and how they had come to know Ival. Ling frowned. Why had it occurred to them to go to Maiera after the queen told them they were only to go to Mai?

Instead of answering, the girls told her they had seen Miss Boulder with the Gelgelians. That interested Ling, who said they must be right - when Miss Boulder was sucked into the crack in the mirror, she continued on until she stopped in Gelgel.

Anna told her they were going to go to Catalonia soon, a place where almost everyone spoke Maieran and so they would have a better chance of finding the other person of the manuscript.

"You have to make sure that he was seen by the Lord of Rocdur," Ling reminded them.

"No, Ling! That he saw the Lord of Rocdur!" said Anna. The witch giggled as she always did when she made a mistake.

Alison, who had brought a camera, took a picture of Ling. But when they returned home and developed the film, no picture of Ling came up, only a white luminous blotch as if she had photographed a pure white space.

As soon as school was over, Anna and Alison were on a plane to Barcelona. During the flight they discussed the Manuscript of the Interference. It wasn't for the first time, but now they felt freer to talk about it and besides, it passed the boring hours flying.

"It doesn't make sense," said Alison as she finished her tasteless dinner. "I don't understand what the Manuscript says, not even each separate section of it, and all together it's a mess. The part about what happened to you seems to make sense, except for the voice that spoke to you in your dream, but not that of the Potian with the cat and the Trail to the west. What Trail? What does that mean?"

"Yeah, and the Queen said there aren't any cats in Pot, so a Potian with a cat makes no sense at all, whether there has to be a Trail to the west or not."

"And what can you tell me about the problem we have to solve?" asked Alison. "Finding someone from our world who has gone to Maiera?"

"That'll be really hard, even if he's someone who speaks

Catalan, because the manuscript says that other person saw the Lord of Rocdur and..."

"The Lord of Rocdur is at least two hundred years old..."

"And the person who saw him could be dead," Anna finished off. "What happens if someone saw him a hundred years ago or more?"

"Right. Then we can't find him," said Alison. "And even if he's still alive, who's to know who he is among all the people in the world who speak Catalan?"

"Yeah," said Anna. "Because who says that we'll find him in Catalonia? They speak Catalan in Valencia and the Balearic Islands and Andorra, too, and even in the south of France and somewhere in Sardinia... And it could be someone who speaks Catalan but lives in some other place in the world. Whew! Everything is so mixed up," said Anna and yawned; it was already very late and the plane was travelling through the black sky over the Atlantic. "Alison, where do you think the other world is?"

"I don't understand a thing about it." And she settled her pillow comfortably into her seat to sleep.

They had to wait in the airport at Amsterdam and take another plane. In no time at all they were in Prat Airport in Barcelona where Grandmother Montse, Jordi Roig's mother, was waiting for them. They were to spend around ten days with her in Barcelona before going to the small town where Anna's other grandparents, Nuria Manent's parents, lived.

Grandmother Montse was an old lady, but she was quick and active. She had very dark eyes, still beautiful and lively, much like Anna's. The girls got into a taxi with her that took them to the Gràcia district, to a little street near the Lesseps subway station where Grandmother Montse had an apartment. It was Apartment 1, second floor, in an old building that didn't have an elevator. Alison grumbled her way up with the suitcases and stopped at the second landing.

"One more," said Grandmother Montse to her.

"But this is the second floor," protested Alison.

"No, because the first floor is called the main floor and the second is called the first," explained Anna.

"You're all crazy," said Alison softly and kept on climbing.

When she walked into the hall, Alison wrinkled her nose; it must have seemed too little and simple. But she quite liked the bedroom where she would sleep with Anna, since it had a beautiful balcony full of geraniums.

Grandmother Montse was a busy woman. She went to French and English classes, which she was skipping while the girls were with her, and in addition, in the mornings she took care of the child of a neighbour who had to work and couldn't afford a sitter for him for the whole day. Grandmother Montse also looked after the apartment below.

The tenant in that apartment was a young woman named Elisenda, who was a writer. Anna had met her when she was a little girl, and when she came in the summer in those days, Elisenda used to give her books of fairy tales and adventure novels. Now Grandmother Montse watered her plants, did a little dusting, and collected the mail. For Elisenda had disappeared and her only family was a wealthy cousin. For the time being, he was paying the rent for the apartment.

"I don't know how many more months he'll pay," Grandmother Montse was saying to the girls after dinner. "The police haven't been able to find a trace of Elisenda; it's as if she went up in smoke. The cousin has been paying for the apartment for almost six months in the hope that Elisenda will turn up, but it seems to me that he's getting tired of it. Maybe the poor girl has been killed; that's what I think most of the time and I'm very worried. Poor thing, so kind and pretty. Do you remember, Anna, that whenever you visited she gave you books?"

"Yes, grandmother," said Anna, who barely remembered the woman, and besides, was getting all the stories her grandmother was telling her confused.

Her grandmother talked about the disappearance of the writer and about the woman whose little boy she looked after in the morning. She, poor thing, could not solve her predicaments on her own. And she talked about her own children. Jordi, away in Canada, who worked all the time at the university and only travelled to go to conferences and never to see his mother; her youngest son who was in Sweden with that girl architect who didn't look after him at all; and her oldest daughter who lived in Argentina and she, their grandmother, never saw her grandchildren unless she went to Buenos Aires herself. And Grandmother Montse talked and talked and talked about cousins and the children of cousins and grandchildren of cousins and friends and neighbours...

They were in the living room and Alison appeared totally out of things. Between grandmother Montse's rapid speech and Alison not knowing who anyone was in the entire list of people, she didn't seem interested at all. She was leafing through magazines, doubtless hoping that Anna's grandmother would finish giving them news of the entire population of Barcelona and the rest of the world. But now Grandmother Montse was telling them what was going on in the government of Catalonia, the city government and the government of Spain, and giving them her opinions on television programs, which were, she was saying, getting worse by the day.

"Grandmother," said Anna, at last able to interrupt, "Alison still hasn't seen anything of Barcelona. Why don't we go out?"

"At this hour?"

"Why not? We've slept all afternoon and we're not tired."

"All right, but only for a little while. Today, because it's your first day. But from tomorrow on you have keep Barcelona hours. Come on, then, let's go out for ice cream."

That night, since the girls were still on Toronto time, they weren't sleepy at all and ended up reading in bed until the early hours of the morning.

"I hope Ival is all right," said Anna, stopping reading for a moment. From time to time she worried about the boy they met in Gelgel. "If the Rocdurians find him he'll be in a real mess. Do you think maybe we should have brought him with us?"

"He ought to be able to get himself out of it," said Alison

without raising her eyes from her book. "He looked like he knew exactly what he was doing."

They said nothing more and kept on reading.

In the morning, Grandmother Montse left them sleeping while she went to look after the neighbour's little boy. When she came back at lunch time, she told them the neighbour's baby-sitter was sick and, although she was very sorry, she, grandmother, would have to spend the whole afternoon there and the girls would have to stay home until dinner time.

"Can we go out? Alison and I?" asked Anna. "Now?"

"What ever are you thinking of? In this heat? But of course you don't have to stay in the apartment all the time. Where do you want to go?"

"I don't know. Maybe to Güell Park. It's not that far and I know how to get there."

"Do you know which bus to catch? You won't get lost?"

"No, grandmother. I'm twelve and Alison's thirteen."

"All right, as you like. But you have to be back in time for dinner."

Later, Anna and Alison were at the Güell Park. Alison seemed to quite like it; she never stopped taking pictures. There weren't a lot of people in the park, just the odd lost tourist or two; they had chosen a good day to go. In a few days it would be July, and the park would be jammed with hordes of tourists. They climbed the endless stairs up to a place where there were arches and columns everywhere. On one side you could see the park through a line of columns and Anna explained everything she knew about Güell Park and its architect, Gaudí, to Alison.

The place was solitary and a little dark. Right in the middle grew a strangely formed tree trunk, just as if the Catalan architect had thought that up too. There was someone standing out of the way by the trunk on the other side, as if he was taking a picture.

"Gaudí built a lot of other things," Anna was saying while

Alison took pictures left and right between the columns. "I must take you to see the Temple of the Holy Family and..."

They had just passed by the twisted tree trunk and Alison turned back to take a picture of it. Instead, she screamed in fear.

Before she knew what was happening, Anna felt a hand on her arm grabbing her. It belonged to the man with eyes like storm clouds, the one she had seen in the computer and then in the cracked mirror in the school washroom. Anna's legs crumpled under her. Alison had started to run, but turned back and gave him a push. He didn't move. He grabbed Anna's neck with his other hand and began to squeeze.

Suddenly the man cried out, let go of Anna, and fell to the ground where he sat holding his head. Behind him was a boy with a rock in his hand.

"Ival!" said the two girls at once.

"Let's go! Hurry!" said Ival. The man was beginning to get up.

All at once, Anna took out the little bottle of extract of monster, removed the stopper with shaking hands and threw the contents into the man's face. He covered it with both hands, screaming curses. The girls grabbed Ival, one hand each, and headed for the stairs. Ival did his best with his wooden leg, but he couldn't move very quickly. The man was coming along behind, his face covered in yellow and, although he couldn't see very well, he was as fast as the girls with Ival.

They were just starting down the stairs, holding Ival under the arms, when the man - now just behind them - stretched out his hand. The girls stepped to one side. The man missed a step. With a gasp, he fell, rolling down the stairs, and stayed motionless at the foot, lying like a heap of old rags.

Going past him, Ival gave him a little kick with his foot. The man did not budge. The three of them looked at each other and then headed rapidly toward the exit from the park without anyone seeing them.

The return to Grandmother Montse's house was complicated. They went on foot and everyone they passed on the street stared at Ival. Dirty, with long greasy hair, dressed in a sort of short tunic and strange pants and with a wooden leg, he was a sight to see, especially accompanied by two clean, pretty girls.

Anna and Alison had to explain to him that they were in another world. It was not very difficult to convince him of that, because he was overwhelmed at the sight of everything around him. As he limped down the street, Ival told them what had happened after they left Gelgel, but kept interrupting the story with exclamations of surprise and amazement. He stared at everything with his eyes open wide and stopped dead in a panic each time a car went by.

When they reached Travessera de Dalt, Ival refused to go across the street on the light. When the light went green for the fifth time, the girls succeeded in getting him to cross; startled faces stared at them from the stopped cars. Then walking slowly, they went on listening to what the boy was telling them. When Ival arrived at the point where he had been freed from prison, the two girls stopped.

"A Potian with a cat! And he was going to the west!" Anna shouted, and she and Alison started to jump up and down in the middle of the street.

"Watch it! You'll make me fall," Ival was saying, propping himself up with the wooden leg, because the girls kept jumping while holding onto him with their hands.

"It was a really big cat," added Ival.

"How big?" asked Alison casually; they were walking again.

"As big as... Maybe as big as you, Anna." The girls looked at him, disconcerted. Ival added, "It was a different sort of cat, very yellow and shiny."

The girls looked at each other, evidently with the same thought.

"Do you think...?" said Anna to Alison.

"It couldn't be."

"My grandmother has a book about different types of cats, I'm sure of it. We'll show it to Ival when we get there... Okay, Ival, what else happened?"

The boy went on with the story until he got to the moment in the Hall of Mirrors.

"That's how it's done," shrieked Anna. "With mirrors."

"But how? What kind of mirrors are they, Ival?" Alison asked him.

"I don't know. And there might not be any now. Tajun broke five of them. All completely smashed, with only little tiny bits left. As I was going I heard the last mirror falling."

Then Ival explained everything that had happened in the Hall of Mirrors and how he was sucked into the crack in the mirror with the man with eyes like storm clouds hanging onto his leg.

"I woke up there on the mountain where we were, beside the trunk of the tree that looked like an animal, with the sun high in the sky. I saw the man with eyes like storm clouds stretched out beside me sleeping and I hid nearby without making a sound. I felt so tired and everything was so strange that I thought I was dreaming and I closed my eyes and fell asleep, but I can't have been dreaming. I woke up when Alison screamed.

Between Ival and all his stories, and the girls explaining what happened to them, the walk to Grandmother Montse's took a very long time. When they arrived at last, there was no one around to see them, in the street or the building. Anna's grandmother was still taking care of her neighbour's little boy and the apartment was empty. With money that Alison gave her, Anna went to Gran de Gràcia Street to buy a toothbrush, a comb, clothes and sandals for Ival. They had measured him pretty well, but Anna was embarrassed at having to buy underpants.

When she got back, Anna filled the bathtub while Alison opened the balcony doors and windows to air the apartment. Ival was giving off a strong odour. They took the boy to the bathroom.

"Can you take off that wooden leg?" Anna asked him.

"Yes. It's tied on with leather straps. Why would I have to take it off?"

"Because you have to take a bath. You smell," said Alison. "In our world you can't go around dirty like that."

The girls put a chair beside the bathtub as a support for Ival, and while holding a bath towel up in front of the boy, told him to get undressed. The boy didn't understand them.

"Come on! Do you want to take a bath with all your clothes on?" Alison asked him.

They gave Ival a bath. What with the boy being terrified, and them having to help him get in the water now that he wasn't wearing his wooden leg, and him yelling and wanting to get out of the bathtub when they put him in, and the girls being shy and wanting him to cover himself with the towel, it was not at all easy. As a result, they all ended up soaking wet and the bathroom was awash in water. The most difficult part was getting him to soap himself and wash his hair. They had to forget about covering him with the towel and put all their efforts into keeping him in the bathtub and soaping his hair. He yelled like a condemned man.

"Close your eyes," said Anna who was rather upset at seeing the stump of his severed leg for a moment. "And don't yell any more or everyone will hear you."

"Anna, put conditioner on his hair or we'll never get it combed."

They finished scrubbing him, combed his hair and cut it, leaving it a little long so that he wouldn't be too frightened. They took him out of the bathtub and left him sitting on the chair with a towel.

"Dry yourself off well and put on those clothes," said Anna.

Shortly after, Ival came out of the bathroom dressed, with one sandal and the wooden leg. As soon as they saw him, the girls fell into fits of helpless laughter. He was wearing the underpants over his trousers.

Just before dinner time, the girls had cleaned up the mess and had put all the boy's smelly clothes and one sandal in a bag in the garbage bin down on the street. Alison had even wiped a cloth moistened with cologne over the wooden leg. They had also shown him how to brush his teeth. Now Ival was all polished up, seated on the sofa eating cookies. He looked very different. His curly hair shone and his features looked attractive. The girls had brought him a book with some lion photographs in it and

Ival was looking at them astonished. How could anyone draw cats so well?

"Was the cat with Tam the Potian like this, Ival?" Anna asked him.

"Yes, like this one here, only very yellow and gleaming." Ival pointed to a picture of a young lion.

"It has to be a lion from Mai," said Alison.

"How can it have got to Rocdur?" Anna wondered. "Do you think it could be a cub of the lioness that Ling was talking about?"

"You mean the one that was taken by the pirates?"

"Yes. I can't imagine anything else that it could be... Ival, you say that the Potian Tam was a child. Was he very young?"

"No. It's hard to say, though, because Potians are small. Maybe the same age as you, Anna, or more likely, a little younger."

"And who was the Suran, Tajun?"

"Someone who was fighting on Abledeer Plain, the same one that killed Raven, according to what I heard when they took us prisoner."

"Wow!" exclaimed Anna. "And you say that the Rocdurian girl was the Suran's girlfriend...? That's a real mess."

"At least the Lord of Rocdur won't be able to find us with the mirrors any more," said Alison, who was putting half of her extract of monster in Anna's empty bottle. "And we know who the Potian with the cat is and we know that he's gone to the west, so one part of the Manuscript of the Interference is solved. But we still have to find the other person, obviously."

"Ival, don't you know anything about this manuscript?" Anna asked him; the boy shook his head.

When Grandmother Montse got home and saw the boy she was not at all happy. The girls said he was a boy from North Africa whose name was Ival. Her grandmother, furious, took Anna into the kitchen. "How silly can you girls be? And what is that Moor doing here?"

"He's not an Moor, grandmother. Well, he is from North Africa, but... Anyway, he speaks Catalan."

"He speaks Catalan? From North Africa? But what is he doing here?"

"He hasn't anywhere to go. Can he stay here?" asked Anna quickly.

"You must be joking! No. Not on your life!" her grandmother snapped angrily. "And where did you find him?"

"On the street."

"Heaven help us! Why, he could rob us all!"

"No, grandma, he's a very nice boy."

"And how would you know? Eh? These North Africans all carry knives."

"Grandma! Why do you say things like that? It's not true."

"Then how is it he only has one leg?"

"And what does that have to do with anything? Except that they cut it off."

"My God! Who cut it off?"

"No, grandma. He had a cut and it got infected and they had to cut it off. Can he stay for dinner?"

Grandmother Montse looked over at the living room. Ival was sitting on the sofa with Alison, looking at the book on cats. Clean, quiet and with a wooden leg. Grandmother Montse sighed.

"All right, Anna. He can stay for dinner. Poor creature, he must be hungry. How old is he?"

"Fifteen."

"And all alone on the street." She sighed again. "He has no family?"

"I don't know."

Dinner was a real spectacle, because Ival had no idea how to manage knives and forks, just the spoon that he used to eat his gazpacho, slurping it up. The potato omelet and the breaded cutlet he gulped down very noisily, using his fingers. Alison, moving like lightning, made him wipe his hands on his napkin, since the boy was about to use his new shirt. Grandmother Montse frowned, even though without a doubt she felt very sorry for Ival, especially when the boy said that he had no family: two little brothers and one little sister had died of fever, one little brother died at birth, taking his mother's life as well, and his father died fighting against the Rocdurians.

"Who?" asked Grandmother Montse, confused and obviously upset listening to so much tragedy.

"A group of bandits in North Africa," interrupted Anna before Ival could say anything else.

After dinner, Grandmother Montse wanted to watch the news. Anna began to feel uneasy. What would happen if Ival was afraid of television? If he began to yell the way he did in the bath? But he didn't yell, he just stared with his mouth open in amazement. The girls had told him not to say a word if he saw things he had never seen before when there were other people around, and Ival did what he was told. It was the girls who cried out when they said on the news that a dead man had been found in Park Güell.

"And today!" exclaimed Grandmother Montse. "When you were there!"

"We didn't see a thing," said Anna quickly.

The news went on to say that he seemed to be homeless; tall, around forty years old, red-haired and dressed in a red tunic with a black dragon embroidered on it. Possibly mentally disturbed. If anyone knew who the man was etc., etc. But Anna was thinking that the interference between the two worlds was getting stronger all the time. It had all started with a dream and now not only could you go from one world to the other, as they had, and Ival, but someone could even die in a world that was not his own.

It took a lot to convince Grandmother Montse, but they succeeded: Ival would stay for a few days. He wouldn't sleep in her apartment, but downstairs in the apartment belonging to Elisenda, the writer. After all, as Anna's grandmother said, when it came down to it the poor woman might never return.

The girls had thought about taking Ival to Mai when they had a chance, but the boy wanted to stay in the girls' world. Since they didn't want to spend all day locked up in the apartment and it was better not to take Ival out on the street, they left him in Elisenda's apartment while they went to see the city. Ival spent the day doing two things: watching television, which he now knew how to turn on, and flushing the toilet, an activity that he found fascinating.

One day, when the girls came back from outside, they found him with a photograph in his hand, looking amazed.

"This woman lives in Maiera," he said. "She's a witch."

"What?" Anna and Alison cried out, looking at a photograph of Elisenda.

"I saw her from a distance, this winter. She lives on the coast, and no one can come near her house because there's a sort of invisible wall that keeps anyone from approaching it."

"Maybe... maybe she's the other person in the Manuscript."

"She shouldn't be," interrupted Ival. "From what you've told me, this person of the Manuscript saw the Lord of Rocdur, and he has never been to the coast of Maiera that I know of, and if he has gone there, it had to have been years and years ago."

"I don't think the witch was the woman in the photograph," said Alison. "If you saw her from a distance she could be anyone."

"Maybe," said Ival, looking at the picture of Elisenda. "But she looks Maieran."

"So do Alison and I," said Anna, vaguely. She was thinking about an idea that she and Alison had come up with. Once they were at her Manent grandparents' house, they would make up some sort of excuse and get Grandpa Roger to help them send off an advertisement to a whole lot of Catalan papers: "Searching for someone who has been to Maiera."

Chapter Twenty-One

BEYOND

Tam, Tariana, Tajun and Groc are already in Sura. They weren't exactly bothered at the border, since the point where they crossed was guarded by no more than thirty or so Rocdurian soldiers who probably knew nothing about the fugitives. Tariana told them, quite firmly, that she was going to Sura as the Lord's emissary and, although they probably didn't believe it, the soldiers looked fearfully at Groc and let them pass.

The regions of Sura the fugitives are now travelling through are quite dry, and the land is full of red rocks, boulders, and heights. Tam and his companions sleep by day in the shade of a rock and set out when the sun goes down; Tajun on one horse, Tariana and Tam on the other, and Groc walking; when the cat tires they fasten on the poles and pull him. Water and food are scarce.

One night, as they travel through a gorge where on each side walls of rock rise and create ghostly shapes under a huge half moon, they hear the cry of a bird resonating and echoing in the gorge. Tajun stops. The two horses shift restlessly. Groc sniffs the air, showing his eye-teeth, and his eyes gleam in the half-light.

A short distance away three riders appear and Tajun approaches them. Tam cannot hear what they are saying, but it looks as if all is well. Finally Tajun comes back, accompanied by three Suran horsemen. They say nothing, looking at Tam, Tariana and Groc.

"They are Coixan's warriors," explains Tajun. "They will take us to their camp."

They arrive early in the morning, when the sun has just risen and it is not hot yet. The camp is rather small and climbs up a rocky height beside a stream; not far from the tents Tam sees a herd of horses and, higher up, some goats. Girls, wearing shirts of thin leather without sleeves and blue skirts, are filling pottery jars at the stream and other women are heating food over the fires, but the most of the people they see in the camp are men who look like warriors, Coixan's men, one of the most active groups of guerrilla warriors in all Sura, as Tajun has told them.

Everyone is looking at Groc. He has been drinking from the stream; once more his fur is gleaming. A very little girl is hiding behind her mother, watching him, open-mouthed, her dark eyes wide, wide open. Just after dismounting from the horses, some women offer them water, a little roasted meat and goat's milk. Tam gets a freshly caught rabbit for the cat. Even so, the people are not only staring at Groc, but at Tariana and Tam as well. A few women smile at them, but Tam suspects that they might not like Potians and that they certainly don't like Rocdurians.

After they eat, Tajun goes to meet Coixan at his tent. He is a very long time coming out and Tam begins to wonder if there is a problem. Maybe they don't want them there or at least they only want Tajun. What reason would they have to want a Potian boy who is of no use to them, or a cat that eats a lot, or a girl from an enemy country?

Finally Tajun comes out of the tent with a Suran who is rather old but appears strong and war-like. His hair is grey and wrinkles surround his dark eyes that seem to penetrate everything he looks at. Tam gets a little nervous when he feels that gaze fall on him and holds his breath from fear. Suddenly the man smiles and the eyes seem to smile as well. Tam begins to breathe again.

"Welcome," says Coixan to them, for he is the famous Suran warrior. "Having heard what Tajun has told me of your flight from the Castle, I must tell you that having you here is an honour." He goes over to Groc, who is sitting on his haunches beside Tam, and scratches his neck; the cat licks his hand. "It is also an honour to have among us this golden cat."

Tam spends the whole morning helping to put up tents for himself and his companions and meeting the people in the camp. Many of them have never seen a Potian before and seem very interested in his green hair, but they admire his stories even more. When the sun is high, everyone sits in the shade, doing nothing, and Tam tells them many things. He describes the flight from the Castle very well, with a whole string of details and praise for his friends: Tajun fighting, he says, against nearly a hundred soldiers from the Castle; Groc roaring at the Lord of Rocdur so that he drops his sword, which is as long as a man is tall; and Tariana fighting against a man of the Castle whose eyes are the colour of fog and inspire terror, although not as much as the Lord's, which are red and make you feel as if you are burning. And Tam continues with that story and other stories of Rocdur and Pot and Fosca. The ones about Fosca leave everyone open-mouthed in amazement, because none of them except Tam has ever been there and Tam realizes how much he knows about different places. Even Coixan looks fascinated and almost respectfully at him.

When he finishes the stories they sleep a little and in the evening Tariana and Tajun are married under a red sky that seems filled with the sound of the drums and the singing of Coixan's people. And after the ceremony and a splendid feast, Tam and Groc are sitting on a rock high on a hill from where can be seen a great spread of land, now dark, and the silhouette of the hills here and there. Everything seems to be falling asleep under a sky filled with stars, and everything is very pure, calm and silent. Tam thinks that here he will have a different life. Perhaps it will not be a smooth one, but never again will he have to kneel before anyone and he and Groc will be happy together.

He hears footsteps climbing up towards them. It is Tariana,

who sits down beside them. Her smile looks as if it will never leave her face. They sit for a long time without saying anything, just looking at the shadows outlining the hills and the numberless stars.

"Tariana, do you believe my family is safe in Pot?"

"Yes. Don't worry. No one in Rocdur knows anything about them. And although they might question my father, he does not know that they went to work at the plantation."

"And they won't harm the Chief?" Because, even though Tam knows the Chief has great power in Rocdur, and in no time at all can make the whole army move, and in addition has an evil temper when he hasn't slept enough, the boy can't help feeling a certain affection for Tariana's father.

"No, Tam. The Lord can't do without my father. He won't harm him. He needs him too much."

"And if he goes with the army to Sura? Will we have to fight against him?"

"The Surans don't have a real army, just guerrillas, and my father only goes to great battles. If there were an invasion of Fosca, he would have to go, and maybe Maiera, even maybe Gelgel, but never would they send a big army to Sura."

Tam feels calmer, looking at the stars and the great spread of dark land down below while he thinks. "Tariana, do you remember the Maieran boy who went with us to the Hall of Mirrors?"

"Ival. Yes, of course I remember him."

"I was wondering where he went when the crack in the mirror sucked him in. Him and that man from the Castle."

"Who knows? Maybe to Maiera. I hope so, anyway. Those girls in the mirror were Maierans, so he must have gone there. Where do you think he went?"

"Well... I was thinking that maybe he went beyond."

"Beyond? Beyond where?"

"Beyond the whole world and the sky and all. Maybe... maybe beyond there is another world."

In the Castle of Rocdur the Lord has become more tyrannical

than ever. He strikes and screams at everyone. The Potian servants who live in the Castle are more terrified than ever and try to keep as far away from the Lord as they can. Even the soldiers of the Castle try to get away when they hear the Lord nearby. The wise men, though, cannot flee and the Lord's anger has been let loose on them more than on the others. When they told him that nothing was left of the mirrors, he caught them by the hair and one by one threw them against the walls or whacked them on the back of the neck, leaving them half-stunned. The Keeper of the Mirrors, the oldest of them all, came close to dying after being beaten.

The Lord ordered them to make new mirrors, but they didn't know how. They only knew how to use the old ones to spy with. The mirrors had been in the Castle from remote times, before the Lord of Rocdur, and the only thing a wise man had ever discovered - and he was the first wise man the Lord ever had - was that you could see where someone was if you had his blood and put it on the mirror. From this was created the Caste of the Wise Men of the Mirrors. There were always six of them since there were six mirrors.

Now, though, the wise men are only five, since the wise man with eyes like storm clouds has disappeared with the Maieran prisoner. In addition, now they don't have mirrors or the blood they used to have after it all got mixed up on the floor. Since the wise men realize that in Rocdur everyone has to be of some practical use, otherwise they cut off his head, they have told the Lord that they will try to remake the mirrors from the nearly pulverized fragments that remain. When will they be done? They don't know.

The Chief has escaped execution, not because it is clear that he knew nothing of what his daughter and his servant had done, but because his services are essential to the Lord's passion for expansion and conquest.

The Secretary always escapes from it all. He bears the Lord's rage without any expression on his face and without a word. Right now, he's in the tower with the Lord, who is reminding him, as he has done many times since the prisoners escaped, that it is all his fault.

"You didn't want us to execute the Suran Tajun! You were the one who said that we needed him to listen to the Gelgelians, that it would be better to keep him in prison to spy on Calpor than to cut off his head!"

"I only wished to help, Lord."

"Damnation! Your help has made us lose the mirrors, you worthless nobody!"

"I, at least, will always be able to find you."

"Oh, yes? And maybe you found me in the unknown world?"

"The girl interfered when I looked inside, Lord."

The Lord stopped talking for a few moments. The girl! Always he had to go back to that cursed girl from the unknown world! "Have you had any news of the fugitives?" he asked, changing the subject.

"Nothing more, except that they crossed the frontier into Sura. Doubtless they have joined up with the guerrillas and so it is impossible to find them. They can be anywhere. Sura is very big and the guerrillas help each other. Besides, they know the territory and we don't."

"Nothing is impossible for the Lord of Rocdur!" And in saying that he seems even taller, more frightening, more powerful.

"Certainly, Lord, it is not impossible. We will send troops to Sura and..."

"Garbage! It won't do any good. We have to find some other way."

"A more devious way, Lord? Spies?"

"Maybe. Can you think of anyone?"

"No. Not right now, Lord. But I will think about it."

"Then think fast. And have they found any trace of what that cat was?"

"No, Lord. Nothing at all. There are no cats like that anywhere. It's inexplicable."

"Inexplicable? Well, I want an explanation!"

"The soldiers found a cave at the river, under the waterfall, where it is clear they had hidden the cat. There were tufts of golden fur from the beast. There was also a man's skeleton..."

"And what use is it for us to know that? Eh, you dolt? How is it going to help us to know that they kept the cat there or that an idiot died in the cave?"

The Secretary says nothing.

"And have you found out how the fugitives got out of the Castle?"

"No, Lord. They disappeared in the dungeons. Magic is the only explanation."

"I have already heard enough stupidities! Get out of here before I cut off your head myself!" he yells, grabbing one of the swords.

The Secretary gets up and leaves the room. The Lord stays alone with the sword in his hand. Through the window of the tower can be seen shadows of houses in the Town; there is only light in the window of the Chief of the Army's house, and the light from the infinite stars high in the heavens.

The Lord is not at all interested in the stars and looking out the window, he thinks about what has happened recently and clenches his fist, enraged. He has no mirrors and who knows if those useless clods, the wise men, will ever be able to make them again? Now they have no way to spy on the Gelgelians or on anyone else; anybody in Rocdur could plot against him and it would be much more difficult to find out about it; now he knows that it isn't impossible to have Rocdurians against him, since the daughter of the Chief himself has done it... And Fosca! Fosca has practically spit in their faces. His entire plan to deceive them and accomplish an easy invasion has been thrown to ground by that woman, the Counsellor. Besides, who would have thought that the Foscans were such friends with the Maieran rebels, friendly enough to laugh at Rocdur? And along with everything else, that cursed girl from the unknown world appears in Gelgel. It had to be her, the girl wearing strange clothes seen by the soldiers. And then afterwards the wise men said the fugitives could see her too in the Hall of Mirrors. And not in one, but in two mirrors! What is the connection between the fugitives and that girl? How could the Maicran prisoner go through the mirror and take the wise man with him? And how did the Suran, Tajun, the daughter of the Chief, a Potian servant and a cat flee the Castle? A cat like one that has never been seen before, and inside the Castle!

The Lord continues looking out the window without finding answers to anything. He caresses the pendant that he wears under his tunic; it hasn't done him much good. He, the Castle, and Rocdur have been deceived by a cat, a Potian boy, a Rocdurian girl and a skilful young Suran who knows too much. He turns his back on the window and in rage and with one single blow cuts the table in two. If only he could do the same to Arnom and Tajun and the girl from the unknown world!

Still tightly clutching the sword he returns to looking at the night full of stars. Oh, how he would like to extinguish them with his look, so that everything would be in darkness: the sky, the Chief's window, the entire world, and the other world of the girl and everything there is beyond and beyond and beyond...

Anna, Alison and Ival arrived in the evening at Montvell, the town where the Manent grandparents lived. Some days before, Anna had called her grandfather to try to convince him to let the North-African boy, Ival, stay with them in the farmhouse in Montvell. Her grandfather told her that if the boy didn't have any papers it meant he was an illegal immigrant and so it would be a heavy responsibility to take charge of him. But Anna's grandfather, Roger Manent, had never known how to say no to his granddaughter and besides, the story of the orphan boy with a wooden leg was breaking everyone's heart.

Grandfather Roger collected all three of them from the Barcelona bus in his little car that was almost an antique, and brought them to the small farmhouse on the outskirts of Montvell. Grandma Maria was waiting at the door for them. Anna resembled her a great deal, except for having Grandmother Montse's eyes and, as she explained to Alison, her grandfather Roger's personality.

Anna and Alison were installed in the top of the house, in the attic, renovated as a large bedroom. It enchanted Alison even more than the room with the lovely balcony in Grandmother Montse's apartment. Anna explained that it was her bedroom at the farmhouse. "Years ago," she said, "it was just an attic, but I liked it a lot because it smelled like sunshine."

"That's nonsense. Sunshine doesn't smell. The sun doesn't have a smell," she said, blinking.

"Well, the attic always smelled like the sun," insisted Anna, frowning with annoyance. Alison always had to look at things from the scientific point of view.

Ival was given a room on the first floor so he wouldn't have to climb stairs. It was the guest room and had a tiny bathroom that Ival looked at nervously - he was still not used to baths - although he certainly would amuse himself a lot by flushing the toilet.

While they were eating dinner, Ival, now able to cope, more or less, with a knife and fork, went back to telling his family history.

"And what's your name, besides Ival? What's your family name?" asked Grandma Montse, smiling like her granddaughter.

"His name is Ival of Maiera," said Alison to help him out, since the boy seemed lost.

"That doesn't sound like a North African name," said Anna's grandmother, puzzled. "And how did you get to learn Catalan?"

"From the tourists," said Anna. "Before coming to the peninsula he was a tourist guide in Morocco, and sometimes they have Catalan clients."

"He must be a very clever boy to have learned it so well," said her grandmother, smiling at Ival. "Don't you think, Roger, that he speaks it very well? He doesn't even have a foreign accent."

"He came on a boat," said Anna before her grandfather said anything. It occurred to her that it would better to get off the subject of Ival's history in order to avoid questions the boy couldn't answer. "They took his papers from him... his passport, visas, everything, on the way to Barcelona, uh... when he was on the train, that's where they took them from him."

"Poor boy. So young and all alone and without papers and..."

Her grandmother didn't continue, but Anna knew she had been going to say, "and with a wooden leg."

For dessert, her grandmother had made a caramel custard and Ival had three helpings. While they were waiting for the boy to finish, Anna asked, "Grandfather, couldn't you fix Ival's wooden leg? It's too short for him and his back aches because he's twisted over to one side."

"Well, of course I could do it, but if Ival went to the hospital they could make him one of the up-to-date ones that can move and everything."

"But, grandfather, Ival can't go the hospital. He doesn't have any papers."

"Anna, sooner or later he will have to get in contact with the authorities. He can stay here for a few days and rest. The poor boy needs it. After that he has to put his legal situation in order."

"But, grandfather! They'll send him to North Africa! Couldn't you give him work here at the farm? I'm sure he could help you with the tomatoes."

"I don't need help with the tomatoes," said her grandfather, laughing. "And how do you want me to give work to a boy of fifteen?"

"At least, maybe we can pay for a lawyer for him," her grandmother interrupted. "We would have to help him, poor thing."

"Maybe, yes... And pay for a good leg for him. The one that you're wearing, lad, isn't much use."

"Yes, it is," interrupted Ival suddenly and angrily. "Arnom said that they made it for me."

"Who?" said Anna's grandmother.

"Arnom is the chief of his people," said Alison.

"Doesn't Ival know how to talk?" asked her grandfather. "Do you two have to say everything for him?"

After dinner, the grandparents took all three of them to a shed near the house to see their dog's puppies. Grandpa Roger and Anna left them looking at the puppies and went for a walk. It was a custom that grandfather and granddaughter had followed since she was a little girl, going for a walk after dinner, just the two of them. They walked a while and sat down on a rock high on a little hill and looked at the night landscape.

This evening as they went they talked about Toronto, school, Puff... Anna wanted to stay away from questions about Ival. She knew how intelligent her grandfather was and she had already noticed the suspicious look on his face during dinner. Grandfather Roger talked about things that he had been reading - he read a great deal on different topics and in a disorganized way, a little bit of everything. He also told her that he wasn't terribly well.

"What's wrong, grandfather?"

"Nothing very important. Little things that doctors like to exaggerate. A good group they are, doctors, always giving warnings in large helpings and frightening everyone. Don't worry if your grandmother says something about it to you. What one has to do is live, Anna, really live until the last moment and have a stout heart in face of adversity."

They went to the top of the little hill from where they saw the lights of the farmhouse and the village down below and the shadows of the distant mountains. It was a beautiful night with a great many flickering stars, and some gathered in clusters or in streaks of light. Anna hadn't really understood what her grandfather had said about doctors and living and all that, but she didn't want to ask, not while they were looking at the landscape partly hidden in the half-light and all those stars high in the heavens. Besides, what could happen to her grandfather? He seemed to her as strong and certain as always. Then, his eyes still fixed on the stars, her grandfather said casually, as if it didn't matter, "Ival's name isn't 'of Maiera', is it? He's from Maiera."

Anna opened and closed her mouth several times without being able to say anything.

"Have you been there, Anna? Have you gone to Maiera?"

"Yes," was all the girl could say. Her mouth felt very dry.

"I, too, have been there."

Grandfather and granddaughter needed some time to explain themselves to each other. Anna told him all her history in detail, from the dream of the battle in the Valley of Can up to the encounter with Ival and the man with eyes like storm clouds in Park Güell. And everything that Ival had told them about what had happened at the Castle of Rocdur. Her grandfather looked at her amazed, but listened without interrupting her except to clarify a few things.

When Anna finished her story it was her grandfather's turn to explain himself. He said that one night in August, more than twelve years before, he dreamed he was in a forest and through the trees he saw a clearing. There was a house in it with children playing outside, a woman hanging up clothes to dry and a man cutting wood. Everything seemed as real as if he had actually been there: the images, the smells, and even the laughter of the children, the blows of the axe on the wood... Suddenly he heard the hoofbeats of horses coming through the forest and he hid behind a tree.

"Like you, Anna, I also hid behind a tree."

"Did you see a battle? Could you hear someone speaking to you inside your head?"

"No, I didn't hear anything like that and the family in the house was no army, but yes, there were a group of warriors crossing the forest, at least a band of about twenty soldiers dressed in scarlet with a dragon..."

"Rocdurians! And were there Surans?"

"There weren't any soldiers like the ones you say are Surans, but yes, they were Rocdurians. And leading the soldiers was a tall broad-shouldered man dressed in a black tunic."

"The Lord of Rocdur!"

"The group of riders went toward to the house and when the family saw them they screamed: 'Rocdurians! Rocdurians!' The woman gathered up the children and rushed into the house with them. The man was farther away and the Rocdurians surrounded him. He pulled out a sword he was wearing and the warrior in the black tunic laughed. The man of the house seemed unable to look at the face of the warrior. Each time he tried to strike he had to lower his head. It was like looking straight into a light - that's what was happening to the man."

Her grandfather continued, telling her what the rider in the black tunic said: "'Do you dare face the Lord of Rocdur?' and killed him with the sword. From the house you could hear a scream and the Lord of Rocdur ordered them to burn it. Before long, the soldiers had done it and the woman and the children came out half-suffocated from smoke. The Rocdurians ran all of them through with their swords."

Anna caught her grandfather's arm. That dream was worse than hers.

"The Rocdurians left and I ran up to the house to see if by some miracle someone was alive, but the galloping of horses coming from the other direction made me hide again. Three riders arrived at the house. They seemed very young, between eighteen and twenty, more or less."

"Rocdurians?"

"No, no. These wore short tunics or shirts, I wasn't sure which, and a type of trousers."

"Like Ival. That's how he was dressed before."

"One of the riders threw himself on the dead bodies on the ground, embracing them, full of bitter grief. When he got up, he drew his sword and raising it, cried out: 'I shall avenge you, my parents and brothers and sisters! I, Arnom, shall avenge you!'"

"Arnom? And was his hair tousled and did he have a beard and really bright eyes and was he very strong?"

"Yes, his hair was wildly tangled and I believe I remember that he had a little beard. I didn't see his eyes, though, and I don't know if he was strong. He seemed to me to be a very unhappy young man, full of hatred, who was either very determined or a fool, because when he finished his vow of vengeance he turned to those who were with him and said something like this: 'Gather up all the Maierans who wish to follow me. We will form an army in Maiera; never again will the Rocdurians murder defenceless Maierans. They will have to fight against our army and we will drive them out of Maiera!'"

"And what else happened?"

"I don't know, because I woke up. But I have never forgotten that dream, never. Not even with the surprise that your grandmother and I had that night."

"What happened?"

"A telephone call from Toronto. You had just been born, Anna."

Anna curled under his arm. Her head was a jumble of all that her grandfather had told her, but she was slowly taking in everything she had just heard and sorting it out in her mind. "Grandpa! Then you're the other person in the Manuscript of the Interference, the person I had to find!"

"Probably."

"Oh! Then I have to tell Alison and Ival! And Ling. I have to go to Mai and tell her..." Anna ducked out from under her grandfather's arm.

"Yes, Anna. You'll do that." Considering everything they had just told each other, her grandfather seemed rather calm.

"And you will come to Mai with us?" she asked anxiously. She so wanted to show Mai to her grandfather.

"Of course, I'll go. And we will have to find a good excuse to be away for several days. We don't want to keep on making such short trips to the other world. We'll go on a holiday to Mai. Does that sound good to you?"

"Yes," said Anna, smiling. "And Ival, grandpa? What will happen to him?"

"Well, since the boy wants to stay in this world, then here he'll have to stay. Your grandmother and I will take charge of him. We can get him a lawyer, as your grandmother said; I'll dream up a convincing story that will make everyone believe that he comes from North Africa. He can stay and live here at the farm and I will teach him to read and write as well as other things. And of course, they'll have to make him a new leg."

"And what if he ever wants to go back to his world?"

"Does the Kingdom of Mai seem very beautiful?"

"Oh, it does! And we can go to Mai using the compass whenever we want, now that the other world isn't going to disappear!"

Suddenly she felt very happy and curled up again under her grandfather's arm. They stayed there in silence under the night sky filled with stars.

"Grandfather?" said Anna, half asleep. "Where do you think the other world is?"

Her grandfather sighed. "What do you think?"

"It ha..." Anna yawned. Everything was very still, except for the chirp of crickets and the rustling of leaves in trees shaken now and then by a slight breeze. "It has to be beyond the dream."